MERLIN'S WOOD

Merlin's Wood — The Battle of the Trees I

© 2017 Anne Hamilton

Published by Armour Books
P. O. Box 492, Corinda QLD 4075, Australia
www.armourbooks.com

ISBN: 978-1-925380-08-8

Photo Credits:
Front Cover — © prometeus | Can Stock Photo Inc
Back Cover — © romko | Can Stock Photo Inc
Chapter Headings — © believeinme | Can Stock Photo Inc

Interior design: Book Whispers
Cover Design: Anne Hamilton

First published in 2003 by Evergreen Books (ISBN: 1920796282)
Updated second edition — first published in 2017 by Armour Books

National Library of Australia Cataloguing-in-Publication entry

Creator:	Hamilton, Anne, 1954- author.
Title:	Merlin's wood : battle of the trees 1 / Anne Hamilton.
ISBN:	9781925380088 (paperback)
Target Audience:	For upper primary and high school students.
Subjects:	Fantasy fiction
	Time travel--Juvenile fiction.

All rights reserved. Except for brief excerpts in critical articles or reviews, no part of this book may be reproduced in any form without permission in writing from the publisher.

MERLIN'S WOOD

ANNE HAMILTON

Dedication:

Rosie S.K.
and
Melissa W.S.
for 'wrighting' the 'trees'.

The Tree
of
Hands

'Murder?' Holly scowled as she looked out the bus window at the heat haze blurring the distant mountains. The sun-scorched paddocks by the roadside jiggled up and down as the bus dipped from one pothole into another.

'It's true!' Reece lowered his voice. 'That's what she said she saw. By midnight tonight, he's going to be arrested for murder. *Our* murder.'

'Be serious, Reece!' Her voice was loud enough for the bus driver to shoot a curious glance over his shoulder. 'Gran wouldn't say that! And even if she did, you've never believed her stories before.' She jerked away to gaze out the bus window once more.

From the highest reaches of the sky, a rainbow spiralled down into the shadows of the distant hills. *Rain!* Holly caught her breath, distracted by the promise in the radiant colours. For a moment, she imagined her dad's depression lifting and her mum singing again. But the shape was wrong. *It must be a trick of the light. A reflection off the window. Rainbows don't…*

'The delusions of grandma are just—delusions.' Reece tugged

at her sleeve to gain her attention. 'This is different.'

'It's delusions of grand*eur*.'

'Those, too.' Reece grimaced. 'How anyone could believe I'm the sole heir to an ancient title and vast estates, I don't know.' He glared. 'But this is different.'

Holly returned his glare. She was unsettled by his insistence. *Gran really is uncanny sometimes.* She stared at the long ribbon of road ahead. In the smelter of late afternoon, it rippled with heat. The dusty fenceposts along the edge seemed to sink momentarily into the summer haze. At last, a pair of blue gums materialised out of a wavering, airy shimmer along with an old painted milk churn that served as a mailbox.

Reece was on his feet as the bus lurched to a halt. 'See ya, Mr Jenkins.' He swung down the front steps.

'Bye, Reece,' the driver said. 'Happy holidays! Are you lot going away?'

'*I* am.' Reece winked. 'Don't know about Mum and Dad. My time machine's only built for two, you know. And I've promised Retro he can have the first trip.'

'Now, hold on a minute!' Mr Jenkins wagged his finger. 'Retro can just join the queue. How many years ago was it—five, six?—when you said I was down for the very first trip. History, you said, would remember my name.'

'That was when you promised to invest in it.'

Mr Jenkins snorted and rolled his eyes. 'Bye, Holly!'

'Bye, Mr Jenkins!' Holly went down the steps with care, clutching several bulging plastic bags.

'Do you need help with those?' Mr Jenkins eyed the bags with a frown.

'They're not heavy.' Holly smiled. 'It's only paper inside.'

'Well, then.' Mr Jenkins revved the bus engine. 'Have a beaut

Christmas, lass! You keep that little brother of yours out of trouble, eh?'

The bus roared off, puffing cloudlets of smoke as it hurtled down the road like a hornet released from a trap. Holly coughed, then blinked. Her eyes stung from the dust blowing backwards. *Mr Jenkins, you'll lose this bus run if you're not careful. Some parents think you drive like a maniac all the time, not just when the last kid is gone.*

Rubbing her eyes, she saw the rainbow again, coiling and twisting, red over blue over green. It shafted down from the highest reaches of the sky. *It isn't a reflection.* Holly blinked at the writhing serpent of colour. 'Reece, look!'

But he was already halfway to the farmhouse and didn't hear her. Or if he did, he was ignoring her.

The rainbow vanished.

Holly stood beside the milk churn, puzzled. Glancing down, she noticed her sapphire-dark shadow pooling with the faint shadows of the blue gums. *Gran didn't say it. But I almost believed it. You're getting far too good at dressing up the truth, little brother.*

A horde of flies appeared, circling around her with a taunting buzz. Flicking them aside, she watched Reece reach the fork in the track. A flattened rippling in the bone-coloured grass was the sole sign he was being stalked.

Only the zinging of the flies interrupted the silence. Holly watched, fascinated, as the grass seemed to pause in its deliberations. *Waiting...*

Retro sprang. With a flash of black snout and a wild wagging of his tiny tail, the puppy leapt straight for Reece's legs. Reece lost his footing and tumbled, Retro scampering around and yipping with delight.

'Re*tro*!' Reece lunged for the puppy. But Retro was nimble and sped across the fields towards the dam. Reece, laughing, set out in pursuit.

By the time Holly reached the house, she was tired, dusty and surrounded by bob-dancing flies. She could hear Retro and Reece splashing and belly-flopping in the muddy waters of the dam.

'Hello, honey,' mum called from the kitchen. 'How was your last day?'

'Fine.' She opened the screen door to the sitting room and hid her plastic bags behind a faded curtain. 'Retro finally got Reece. Snuck up on him a beauty. You should've seen it.'

'Sorry I missed it.' Mum's laughter echoed down the hallway.

Holly was dumping her school bag when she glimpsed a darting beam of parti-coloured light. A lancet of red, blue and green shimmered through the window, angling onto a display cabinet where Reece kept the best of his rock collection. Holly stared at the spot where the light had fallen. Part of a fossil fern had melted into a slush of mud. Half the fossil was solid rock, the other half was brown sludge with green tips of fern-frond showing. Holly was so startled it took her a moment to realise the once-perfect fossilised dinosaur egg next to it had cracked and the end of a claw was showing. Her shriek was so tiny it was almost soundless.

'Mum!' Holly raced to the kitchen. 'The fos…*sils*…!'

'Yes, I know.' Mum shook her head. Her hands were white with flour as she rolled out a sheet of pastry. 'I don't know what's with Reece lately. I'm sick of the practical jokes—and the mess they're causing.'

Practical joke? Holly wanted to thump herself. *Fell for another one.*

'Time for chores,' Mum said, as Holly went to the fridge to get a cool drink. 'Where's Reece now?'

'Down playing with Retro in the dam.' Holly reached for the biscuit tin. There were only two biscuits left. She bit into one, then hesitated only a moment before palming the other. Pushing open the screendoor at the back of the kitchen, she stood and listened for the groans of a tractor.

'Don't let the flies in.' Mum flipped a pastry cover onto apples in a pie dish.

'*Reece!*' Holly closed the door behind her. 'Chores!' she yelled. There was no answer. 'Reece!' She scowled. *Practical joke!* She was angrier with herself for falling for it than with Reece for devising it. *As if a dinosaur would be hatching!*

She took a bucket of feed to the chickens and checked the water troughs. They were empty and the chickens were obviously distressed. *You owe me, Reece.*

The sun was a giant red eye, taking one last indifferent look across the darkening heat-hammered hills as she finished the chores. Puffing and sweating, she reached the back door just as Reece came along, his hair dripping with water. Retro, his sleek wet fur like polished coal, followed at his heels. 'You owe me the washing up.'

'Do not,' Reece snapped.

'Do so.'

'I didn't agree to anything.'

'Doesn't matter.' Holly pushed the door so that the screen slammed back in Reece's face. She flounced through the kitchen, ignoring her mother's disapproving look. 'I did *his* jobs.' She went into the hallway and opened the top drawer in the desk. 'Fair's fair.'

As she removed a pair of scissors, a yell came from the kitchen. 'Holly, ya lousy thief, where's my biscuit?'

'It was down-payment on those jobs of yours I did.' Holly opened and closed the scissors several times. Satisfied they weren't stiff, she headed for the sitting room.

'It was *full* payment,' Reece bellowed. 'I'm not doing any washing up for you now.'

'Says *who?*'

'Says me.'

'Stop it, you two.' Mum's exasperation was plain. 'Reece, thank your sister. You've enjoyed yourself while she's been working. Now get ready for dinner.'

Holly waited, one ear cocked in the hope Reece would get more of a dressing down. She wondered why Mum didn't mention the mess in the display cabinet. Her other ear was alert to the sounds of sunset. Crickets had already begun to rasp their songs to the night; a hunting owl hooted overhead; the signal calls of marauding foxes echoed between the hills.

When Reece's 'thank you' failed to materialise, she shook her head without surprise. Going to the faded curtain, she pulled out the plastic bags. She sat down in Gran's armchair and reached into the first bag. Taking out a piece of paper, she began cutting out the shape on it.

Reece came to stand, hands on his hips, at the entrance to the sitting room. Retro crouched at his feet wearing the same pugnacious, snarling expression.

'Oh, grow up and show some maturity and gratitude.' Holly didn't bother to look up.

Reece stalked over to her and shook his head. Droplets of water flew from his hair.

'Go away!' Holly screwed up her eyes and hunched over to protect the paper she was cutting. Retro bounded up, shaking himself in imitation of Reece. 'Stop it!' she yelled. 'Go *away*, both of you! You're ruining my tree.' *Something is seriously wrong with you, Reece. You've been spoiling for a fight for the last two days. What's eating you?*

'Tree?' Reece stopped. He peered at Holly's work. 'That's not a *tree*. That's a hand.'

'I know it's a hand.' Holly turned the paper over to show a

name. 'As a matter of fact, it's Lissa Wheeler's hand. But it's going to be part of a *tree* when I'm finished with it.'

Reece sneered. 'You went around all lunchtime tracing people's hands just to make a *tree?*' His eyebrows narrowed, coming together in a disbelieving frown. 'Yeah sure, sis, the truth now.'

Holly sighed. *The only reason you don't know the truth when you hear it, Reece, is because you're always busy improving on it.* 'I am making a tree. A *Christmas* tree, if you must know.' She dropped her voice. She didn't want to refer directly to the fact she'd overheard Mum and Dad saying they wouldn't be able to afford much of a celebration this year. 'I got the idea from Nerida. Everyone had to make a card for their final art project, showing what Christmas meant to them. She got her family to put a handprint on a piece of bark. Then she made the hands into the shape of a tree. I know it doesn't sound much, but it was just fabulous.'

'Hmpph.' Reece glowered as Holly finished a cutout. 'You didn't ask to trace *my* hand.'

'You,' said Holly, 'are not in my class. Besides, I can get yours any time. Sometime between now and never, I'll ask for it.'

'This is stupidest idea I've ever heard of.' Turning on his heel, Reece disappeared down the hallway. Holly had just finished her tenth cutout when he arrived back, dangling a piece of silver baking foil from his upraised hand. 'Da da, drum roll please. I have the piece of persistence.'

'It's pièce de résistance.' Holly stared at the flickering foil. 'What is *that?*'

'It's *my* hand in silver. The perfect decoration for the top of your tree.'

'Get out.' Holly grimaced. 'What makes you think I'm putting your ugly paw anywhere?'

"Cos I'm not doing the washing up unless you do.' He put the silver hand down on the wing of her armchair and went off, whistling.

Holly heard the sound of the tractor coughing its way up the hill. 'Dad!' She jumped up and ran to the door.

The phone rang. A few seconds later, Mum's voice rang out from the hallway. 'Reece, Holly, it's your gran. Come quick—she's only got a few minutes.'

Holly raced to the phone, but Reece was already there ahead of her. 'Of course I got your postcard, Gran. So that's *my* castle, hey?' His serious tone contrasted with the mocking gleam in his eye. 'What's it called? Really? After little old me?' He sounded so derisive Holly wanted to hit him. 'And you hiked all the way to the top? Better have photos, Gran, or we won't believe you. Can't you email them, you old fraud?' Reece leaned back against the wall. 'Of course I'll be careful. You know me.' He winked, like a conspirator, at Holly. 'See ya, Gran.'

Holly didn't know what to make of Reece's wink as he handed the phone to her. 'Hello, Gran.'

'Is that you, Celyren dear?' There was a background buzz of static.

'Yes, Gran.' Holly grimaced. She never used her real name, but Gran always insisted on it. *An old name on our side of the family,* Gran would say with pride. *Always given to women of great courage and daring.* 'Where are you today, Gran? Have you visited any more Welsh castles?'

'Oh no, dear. I've been doing something much better. I've finally done something today I've always wanted to do. I've climbed Cader Idris and stayed overnight on its summit. It was freezing. But it's my last chance to stand where Merlin once stood and catch a little of his magic.'

'Merlin was there?' *I bet she told Reece she climbed it just because he's named after Merlin. He'll be even more unbearably smug—if possible.*

She raised her eyebrows at him as he lounged, one hand behind his back, against the wall.

'Of course Merlin was at Cader Idris,' the husky voice came down the line. 'Some call it Arthur's Seat, but there's no round table anywhere in sight.' Gran chuckled at her own joke while Holly groaned inwardly. 'It was worth it, dear. Even though I've got a bout of arthritis you wouldn't read about. The winter gremlins have certainly been working overtime on the frost lately.'

'Send some cold down here then.' Holly kept a wary eye on Reece. 'It's been a sweltering day.'

'Well, I would if I could, dear! Oh I'm so *very* glad I'm in Wales again, even though I miss you all very much. But it won't be long now until I'm back again. Only five sleeps to go, Celyren!'

Holly stifled a groan. If anything was worse than being called by her real name, it was being treated like a baby. *Five 'sleeps'! Please!*

'So what are you doing right now?' Gran went on.

'Dad's just come in and we're about to have dinner.'

'Dad's just come in…' Gran repeated the words in a strange, dull monotone.

There was a long silence. 'You still there, Gran?'

'Yes, dear. I've been thinking today, Celyren. Worrying about something.' There was a crackling pause. 'Did Reece tell you? About the death in the seeing? I didn't know what to make of it, but I… I… well, I couldn't say nothing.'

Holly felt as if she had turned to stone. 'Gran?'

'I had such a fearful night last night, Celyren. Up on the mountain. I thought perhaps the seeing was wrong, but …' The line echoed, magnifying Gran's voice abruptly. 'Celyren, you're old enough to handle the truth. Ask your mother who your real father is.'

Holly stood there, the phone at her ear, feeling faint. *Real father?* She gripped the phone so tightly her knuckles went while.

Old enough to handle the truth? She was dizzy enough to fall. She stared at Reece who stood watching her, one hand behind his back.

'Celyren—are you still there?'

'Yes, Gran,' Holly managed to say.

'Be careful, dear. Trust…' A long burst of static drowned out the next words. '…and then the mountain said he would kill time … time itself…' Gran's voice returned to normal. 'I'm going on to Cardiff this evening, Celyren. I'll be in touch as soon as…' The connection was lost, cutting the call mid-sentence.

Her thoughts reeling, Holly replaced the receiver.

At that moment, Reece struck. Whipping out a water pistol from behind his back, he squirted her straight in the eyes.

'Arghh!' Holly darted after him as he fled to the kitchen and put the kitchen table between them.

'Now come off it, you two. Just what's going on here anyway?' Dad came up behind Holly and folded her into the protection of his arms.

'She wanted to get cool,' Reece said. 'She said so to Gran. I was just trying to help.'

'Help?' The sarcastic edge to her dad's voice was a great comfort to Holly. Reece wasn't usually caught out like this, red-handed and defensive. Right at the moment, standing in the circle of Dad's arms, she just wanted to forget Gran's words. 'Sometimes, you know, I forget that you two are twins.' Dad glared at Reece. 'Start acting your age, son, and not your shoe size. Have you done your chores, young man?'

'They're done, Dad.'

Holly's head tilted as she frowned at Reece, daring him to tell a less slippery truth. Reece stared back, a look of complete innocence on his face. He didn't say another word.

'Holly did Reece's jobs,' Mum said.

'They're still done!' Reece's face twisted into a mutinous scowl. '*And* I'm going to do the washing up instead.'

'I'm here to make sure you do, young man.' Dad sighed and went to sit in his favourite chair. 'What did Gran have to say for herself?' he asked. 'Gallivanting around at her age, I still find it hard to believe she's gone back to the home country at this time of year.'

'She climbed Cader Idris and took photos of moonrise on the snow,' Reece said.

'Cader Idris?' Mum asked. 'Really?' She smiled. 'That's a mountain in Snowdonia National Park. Legend has it that, if you spend midsummer night on the mountain, in the morning you'll be either mad or a poet. A poet good enough, perhaps, to win the coveted Silver Chair of a Chief Bard at the National Eisteddfod.'

'Don't know if I could handle your mother being a poet, Mrs Morgan,' Dad said. 'And where would we put a silver chair?'

Reece's brows beetled into a deep frown. 'I can't understand it. She's been on about this castle of mine long before she went up the mountain.'

'You're afraid she's gone mad?' Dad asked. 'No fear of that, son. You put your finger right on it when you said "long *before* she went up the mountain". She's been off her rocker for years already.'

'*Sam!*' Mum snapped. 'It's my mother you're talking about. And didn't you listen? It's mid*summer* night, not midwinter.'

'It's midsummer *here*.' Dad laughed and slapped his knee. He stopped, his tone changing to mild and placating. 'Just a little joke, darling. Just a joke. The silver chair, too.' He moved his head so that he could look down at Holly. 'So what's all this paper you're cutting up in the sitting room, Holly Polly?'

'I'm making a Christmas tree.' There was a lump in her throat that hadn't been there a minute ago.

'Things aren't so bad that you have to…' Dad began, before

sighing and breaking off. 'You really are a helpful girl, Cerylen. Just let me have a word to your mother and then you can tell me about your tree.'

'Sure.' Holly took a deep breath. *Cerylen. I'm so glad Gran isn't here right now—she gets so fired up when Dad calls me Cerylen and not Celyren.* As she headed back to the sitting room, Retro came out of the corner and assumed a stalking pose. 'Don't even think about whatever it is you're thinking about!'

The puppy slunk straight back into the corner with a plaintive yip. She ignored the huge brown eyes and tiny quivering jaws and began cutting out the tracings with swift, savage hacks.

She was so caught up in misery and foreboding that she didn't notice Retro sidling along the wall until he was reaching upwards. She snatched the foil hand away at the same moment as he swiped. A section of the middle, the shape of a large teardrop, tore in one of his claws. The rest remained with her.

'*Retro!*' Dad exclaimed, as he came into the room. 'Who's been teaching you bad habits?' He hustled the puppy out the door and switched on the television. A spluttering grey haze appeared on the screen. 'Worse than ever. Ted Wheeler said he's having reception problems, too.' He sighed and turned to Holly. 'I thought you said this was a tree.'

'It is.' Holly's voice was low and wistful as she explained.

Dad picked up one of the plastic bags and peered inside. 'So these are tracings of all your friends' hands? That's wonderful, Holly Polly!' He smiled. 'It makes Christmas into something personal. None of the usual trashy commercialism.'

The lump in Holly's throat tightened. Her thoughts kept spinning backwards, in ragged turbulent fragments, towards Gran's words. *REAL father?*

Feeling Dad's eyes on her, she concentrated on Matthew

Murchison's fingers as if they were the most important things in the whole world.

'It'd be so much more convenient,' Dad said, 'if people weren't individuals, wouldn't it? Then you could put all these paper sheets one on top of the other and cut them all out at once.'

Holly said nothing. She stared at the scissors in her hand, unable remember how they worked.

'Are you sure something isn't wrong, Holly?' Dad asked. 'You're very quiet tonight.'

'Dinner's ready,' Mum called from the kitchen.

Holly was grateful for the interruption. She put down the scissors and hurried from the room. Dinner was already on the table, the vegetables steaming.

'Lamb chops!' Reece licked his lips. 'C'mon, Dad! You're being a slowpoke! We're gonna start without you.'

There was a delay. 'Sam!' Mum called, sounding irritable. 'Dinner's getting cold.'

'On a day like today?' Dad sauntered into the room. He sat down, gave thanks and then started to talk about Holly's tree. 'I really like your idea, Holly old Polly.'

Holly fiddled with her food while Reece wolfed down everything on his plate.

'What's up, princess?' Dad asked.

'I'm just not feeling well.'

Reece eyeballed her uneaten chop so steadily Holly thought he would stare a hole right into it. 'Don't want that to go to waste, do you?' he asked. 'There are starving children much closer than Africa who are dying for it.'

'Star*ving*!' Dad half-rolled his eyes at Reece. 'Dying? As if, son. As if!' He divided Holly's chop in two, as Mum brought out the apple pie for dessert.

When dinner was over, Holly cleared the table and Dad went back to the sitting room.

'Where's Reece?' Mum asked as she rinsed the dishes ready for the washing up.

'Gone to give the bones and scraps to Retro,' Holly said.

'Well, he's taking his time.'

'I'll go look.' Holly half-wondered if he might have joined Dad in the sitting room. The stone that was sitting in her belly seemed much heavier and larger. But when she entered the darkened sitting room, her heart instantly lightened. 'Dad!'

'Nice, isn't it?' Dad stepped back, surveying his handiwork.

'It's *lovely!*' Taped to the window, starlight winking through the fingers, half the tree of hands was already up. *It's even better than Nerida's.* Holly was utterly charmed. *It's so... so real. I could almost believe there was an actual tree just inside the window, not just a collage of paper cutouts.* Reece's silver hand was on the top, the teardrop hole in its centre allowing the light of the rising moon to chase the shadows through the room. 'It's magic, Dad!'

'All the credit is yours. I hope you don't mind I put Reece's hand on top.'

Holly gazed upward, enchanted. She did mind, but she didn't want to argue. *Just for you, Dad. I'll put up with his stupid hand, just for you. But he better treat me with a bit more resp...* Her mind seized, mid-word. *She told him,* Holly realised. *Gran's told Reece already about Dad. That's what's eating him...*

Her skin began to tingle. As she continued to look up, patterns began to work themselves across the surface of the silver hand—the foil itself seemed to thicken into a three-dimensional gauntlet. *It must be a trick of the moonlight.* She blinked, trying to clear her vision. But it didn't clear. A shiver of dread spread up her spine, as cold—a strange comparison fixed itself in her mind—as cold as the snow-crusted rocks and the windswept ice on Cader Idris. *Cold, so cold… in this sweltering heat.*

As she blinked again and shook her head, the strangeness in the room disappeared. In an instant. It was just the front sitting room—as normal as ever. 'Has Reece been in here?'

'Trying to avoid the washing up, is he?' Dad asked. 'Here you keep on with this while I go find him. He's not getting out of anything. If it's not to do with the tractor, he seems to think it's beneath his dignity these days.'

As soon as he'd gone, the strangeness returned. She stared at the tree of hands, feeling more overwhelmed with fear every passing moment. She couldn't move. The silver hand had become a living thing. *It's real.* As she gazed at the intricate tattoos, the fingers flexed. A twining helix of light, like the glistening rainbow she had seen in the sky before sunset, reached out of the hole in the centre of the hand. Frost crystals began to form around the outline of the paper tree.

A shrill crackle startled her and as she turned towards the noise, she could have sworn she saw a second taloned claw begin to thrust its way out of the fossil dinosaur egg.

The spiral of light lanced through the room and began to unravel. It separated into long undulating tendrils and shimmering tremulous threads. Moon-white, sun-gold, diamond-glitter filaments coiled over the furniture and slither-climbed the walls, reaching towards her.

Holly turned and ran.

The Tree *of* Time

Holly slammed the door and raced outside into the darkness. 'Dad?' Her throat was dry with fright. 'Where are you?'

A deep growl rose from the ground just in front of her. Startled, she had jumped backwards, before realising it was Retro. The puppy's fur was on end. His stance fierce and his teeth bared, he was staring at the sky. Holly looked up but she couldn't see any obvious menace—just the Southern Cross and its two Pointers twinkling with unusual brilliance.

She glanced back at the house. The dark form of her mother's silhouette walked into the sitting room, stayed a moment, then returned to the kitchen. No cry of alarm or call for help. *It's stress. Caused by Reece and his stupid pranks, Gran and her babblings. I didn't see Reece's hand come alive. I just imagined it.*

Retro's barking became incessant. She reached down to pat him, but he snapped at her fingers before resuming his watch of the sky. 'What is it, Retro?' She looked around. 'Where's Dad?' A torchlight was bobbling up and down in the distance. As she set off towards it, it disappeared behind a looming shadow. *The oak tree. Dad's gone down to see if Reece is in his cubby house.* 'Come on, Retro.'

A rumble emanated from Retro's tiny throat as he snarled at the sky. Holly left him and went down the hill, heading for the tree. The glow of the torch lit up the hollowed-out interior at its base. 'Dad?'

The torchlight cut out so quickly her suspicions flared straight away. 'Reece! Come on out, I've got to talk to you.' No answer.

Holly stomped forward.

'Don't touch anything!' Reece's voice was fierce. 'If you break anything, I'll slug you. Everything in here is fragile and state of the ark.'

'That's state of the *art*.'

The torchlight clicked back to life, revealing a tangle of wires and wheels. An old television console was perched on a tree root and held steady with a harness of fishing lines. In front of it was a wooden crate with knobs, light bulbs and buttons on top, a computer keyboard in front and multicoloured wires dangling underneath with old watches attached to them. Everywhere there was space, a clock was perched.

Behind it all was Reece, standing in a golden glow, his hair a wild aureole of light. He glared at her like a mad scientist.

'No, you're right, this is state of the ark. Maybe even long before Noah's Ark.' Holly stared at the jumble inside the tree. 'Come out. I need to talk to you.'

'About the washing up? I'd be diluted to do it.'

'That's *delighted* to do it.'

'There's no delight about it.'

'Reece, this is not about the washing up.' *It's about Gran. About Dad.* 'You gave a promise, I expect you to keep it.'

'I will keep it one day, sis. But I never promised for *tonight*.'

'Dad won't let you get away with that.' Holly struggled to keep her anger from rising.

'Wanna bet? In this dog-eat-dog world, it's survival of the glibbest.'

For a moment, she was speechless. '*Fittest*,' she corrected. Her lips twisted into a menacing half-smile. She leaned over, taking hold of the largest knob on the fruit crate. 'What does this do?'

'Don't touch it.'

'Why not?'

'I can't answer on the grounds it might incinerate me.'

Holly took a deep breath. *That was his last chance.* 'Not *incinerate*, *incriminate*.' She smiled. 'I'm guessing your time machine won't work without it?' Her voice was so honeyed it was sickly. 'Good!' She reached for one of the dangling watches, yanking as hard as she could. The instant screech of grinding metal set her teeth on edge.

'Don't bring the tree down!' Reece yelled. 'Okay, okay, I'll do the washing up.'

'How kind,' Holly sneered.

'Just get out of my lab and don't touch anything—there's stuff here more valuable than it looks.'

Holly snorted in disbelief. 'Reece, I've got to talk to you…' She paused. '…about Dad. And what Gran said.'

Reece's face was like stone.

'You don't believe Gran about the murder, but you do believe her about Dad not really being…' She hesitated, not sure how to go on. A muscle at the side of Reece's mouth began to spasm. *He's terrified.*

Gathering her thoughts, she turned to gaze out into the darkness beyond the torchlit interior of the tree. Retro had come down the hill but he was still growling at the stars.

'What's up, Retro?' Reece ignored Holly he manoeuvred his way around the jumble of his time machine. He looked out at the night sky. 'That's strange.' He gestured towards a star above the silhouette of the house. 'There's fireworks on Alpha Centauri tonight.'

'That's Alpha Centauri?' Holly stared at the orange star as it pulsed in rapid, brilliant bursts. *He's trying to change the subject.* 'What did Gran say exactly?'

Reece didn't answer for so long Holly thought he wasn't going to reply. 'You remember that man?' His voice was a strained whisper. 'The one who … who… ?'

Holly cut off his stammering. 'Who what?'

'Mum's friend. Remember? The one who was so rich and effluent.'

'That's *affluent*. *Aff*luent: comfortably wealthy. *Eff*luent is what flows out of the toilet.'

'Yes.' Reece nodded. 'Like I said, *effluent.*'

It took her a moment to make the connection. '*That* man?' She bit her lip. *The one who made Mum laugh. And sing.* She and Reece had met him just once three years ago, when he'd come half way across the world to visit. 'You didn't make it easy for me to track you down,' he'd said, kissing her mother's hand and holding her gaze far too long. He'd been a swift and brilliant meteor, giving the twins expensive gifts and making their father cold, watchful and silent for months. For the first time, it occurred to Holly that that was when Reece started visiting his cubby each day—almost hiding out.

'It's his castle on the postcard.' Reece took a deep breath and pointed to the throbbing display of wildlight in the night sky. 'Alpha Centauri…' His change of subject was transparent. '…is the closest star system to the sun.' The star pulsed faster, like the strobe-flashing of lightning. 'Looks like the party to end all parties.'

'*His* castle? But Gran said it was *your* castle.' *I can't think about this.* Holly was gripped by a new panic. *I won't.* A splinter of ice seemed to stab at her heart. Her eyes fixed on Reece's face then followed his gaze up towards the heavens.

A twining spiral of light, glistening with threads of moon-white, sun-gold, rainbow-shimmer, seemed to reach out of the lantern-orange star above. It was the same strange sort of swirling tendril she'd seen back in the sitting room. With Reece beside her, it didn't seem threatening—just a distant coil of unusual colour. 'Is it going to explode?'

'Hope not. Alpha Centauri's a real long way away, but it's still much too close to Earth if it blew up and became a supernova. We'd all be destroyed by the radiation waves.'

'Well, that would solve the problem of the washing up.'

'Haha, sis.'

Retro began to bark.

'So that's where you lot are.' Dad sounded half-angry and half-relieved. 'Thanks, Retro. Good on ya.'

Without warning, a lightbeam hit.

Like curved lightning, it came out of the stars and arced down onto the oak tree. From her vantage point, all Holly could see was Retro, outlined momentarily like a x-ray, and then—instant overwhelming darkness.

She blinked, her eyes dazzled by the after-flash. A shot of light brought Retro back into view. One second he was a blue-black cattle dog, the next his fur was as white as a polar bear's. As he yelped, his eyes became fire-red coals, the tips of his ears tinged crimson. Dad was bounding towards the tree.

Then he vanished. A cascade of iridescent pastel bubbles appeared and rushed across her line of vision. Reece turned on her. 'Look what you've done!'

'*Me?!*'

'If you'd kept your hands off my stuff, this wouldn't have happened.'

'I wasn't touching anything.'

'We could be adrift in time.'

'Yeah, yeah.' Holly was scornful. A slow-drifting whirlpool of pastel bubbles obscured her view of Dad and Retro. 'Sure thing. Your time machine has actually worked?'

'For your information, I'm doing serious scientific research.'

Holly raised her chin. 'You know what I think has happened?' *He wants to argue. He wants to start a fight so he can distract his thoughts from the man with the castle and who he is and what Gran means.* 'I'd say all these bubbles are from that bucket of detergent up in the tree. You know, the one you set with the tripwire to spill on intruders.'

'How'd you know about that?'

'*Reece…!* I've known you all your life and I've never known you to be less than predictable. It's probably still the same bucket of detergent you put there when you were six.'

'Is not. That evaporated years ago.'

Holly reached forward but, to her surprise, her hands didn't meet with detergent. The drifting bubbles seemed to be charged with static electricity. They gave her a sharp buzzing jolt.

Reece tried to punch one of the larger bubbles out of the way, but was thrown backwards as soon as he made contact. 'Yow!' He picked himself up. 'We're trapped.'

'Dad!' Holly called. There was no answer. 'Dad?' She was starting to feel anxious. 'Retro?' She turned to Reece, pointing to the bubbles. 'What're we going to do? And what is this stuff?'

'Let me think.' Reece took a step backwards.

Think? Holly sat down, hugging her knees. Instead of their present predicament all she could think of was her father's face as he'd watched her mother and The Man walk hand in hand in the sunset. She thrust the image from her mind and concentrated on the bubbles as they expanded and burst in a slow motion ballet, merged with other bubbles, and then swirled again, colliding and combining in an ever-changing display of luminous pastels.

She stifled a yawn. Her eyelids drooped. She could hear Reece's voice, calling her—calling, calling—from a long way off. 'Far away,' she whispered. 'Over the hills and far away…'

'Far away, yes, too *far away*,' a tiny voice near her ear said, '*for you to reach before Dreamfall.*' *Dreamfall?* She shook herself awake. 'Wha…?!' She felt so drowsy.

'Come and help me, I said.' Reece sounded annoyed. 'I think the problem is the battery.'

Taking care to avoid the bubbles, Holly got up and tried to rub the sleep out of her eyes. 'What battery?'

'I think that when you pulled on the wires something snapped, which means the electrical circuit couldn't close even though you jerked the knob to activate the car battery. Except the bucket of detergent seems to have made a conducting pathway anyway.'

'You're trying to blame me for this. But it's not my fault. We bounced off the bubbles. They're like rubber. Rubber doesn't conduct electricity.'

'They might be *like* rubber, but they're *not* rubber.'

'Well, they're your problem. After all, this is *your* tree. Come on. Think of something.'

'I already have. I'm going to disconnect the battery. Now your job is to grab that wheel…' He pointed to one behind a line of clocks. '…and reel the wires in. That way we've got a chance of breaking the circuit one way or another.'

'I suppose it's worth a try.' She reached up gingerly for the old rusty wheel, touching it with a fingertip. Realising it wasn't conducting an electrical charge, she took firmer hold of it. She could see some faint patches of faded pink paint on the wheel and realised it had once belonged, years before, to the trike she'd had as a toddler.

Without warning, she lost her grip as the wheel flew out of her hands. Like a bullet, it sped into the bubbles, forming a hollow as it went. She ducked as it ricocheted back, but it only reached as far as the line of clocks before it was pulled back into the swirling surface. The clocks tumbled and their hands shot off, like wild arrows, into the spinning shape. It flattened slowly until at last it was twice as wide as before. It had become a bright fluid silver.

'Magnetic attraction,' Reece gasped, round-eyed.

'Bubbles aren't magnetic.' Holly stared at the gleaming wheel. The wall of bubbles had been pulled out of shape by its passage— now it was curved outwards, away from the tree. Patterns were starting to form on the wheel, patterns just like the intricate markings she'd seen on the silver hand in the sitting room. *It's a moko. I should have recognised it before. It's a Māori tattoo.* But there were also clock hand shapes in the mix.

'They've became ionised,' Reece said. 'I don't know how—but they're ionised.'

'What?'

'Like an aurora. The bubbles have got an electric charge, and electricity has a magnetic field. That's why it's called electro-*magnetic* radiation.'

A roarer? Holly was baffled. But she wasn't game to ask. Reece could put anything over her by way of explanation and she wasn't sure she believed anything he was saying. It wasn't just that he was good at embellishing the truth when it suited him, he also was extremely adept at making up whatever he needed to fill the gaps in his ignorance.

'I'll just try to disconnect the battery again.'

'If he does that, the Shield will fail. And if the Shield fails, you will be found. And if you are found before Dreamfall, things will go the worse for you.'

'What'd you say?' Reece's face was a picture of incredulity.

'Nothing.' Holly shook her head and looked for the source of the voice. Reece was glaring at her in disbelief, when she felt a peculiar sensation. Her feet had left the ground. 'Reece!'

'What?'

'I'm... I'm floating.'

'Yeah sure. I always knew your head was full of hot air.'

Next to Holly, the fruit crate had also begun a slow ascent. She turned and realised that everything that wasn't attached had lost contact with the ground. At last Reece started floating too. 'It's okay, it's okay.' He sounded as if he were trying to stifle a rush of fear. 'All we've lost is a little gravity.'

'How can you lose gravity?'

'If you're in free space, like aboard a rocket, for instance, then you're in zero gravity ...' Reece flung out his hand, reaching for a knob of wood and seizing it. 'But that's not possible, so ... this must ... just be ... uhhh ... a simulation.'

'How?' Holly felt a surge of terror. 'How did we get from your cubby house to a zero gravity simulation?'

Reece steadied himself against an upright plank. 'If you raise your arm slowly towards me, I'll reach over and pull you down.'

'What if that doesn't work?'

'Then I'll wait until your head hits the top of the hollow and I'll pull you down by your knees.'

Holly considered the practicality of his suggestions. 'But what if the tree's floating too?' She began to raise her arm. '*Reece!*' She was falling in slow-motion, head over heels, out the doorway and back towards the wall of bubbles.

'I'm coming!' Reece looped the strap of the torch over his head and pushed off from the trunk towards her. He fell into a rapid-tumble spin and went hurtling over her head. He bounced, sparking and buzzing, with a painful jolt off the bubble wall. 'Heeeeeeeeeeeeeeeeelllllp!' Bumping into the tree just above the entrance, he plummeted to the ground, shot back up and spiralled towards the bubble wall, and rebounded towards the ceiling. Colliding with Holly, he sent her into a tailspin before heading back in a wild rolling tumble. He finally managed to slow down by taking his water pistol out of his pocket and squirting a jet of water backwards under his armpit. 'Retro-rocket! Just like on a spaceship.'

Holly was startled when he managed to hook his foot into her elbow and they both glided slowly to a kind of floating stop. 'Reece, there are people who say you can't keep your head in an emergency, but they don't have a clue what they're talking about.' It was as close as she dared come to thanks. There was silence. They floated, both staring at the silver wheel in the middle of the bubble wall. It seemed to be larger than ever. 'Any more ideas?'

'Not any that don't involve a fair bit of movement. Which we need to restrict at the moment.'

'Can you squirt us away from the bubbles?'

'I'm out of water.'

'Oh.'

The bubble wall began to sizzle and crackle, splitting down the middle as it melted away. 'Yes!' Holly felt the utmost relief as, with a gentle thump, she dropped to the floor. 'We're free!'

Reece was staring into the darkness beyond the disappearing bubbles. 'Sis, where'd that wall come from?'

A very solid-looking metal wall was standing where once there had been nothing more than an overhang of oak branch. 'Reece, it's got a door in it.'

'I did notice that.' Reece's brow was puckered in thought. 'You reckon we should open it?'

The silver wheel, which had once been part of Holly's pink baby trike, was in the centre of the door. Its strange moko-like engravings and clock hands flickered in the shadowy light. Holly shook her head. 'It's spooky. I don't like it.'

'Well, give me another option.'

'Let's look around. Maybe we can get out behind the tree.'

'I think we should go together. Very strange things are happening here.'

'That's an understatement.'

Reece took a deep breath. 'I'd like to look at the wheel close up. Not touch it, sis, just look at it.'

Holly nodded as Reece shone the torch directly on it. *'Spooky' doesn't even begin to cut it. It's positively dangerous. We've just got to find another way out of here.*

Reece gestured to her to move along the wall. It was seamless dirty metal which went up about three metres to a dark dusky ceiling. Only half a dozen paces to the left they came to a corner. Another dozen to the left and there was another corner. Another dozen and another corner. Then just a few more and they were back at the silver wheel, having gone right around the oak tree. 'We're in the middle of a metal room.'

'How did we get here? With a *tree*?' Holly took a deep breath. 'And more importantly, where are we?'

'Insufficient information to determine at this time.'

'And how are we going to get out of here?' Holly pointed towards a faint glow of light near the floor. 'Reece, look!'

'Careful.' Reece pointed the torch towards the glow.

Holly realised something was wedged tight in the tree's roots. It was a box, covered in symbols. The lid was dented. Reece picked it up and prised it open. There was nothing inside.

'What's an empty box doing here?' Holly asked.

'It's not empty. It's full of air.'

'Is that supposed to be clever?' She spotted a patch of white packing material nestled in amongst the roots and bent to pick it up. 'Here's what was in it.' As she pulled the glistening filaments apart, a thousand tiny stars danced in the torchlight. 'Oh!' She caught her breath as she held up the mesh of silver filigree. A shaped, jewelled collar—threaded with winking gold-tinted diamonds—gleamed like a ribbon of stars. 'Wars would be fought over this necklace, Reece.'

'Put it down.' Reece's tone was sharp.

'Why?'

'It isn't yours.' He scowled. 'Put it down, sis.'

'Boys would swoon over me if I wore this.'

'You're making my skin crawl, the way you're talking.'

Holly held it against her neck. 'It'd make me beautiful beyond compare.'

'Cut it out, sis. You're scaring me.'

'This scares you more than anything that's happened so far?'

'I don't mind admitting I've been terrified tonight. But it's nothing compared to this. Put the necklace back and let's find a way out of here.'

'Take it with you. It is the integrated mesh of a tachyon decelerator. You will need it to pass the wheeltrap and reach Dreamfall safely.'

'Sis, *don't* do that.'

'It wasn't me, Reece.' Holly looked around uneasily. The voice seemed to echo from a distance, and yet still be close at hand. *Someone's watching us.*

Reece closed his eyes and took a deep breath. 'Maybe we should try the door, after all.'

'I don't like that wheel.'

'I don't know what else we can do.'

'Are you still scared?'

'Beyond imag…'

Without warning, Holly found herself thrown to the floor. The room began to tilt. The necklace fell out of her hand; Reece hit the ground beside her.

She tried to get up, but she felt every part of her body getting heavier and heavier. So heavy that after a few moments straining, she was pulled back flat. Her hands seemed like tonne weights, her back felt as if it were trying to press its way through the floor. Even trying to lift one finger needed a superhuman effort. The pressure was enormous.

But where is it coming from?

'Hhhhoooollllllyy…'

She could see Reece trying to say her name. His lips were pulled back, the muscles of his face were distorted by the strange unstoppable force that seemed to come out of nowhere and go on forever. *Are we going to die?*

Then, almost as quickly as it had come upon them, the mysterious pressure ended. Holly had a sudden pounding headache.

'Let's try the door before something else happens.' Reece pulled Holly to her feet.

Together they went to the door. Just as Reece put out his hands to grasp the central wheel, a voice seemed to come from the oak tree behind them. '*Set the tachyon decelerator to stability function and you will be able to escape the wheeltrap.*'

'Stop!' Holly commanded. Reece jerked his hands away from the silver wheel. She glared at him. 'I'm getting the necklace.'

Reece scowled at her. 'It's not a necklace—it's a tachyon decelerator.'

'I'm getting it anyway.' Holly darted off to pick up the jewelled collar. She watched Reece out of the corner of her eye as he glowered at the door and muttered to himself.

'Tachyons…' he was saying. 'The weird voice can't be Holly playing tricks. She knows nothing about the simplest physics, let alone particles with negative mass that travel backwards in time. I don't get anything about this.'

Particles with negative mass that travel backwards in time? Huh? Holly stared at the collared necklace, stroking it gently. *Sometimes Reece's science is stranger than Gran's ramblings. At least when she tells the story about Merlin living backwards in time, I know it's just a legend. But when Reece goes on…*

He was still talking to himself. 'Let me think it out… first, we're floating like in zero gravity. Then we've got so much gravity, it's like atmospheric re-entry. This is the sort of simulation astronauts go through…' He looked at her, his eyes narrowing as he watched her fingering the jewels. 'It's impossible to be aboard a rocket but it's the only thing that makes any sense.' He raised his voice and nodded at the necklace. 'I bet that thing's more dangerous than this wheel. It gives me a really bad feeling.'

'I'm fine with it. I'll wear it.' Too late she realised her tone was far too eager.

'No!' It was a snap. 'Give it to me.'

'Why?' Holly failed to keep the petulance out of her voice. 'What are you going to do with it?'

Reece hesitated. 'I'm going to set its stability function.'

'Yeah? How?'

Again Reece hesitated. 'The thing's obviously made to be worn. So *I'm* going to put it on.'

'Why can't I then?' Holly tightened her grip on the necklace.

Reece sighed, obviously choosing his words carefully. 'Because a feeling of dread creeps up my spine every time you talk about it. It's a trap for you, but not for me.'

'What's that supposed to mean?'

'I reckon it's here to tempt you.' His voice began to sound more confident as he squinted at the mesh in her hands. He laughed, as if trying to ease his own nerves. The sound echoed back, brittle and thin, through the gloom. 'It sure ain't going to enhance my beauty.'

As soon as the words were out of his mouth, Holly felt a surge of emotion, a wave of almost crushing disappointment, emanate from the door. She knew in an instant Reece had stumbled on some part of the truth. The level of seething frustration radiating towards her was stunning. The desire to put the necklace on was replaced by a different compulsion. 'Let's hurry.' She was propelled by a new sense of urgency.

'Right… Quickly, put it on …' Reece was hesitant once more. '…yes … on my head.'

It took an immense effort for Holly to reach her hands up and place the jewelled mesh on Reece's head, rather than around her own neck. 'This crown…' Reece straightened, his sudden smile dark and cold. '…with it, I could rule the entire…'

'Crown?' Holly interrupted. 'It doesn't look anything like … Reece, it's changing…'

'Take it off his head. *Now.* Put it around his neck!'

Holly jerked the coronet-like mesh off Reece's head, half-strangling him as she pulled it taut against his throat. It settled back into a necklace shape. 'I sure hope something about this works.'

'So do I.' Reece coughed and shook his head, as if to clear it. He placed his hands on the silver wheel. Instinct led Holly to put one of her arms around his waist and the other on the necklace. The gold-tinted diamonds in the mesh began to pulse. 'Now!'

Slowly, he began to turn the wheel.

The Tree *of* Clouds

A sudden hiss turned into a rushing roar. The engravings on the wheel flashed golden and the clock hands turned blood red. Reece felt the tips of the clock hands turn into spikes. It was all he could do to hold on. He lurched forward as the wheel warped in his hands and collapsed, almost pulling him and Holly into a dark windswept vortex. The door disintegrated outwards. Fragments hurtled into a cavernous passage swirling with shadows like clock hands and glowing tattoos.

Reece's shirt whipped around him. Holly's hair was a frenzied tangle obscuring his vision as he turned to shout at her. 'Hold tighter.' He was sure she couldn't hear him. He had no idea how he was managing to hold his ground against the pull of the vortex.

Or maybe I do. Maybe this is 'stability function'. The mesh around his throat glowed with increasing brightness. He could see a pulse of light racing faster and faster around the diamond clusters. A steady halo shone above Holly. He could feel his hair standing on end.

He stepped forward.

The dark vortex disappeared and, at the same moment, the light around his neck died. Behind him he could hear Holly's sigh of relief.

A night sky was framed by an open hatchway. Stars glittered across its inky blue expanse. A hot wind rustled through the dry grass on a hillock. Reece took another step forward.

Everything seemed normal—finally. The Southern Cross was right overhead. 'Dad! Dad? Are you here?'

He felt something at his throat and realised it was Holly unhooking the necklace. He glared at her as she wrapped it around her wrist. *Pointless saying anything.* At least the thing seemed far less sinister under a familiar, friendly sky.

'Are we home?' Holly asked.

'I don't think we've come too far.' He gazed out across the starlit landscape and pointed to a line of low hills silhouetted in the distance. 'I think I recognise them.'

'I don't.' Holly shook her head.

Reece peered left and right, trying to make out exactly what the long sleek shape they'd stepped out of actually was. But, in the cloying darkness, he could only see mysterious and dappled shadows. The feeling of reassurance he'd had on first stepping out the hatchway was fading fast. 'C'mon.' He gestured at the slope in front of them. 'Let's go up this hill, have a good look around, and get our bearings.'

Holly followed without arguing. That was a surprise. As he strode off he was became aware of the silence. *Eerie.* The grass beneath his feet felt odd. It bounced aside like elastic.

Holly broke into a run and bounded past him. He flew after her and they topped the hill in less than a minute. He was panting as he reached her, his hands on his knees. Together, as if they were both fearful of what they'd find, they turned to look back the way they'd come.

In the middle of a field—its cargo hold wide open, just as they'd left it, was a double-finned jet. Even by starlight, he could see how enormous it was.

'Whose backyard did you think we were in?' Holly asked.

Reece struggled keep his composure. His thoughts seemed half-frozen. 'It's… an experimental aircraft that … somehow managed to scoop us up by accident.'

'And half a tree at the same time?' Holly was shaking. 'Reece, we were in space, weren't we?'

Reece looked straight up and considered what had happened. 'It must be an orbital shuttle. Fortunately, what goes up must come down.'

'I've been to space.' Holly nudged him. 'No one's ever going to believe it.'

Phone. If only. 'I don't suppose you've got your mobile?'

'I wouldn't have waited this long to yell for help, if I had.'

'Well, let's get some bearings.' He pointed out five stars. 'The Southern Cross and the Pointers form a navigational aid…' But there was only one Pointer.

He frowned as a blush of peach-coloured light spread across the horizon. Sunbursts shafted upwards, as dawn arrived accompanied by a chorus of birdsong.

'Were we out all night?' Holly asked.

Reece shot a pointed look towards the necklace wrapped around her wrist. It had become a jewelled cuff bracelet. 'Tachyon decelerator equals time distortion.'

'You just made that up.'

Before he could retort that it was an educated deduction, sounds echoed up from the landing field. A huge section of the jet's front canopy was raised and a ramp slid to the ground. Several black uniformed figures emerged from the canopy and strode down the ramp. 'Told you it was a military operation,' he whispered.

'No, you didn't. You said it was an experimental aircraft.'

'Same thing.' He crouched down, pulling her with him as he watched the men moving around the jet. Urgent shouting followed the discovery of the open hatchway.

Holly lowered her voice. 'Do we throw ourselves on their mercy and ask for help?' She paused. 'Or do we run?'

It didn't take a second to decide. 'Run.'

They slithered down the far side of the hill. Halfway down, the ground behind his heels exploded. He glanced over her shoulder. Silhouetted on the hilltop against a waste of stars, he could see a group of dark figures. Some had rifles aimed, some were watching their progress through binoculars. Then, as he saw a flash from one of the rifles, a small pile of stones right between him and Holly was hit by a pale bolt of pulsing light. As it burst into a firestorm of hot pebbles, they both jumped aside. 'They're trying to separate us. Stick together, sis.'

'But we make a bigger target together,' Holly panted.

'Maybe.' His own breathing was ragged. 'But they can pick us off more easily if we separate.'

Holly wasn't fooled. She must have seen the fear written all over his face. 'I'm glad you're as scared as I am.' Together they pounded over the top of an incline which hid them momentarily from pursuit.

'Look!' He pointed across a ravine of stone scree to a stand of trees. 'If we can reach that, we might be able to find a place to hide.' Down the hillside they went, sliding on the loose stones. They scrambled up the far embankment and dived behind the nearest tree trunk.

Reece bent over, sucking in deep gasps of air. Turning, he found the tree had long thick aerial roots to peer through. Strange grids of light—winking squares of red and blue—were moving in complete silence through the darkness towards them. For a moment, he couldn't work out what the blinking signified. Then: 'Robots!'

Holly blanched.

Reece stared, trying to come up with a plan. Robots were chasing them: steel men with communication lights blinking in a breastplate array. Long ribbed metal arms with silver skeletal hands were waving up and down as the robots tried to keep balance while tumbling down the steep scree. Above them, black uniformed figures directed them towards their target.

'Maybe we should give ourselves up,' Holly suggested.

Reece stared at the jewelled cuff on her wrist. It had shrunk and now fitted her forearm perfectly. 'They must want the tachyon decelerator.'

'It's mine.' Holly's tone was fierce and protective. '*Mine.*'

'It's going to get us killed.' Reece folded his arms. 'Now is not the time to get into one of your stubborn moods, Hol.' He stared at her. 'Take it off, sis. Maybe we can buy our way out of this.'

Holly snarled at him. 'It's mine.'

'Hol*ly*…' Reece pleaded.

Holly clenched her fists. Then with an obvious and enormous effort, she held out her arm. 'You take it off, Reece. I don't think I can do it myself.'

He ripped the bracelet from her. Stripping off his shirt, he waved it as he stepped from behind the tree trunk. 'Don't shoot!' He held up the silver mesh bracelet in his other hand. The diamonds caught the sunlight and spun it into a shimmering web of palest gold. 'Don't shoot. Please. We surrender.'

On the far side of the ravine, one of the black uniformed men bellowed at him. 'Aghin! Estaisin m'rendi!'

He waved his shirt steadily in what he hoped was a peaceful

fashion. And he held the bracelet even higher.

A narrow beam of searing light shot out from one of the robots. Reece turned his face aside, blinking as he tried to shield his eyes against the stark, white headlight. The man yelled again. Reece half-turned towards Holly. 'I don't think these guys are *our* military.'

Holly sounded incredulous. 'You mean you actually thought they were?'

'Aghin!' the man barked again. The robots stopped in their tracks. The man waved a gauntleted hand, gesturing to one of his troopers. The selected man ran forward but, instead of plummeting down the scree as Reece expected, he leapt high in the air.

Reece stared, open-mouthed, as the trooper executed a perfect somersault across the ravine and landed less than an arm's length away. Speechless, his first thought was to wonder why they needed such clumsy robots. His second was to be afraid. Seriously afraid.

'Here.' Reece held the bracelet towards the trooper. But the man only raised his rifle and pointed it straight at his head.

He waved the bracelet desperately. 'I'm not armed. Except with a water pistol.' He felt rattled. 'You want that, too?' He began to reach for the toy gun.

'*Reece!*'

He froze at Holly's scream. She crashed through the aerial roots and cannoned into the trooper just as he fired. The shot went wide. It hit one of the robots halted on the slope, punching a huge smoking hole through its chest and sending a billow of sparks spraying into the air. The air glistened with a sudden puffball of stars as Holly grabbed for the rifle before the trooper could aim again.

She missed.

Move. She's buying time. Move.

But it was as if his muscles had forgotten how to function.

Before he could blink, three figures came somersaulting across the ravine, just as the first trooper had done. Moments later, he and Holly were surrounded.

'We're unarmed.' Holly held up her hands in surrender. 'And civilians. And if you don't watch it, I'm …I'm …I'm going to scream.' She let out a piercing shriek.

Reece couldn't work out whether it was stupid or an act of genius. One trooper raised his rifle and aimed it at her. He turned, as if waiting for orders from the leader on the far side of the ravine. Half a second later, he was sailing through the air. The aerial roots of the tree had risen in a hissing vibrating mass and were swinging out like lashing hooves. Another trooper hurtled headlong into the ravine. And then the last two more were whipped onto the flinty scree.

An avalanche of stones took them to the bottom. The robots had been re-activated and charging up the slope, striding over the avalanche as if it were an escalator.

Reece sensed Holly's panic and turned to grab her hand and run. The roots, hissing and trembling, were too quick. Musky coils wrapped around them both. A moment later, they were swung up into the air. He expected to be dashed to the ground, but he could feel himself being hoisted higher and higher. The more he struggled, the tighter he was swathed. He felt smothered by a strange smell of earth and decay, and could hear sounds of confusion below as he was passed along and up, from one cocooning root to another. The noises behind him became more and more distant, the hissing changed to a slow soothing murmur like a lilting lullaby. *It's a cradle.* He rose higher and higher to the sound of swaying, hypnotic rhythms. His eyelids drooped, heavy with sleep. He tried to stay awake, but it was no use. *Far away,* a voice seemed to sing inside his head, *far away... over the hills and faraway...*

A cold, freshening breeze woke him, hours later. He yawned and stretched. Holly was already up and sitting near his feet. Rubbing his eyes, he discovered they were in a bowl-like hollow lined with velvet moss. The rim of the hollow was a band of striated wood and, as the leaves overhead were lifted by the wind, he could see starlight piercing the curtain of night above. *A whole day gone.*

Memory came in flashes. *The light from the sky, the experimental aircraft, the troopers, their weapons, the strange roots…*

'Reece,' Holly said, 'I think we're further from home than you thought.' She pointed at the horizon. A pale green moon, surrounded by a set of brilliant white rings, was rising.

Reece, stunned, counted the rings. 'Seven.' Terror rose. And then subsided. *If Holly can take this in her stride, I'm not going to panic. I won't be shown up by a mere girl.* 'Where we are?'

'We're up a very tall tree.'

It wasn't what he'd meant, but he supposed it was as good an answer as any. He took a deep breath and considered the enormity of the fact that they really were—somehow—on another planet. He peered over the edge of the moss-lined hollow. By the light of the seven-ringed moon, he could see the ground far, far below. *Very tall tree? That's an understatement. We must be as high as the clouds.* He gazed out on snow-smudged mountains. As he turned, the glinting peaks disappeared, dropping away to dark rolling plains. Craning his head, he looked up at the shadowy crest of the tree high above her. 'How did we get so high? This can't be the same forest, Holly. I'd have noticed a tree like this.'

'How are we going to find our way back?'

'For a start, what goes up must come down.' Reece grimaced. 'But we're going to need a rope.'

'Rope?' Holly pointed to the huge gap between the branch they were on and the next one down. 'Speak for yourself, Reece. I want an elevator. Nothing less.'

'*One elevator. Coming up.*' A soft whisper seemed to emanate from the leaves.

Reece jumped. 'Holly?'

'Not me.' Holly's eyes were apprehensive as they searched their immediate surroundings.

'Okay, enough!' Reece realised it was the same voice they'd heard on the ship. 'Who are you?'

'*Your coming has been anticipated. It would be advisable to attempt to behave in a manner befitting the fulfillers of prophecy.*'

I'm dreaming. I'll wake up soon.

'*Your arrival on Dreamfall has been awaited for centuries.*'

Proves I'm asleep. Dreamfall must be a dreaming place.

'Where is Dreamfall?' Holly asked.

How can she be sharing my dream? On the other hand, maybe it's not 'where' but 'when'… 'Is it like the Dreamtime? With the rainbow serpent?'

'I saw it.' Holly's eyes were enormous. 'The rainbow serpent. In the sky. Just before this happened. At least, I saw something—it was all different colours and it…' Her lower lip disappeared between her teeth. '…was weird.'

Reece tried to marshal his thoughts. 'We can't have gone back to the Dreamtime. It's impossible.'

'And going to another planet isn't?' Holly asked.

'*Your elevator has arrived. A modicum of dignity would enhance your prospects.*'

'Elevator!?' Holly scrambled back as far as she could, just as two moon-bright eyes appeared over the edge of the hollow.

Reece froze as a silvery-green snout poked upwards and the glowing eyes began to study them. 'Llylli lyy'ev'li?' The voice belonging to the silvery-green snout was as liquid as water cascading over long-smoothed rocks.

The snout came closer and Reece could see the wide lustrous eyes had lilac irises and sweeping long-fringed lashes.

'An honour to meet you,' Holly squeaked, nudging Reece with her elbow.

'Yes. Absolutely.' He tried not to sound as wary as he felt. 'A huge honour.'

'Llyli-uu?' the snout asked.

He shrugged and raised his hands, gesturing his lack of comprehension.

'Glyffy-llyli?' Another snout emerged right beside Reece, satin nose sniffing, lavender eyes wide with what seemed to be astonishment, pewter-green skin wrinkled in a puzzled frown. 'Hmmm…hmm.' The creature gave a snort.

'You wouldn't be here to help us down?' Holly asked.

The creature gave another snort. 'Hmmm…hmm.'

'Does that mean "yes"?' Reece asked. 'Or "no"?'

'Glyffy-didee?' The creature's companion raised its neck so that its full head was over the hollow. 'Koko?' Holly and Reece both leaned away from it.

'Hey!' Holly clicked her fingers. 'I've got it!'

Both creatures jerked away and disappeared below the rim of the hollow.

'Got what?' Reece asked.

'Glyffy's her name.'

'How'd you figure that out? And how do you know it's a her?'

Holly just shrugged. Reece stretched over the rim and got a full look at the strange creatures. They were giraffe-like with long flat ears, immense necks, short haunches and agile, nimble legs—legs so long they reached right to the next branch far below. 'Glyffy.' Reece held out his hand. 'Pleased to meet you. I'm Reece.'

He pointed to himself and repeated his name. 'Reece.'

The eyes of the giraffe-like creature narrowed. 'Leeze.'

'Hey, great!' Reece grinned. 'Houston, our problems are solved. This is like "Me Tarzan, you Jane." We'll be swinging out of this tree shortly.'

'Be sensible, Reece.' Holly squatted by his side. 'Holly,' she said, pointing to herself.

'Olly,' the creature repeated.

'Hi, Glyffy,' Holly said. 'Can you help us down?'

'Hmm… hmmmm.' Lilac eyes narrowed as the snout rose level with her face. 'Koko?'

'What's that mean?' Reece asked.

Glyffy's snout rose higher into the air and came down again, her neck bent in a long sinuous loop. She grabbed Reece in her mouth and, with a quick heft, pulled him over the edge. It was so fast he didn't have time to be afraid before he was deposited against the other creature. Grabbing hold of a ruff of fur at its neck, he felt a ripple underneath him. And then he was sitting—on a crick in the neck of an alien giraffe.

'If you think I'm going…' Holly was cut off as the creature Reece was riding bent forward to grab her. She flapped her arms for a second before being pushed against Glyffy's neck. As she began to slip, the neck folded to support her. 'On second thoughts…' Her whisper was a hoarse, frightened rasp. '…a rope *is* a better idea than an elevator.'

Glyffy jumped.

'Arrghh!' Holly screamed.

Reece stared. One branch, one scream. Two branches, two screams. Three branches. Either Holly's yelling was becoming muted by distance or she was becoming less frightened.

The giraffe he was on waited until Glyffy had made seven

jumps before following. Reece felt himself whooshing downward through the air and landing with a thump on a lower branch. It was almost exhilarating.

Thump.

Whoosh.

Thump.

Whoosh.

Thump.

How many branches are there?

Whoosh.

Thump.

Whoosh.

Thump.

Whoosh.

Thump.

Whoosh.

Thump.

Thump.

Thump.

Thump.

The branches are closer together.

Thump.

Thump.

The last jump brought Reece to the ground in the middle of a herd of willow-green giraffes. The creatures all peered at him and Holly in silence. A wall of eyes enclosed them. The eyes glinted, unyielding and inscrutable, as hard and beautiful as onyx.

'Errgh! What a smell!'

'Ssshhhhh, Leeze!' said Glyffy.

Holly giggled. 'Which in anybody's language means: "keep quiet, Reece."' Her laughter stopped as she cringed under the circling wall of eyes. 'Hello, there. Thank you.'

The wall began to break up to reveal dozens of individual creatures. With long leisurely paces, Glyffy began to move forward. A path cleared before her. Reece's giraffe fell in beside her and, with a few long strides, they were clear of the vicinity of the tree. A dozen strides further, they came to a high precipice.

Below them, Reece could see a wide plain, gentled by moonlight.

'Are we going down there?' Holly patted Glyffy. 'That's where we came from, isn't it? That's where the landing field is?' The giraffe tilted its head, as if considering her words.

'Look!' Reece pointed to a reflection winking intermittently on the plain far below. Strings of tiny black and silver men were fanned out across a wide front, directing scores of robots in a search pattern. 'Uh, oh.' Reece glanced at the sky. Tiny glossy shapes were speeding towards them: black silhouettes, their outlines pin-pricked in red, resembling helicopters, only much smaller.

'What are they?'

In the pin-drop silence which followed Holly's question, Reece could hear the distant buzzing whirr of their blades and a likeness came to his mind. 'Hornets.'

'They're looking for us. Aren't they?'

Reece didn't answer.

'Hmmm,' snorted Reece's giraffe.

'Hmmm,' snorted Glyffy. Together, they turned away from the edge of the precipice and headed back towards the tree. Their strides were so long the kilometre was covered in seconds. They passed under its canopy, the herd following. They turned away from the snow-topped peaks ahead and galloped down into a broad valley.

Sprinting on, they rounded a spur of rock where the valley branched. They continued up a steep, narrow section and were soon walled in by vast overhanging rock faces. The herd moved faster, overtaking them as they headed into a ravine. Darkness dropped like a curtain as they entered it. Not even the light of the seven-ringed moon filtered down to the ravine floor. Echoes of their passage reverberated like thunder from the rock overhangs. They were travelling at a tremendous rate.

'I'm sure we'd win the Indy.' Reece waved at Holly.

She was white-faced but her smile was brave. 'This must be just like wearing seven-league boots in fairy stories. We're eating up the landscape like it's a stroll to the back fence.'

Reece's eyes were becoming accustomed to the dimness in the ravine. Looking back he could just see the huge cloud-seeking tree dwindling into the distance. *Fifty kilometres. Holly's right about eating up the landscape.* Reece could also see swirling patches of dust raised by the movement of the herd. *I hope that's not visible down on the plain.*

He began to suspect they were following a trail. The path led steadily upward, narrowing as it went so the herd could only travel two abreast. He could see the advance guard ahead of them. Glyffy shifted position so that Reece was diagonally in front of her.

They're anticipating an ambush. And they've placed us so that, whatever side an attack comes from, one of us has a chance of being safe. Even as he thought it, a roar came above and, with a wild buzzing whirr, one of the hornet 'copters descended into the gorge. It dived under the rock overhangs and skimmed along the top of the herd. Twin spotter beams, fore and aft of the 'copter, zigzagged across the racing animals. 'Keep your head down!' Reece yelled at Holly.

She buried her face in Glyffy's fur, shrinking against the green skin. He copied her action.

The 'copter swept by overhead and was soon a fading echo. 'He missed us.' Reece watched the lights of the 'copter vanish into the dust haze behind them. His relief was short-lived. The giraffes slipped out from under the shelter of the rock ledges as the path began to ascend the cliff face.

Worse, the pastel colours of dawn were beginning to limn the sky.

Worse still, the track disappeared.

But, sure-footed, the giraffes leapt upward to the nearest outcropping of rock and kept on going. Soon they were nearing the top and a freezing wind was springing up. Reece was just swallowing to make his ears 'pop' when an entire flight of hornet 'copters swept over the rim of the cliff. Soaring in a tight disciplined arc, they whirred up beside Reece and Holly, matching the speed of the giraffes as they climbed.

They were so close that Reece could see the face of the 'copter pilot as he pulled back on the controls of his craft and a pair of snub-nosed barrels suddenly protruded from the front.

'He's going to shoot!' Holly yelled.

A moment later, fire engulfed the side of the mountain.

The Tree *of* Glass

In the sudden smoke, confusion and gouts of spouting flame, Reece didn't realise for a few moments what had happened. Then he saw a giraffe, with a deft kick, send a rock straight into the rotor blades of the nearest 'copter, and it made sense. The machine wobbled for a second before crashing into the side of the cliff. Blazing tongues of fire ripped through the air and fragments of rock exploded from the cliff-face. A flying splinter of stoneshatter tore a hole in the fuselage of one of the other hornets, sending it into the ravine below.

Giraffes scattered as a exploding pillar of flame surged up from the ravine floor.

The remaining hornets pulled back. Once beyond the range of any projectiles kicked by the giraffes, they began raking the cliff-face with short bursts of laser fire. Reece felt a shot whizz past his ear. Panic-stricken giraffes began leaping up the path, trying to elude the deadly 'copters. Looking straight up, he saw three giraffes launch themselves from the very top of the cliff in a desperate attempt to cross the ravine. Their legs hurdling nothing but the breeze, they propelled themselves into mid-air. Out, out they went, legs flailing recklessly, in a wide arc. One by one, they dropped, their long legs suddenly entangling in the whirring blades of a 'copter. Reece stared as blood-splattered limbs stalled the hornets, sending them hurtling to the ravine floor. He was torn between horror at the gruesome death of the giraffes and profound relief so many 'copters had been destroyed.

The hornets swarmed still further back, out of range but gaining on the giraffes carrying Reece and Holly. Just as the lead 'copter got a fix and moved into firing range, a cry came on the far side of the canyon.

Half the 'copters wheeled upwards in tight arcs, rotating to the rear. Reece stared across the chasm, but could see nothing. Only the shadows of the ledges and clefts along the cliff-face. As he watched, the 'copters began to fire into one particular shadow. Flashing bolts of silver immediately speared back out of it. Four of them made their mark—one in the vulnerable fuselage of a hornet, the other three hitting the pilots. Control lost, the 'copters spiralled dangerously in the narrow confines of the ravine. One side-swiped another and both exploded in a violent fireburst.

The heat of the double blast was so enormous Reece felt his eyes were frying and his skin sizzling. He was sure his eardrums had gone: straight afterwards, there was a silence so immense the whole world seemed to hold its breath.

He expected to hear a stampede of frantic giraffes, and further explosive volleys—but there was nothing. Just the eerie silence.

He saw Holly hug Glyffy in relief. 'Thank you.'

Maybe I'm not deaf, after all.

Figures emerged from the shadow of the overhang—human figures. Some of them held silver spears. He realised the shadow was the mouth of a cave and a dozen spear-carrying warriors were standing in the entrance, weapons ready.

'Etus!' A commanding voice rang out from high above.

Reece looked up a discovered a tall spearman, standing astride a crag and glaring down at them.

'Mo ma?'

'Ara tobrit.' Glyffy sounded defensive and apologetic.

The warrior stamped the long shaft of his spear several times.

Holly raised her arm. 'What's your problem?' she shouted. 'It's not as if any of *your* people have been killed.'

I wonder how she came to the conclusion that's what he's angry about.

'Etus!' the spearman snapped. 'Ho ro?'

'Glyffy marbin Olly, Caroon marbin Leeze,' the giraffe said.

Holly turned to Reece. 'They're introducing us. You're sitting on Caroon.'

She understands them? 'I take it first impressions aren't endearing us to anyone?'

The spearman barked again. With his stave, he pointed down the ravine into the smoke-hazed distance where a multitude of black dots could be seen against the sky.

Reece stared. *They're hornet 'copters. Hundreds of them. It wasn't any use destroying these here, because it only let the others know where we are.* And then he stared in even greater amazement: coming up over the horizon was a second sun.

The hornets hovered in the lemon-tinted sky, the light of the second dawn dancing on their blades and muting their darkness to pearl. For a moment they looked beautiful, winking like a thread of gossamer beads across the sky. Then, as the sun rose just a fraction higher, their silhouettes grew deadly and venomous once again.

The spearman gestured to the giraffes. With a brisk wave of

his arm, he indicated for Glyffy and Caroon to follow him. Three long giraffe-steps upward was the crag where spearman stood. One moment he was beckoning them to his side, the next he'd jumped down and disappeared.

'Wha..?' Reece was baffled.

'There must be a door,' Holly said.

Glyffy reached the crag and the open door. The warrior just inside the entrance urged her on. But Glyffy couldn't get in. She contorted her neck, trying to bend low enough so Holly wouldn't be bumped.

'Stop!' Reece called.

'Sstob?' Glyffy repeated.

'Stop. We can walk.' Reece pointed to the height of the doorway. 'Let Holly down.' He patted Caroon. 'And me, too.'

'Olly doun?' Glyffy looked puzzled. 'Un mee too?'

Holly thumped her gently and she seemed to get the message. Reece could see her feet were unsteady as Glyffy deposited her on the ledge. He staggered a little himself as Caroon set him down.

Twilight descended as he walked into the doorway after her. The sound of his breathing seemed strangely loud and ragged. 'Get a move on, Hol. You're blocking the passageway.' He pushed her into the dimly lit interior.

Reece could sense something snaking along the rock ceiling. Suddenly, Glyffy's snout was right in front of him, peering down in the gloom.

'Hey, it's okay, Glyffy,' Holly said. 'You'll be all right.' She turned to Reece. 'I'm not sure about me, though.'

'C'mon, sis. Move along.'

'You take the lead, why don't you? Just squeeze past me.'

'I don't need to prove I'm scared,' Reece whispered. 'Just move so Caroon can get in.'

He touched the wall of the passage. The rocks were freezing. Feeling his way along, he took a dozen steps forward. It was a comfort to sense Holly in front and Glyffy's head above him.

With a sudden hollow clang, complete darkness fell. The door had closed behind them.

Reece gripped Holly's shoulder. 'You can keep it there,' she whispered gratefully.

'We've got to stop sounding as scared as we are.'

'You mean,' Holly said, 'like dogs sense fear, these guys might attack if we show a sign of weakness?'

'Something like that.'

The unrelieved darkness gave way to a faint luminescence. Up ahead, a pale light was flickering with soft blue-white radiance.

'Ettii,' came a voice from next to the light. 'Olly ae-ra Leeze, ko-sto.' It was the spearman. The light came from the tapered head of his stave. It glowed, faint but steady, in the darkness. The spearman pushed past them all.

As soon as he was well clear of Glyffy's snout, he raised the spear high so its light was like a glimmering beacon. Then he strode off.

'Not so fast!' Holly exclaimed.

Reece agreed with her. His eyes hadn't adjusted to the scant blue light and he was sure that, if he went too quickly, he'd fall on the uneven stonework.

'Ka!' the spearman snapped, coming back towards them.

'Ka, yourself!' Holly retorted.

'Holly!' Reece tugged at her sleeve. 'Be polite to the man.' She was taking what he said about not showing fear to the opposite extreme. He interposed himself between her and the spearman. 'Excuse me, sir...' He put his hands in his pockets. 'Could you please go a bit slower?' *Polite, but firm.* 'You're familiar with this passageway, and we aren't—and while we'd definitely like your help, we don't know whether we can trust you. But we don't have much choice, do we? I'm sure that your second impressions of us aren't much better than the first were, but let me tell you, sir, if I may be frank, it cuts both ways.'

If the spearman understood a single word, he gave no sign of it.

'Hmmm,' Glyffy snorted.

'Hmmm,' Caroon repeated.

'Hmmm,' grunted the spearman at the two giraffes. And with a scowl, he added, 'Hmmm,' for good measure at Reece and Holly.

'Hmmm.' Reece creased his face into a ferocious glare and grunted back.

'Hmmm,' the spearman growled back.

'Hmmm!' Reece bared his teeth.

'Oh, for crying out loud! That's enough!' Holly stamped a foot. 'That was the last "hmmm", you hear me? You *all* hear me? Stop acting like savages spoiling for a fight. Stop trying to provoke each other.'

The spearman snarled at her but turned at once and went off down the passage without another word.

Well, we came off rather better there than could have been expected, sis. Reece took a deep breath and followed the spearman. A faint musky smell grew more potent as they moved. It took Reece most of a minute to identify it: the odour of giraffe in a confined space.

There's one good thing about this, though—we're going downhill. The blue light vanished. It took Reece a few seconds to realise the spearman had turned a corner. For a moment, his heart had thudded in a wild tattoo, thinking that they were lost in the dark bowels of a mountain. Rounding the corner, he saw the warrior standing still. The luminous tip of his spear jutted out over a black forbidding space. Reece felt a cold blast of air sweep upwards as he approached. By the dim light, he could only just make out a new challenge. 'Steps!' *Going up. I hope not too far.*

The spearman led the way. Reece followed with caution, Holly just a pace behind him. A misty greyness lay beyond the faint halo of blue lighting their way. As they ascended the stairwell, a brighter outline appeared in the greyness and the air in the passage gradually lost its bitter edge.

At last the spearman stepped into a patch of sunlight and stood, waiting, as Reece and Holly caught up with him. Reece blinked at the sudden brightness and reached up to shield his eyes.

'Olly! Leeze!' The voice of Glyffy came from far back on the stairwell. 'Iszy toe!'

Reece was surprised to realise the giraffes hadn't been right behind them. 'They must be stuck.' He turned and yelled, 'I'm coming!'

Before he could take a single step, the spearman grabbed him, swung him around and pushed him, together with Holly, out of the entrance and into the full sunlight. They were standing on a wide stone pavement. It stretched out in a series of blue-black terraces hewn into the bowl of a natural amphitheatre. It was a bare, desolate place with only a single stunted tree in the middle.

Cold and silent, rain-starved and windless, it seemed to be a plugged sinkhole whose high rocky sides had been carved into tiers. Reece felt his spine tingling as he gazed at the empty terraces. *I don't like this. Who sits on those tiers and why? This is an arena of some kind, but what happens here? Let's get outta here fast.*

His eyes drifted to a black expanse at the far side of the amphitheatre. *A pool. We may not be able to drink the water here, if that's a normal spring.* He looked up with anxiety at the morning sky. It was a ragged, stone-washed blue. *What happens if those hornet 'copters appear?*

He began to fret over a dozen worries when his thoughts were interrupted by a sudden tremendous rush behind him. Glyffy, skittering feet first out of the entrance, landed in an awkward sprawl on the pavement. Seconds later, Caroon followed.

Both giraffes, after a few moments of stunned silence, crooned a low howl of pleasure at the sky. Then, with ungainly shakes, they scrambled to their feet. 'Hmmmph,' Caroon snorted.

The spearman scowled once more, but made no comment as he led the way across the pavement. He had only gone a few steps when Reece heard a delicate tinkle of windchimes.

'Look!' Holly pointed a shivering finger towards the stunted tree in the middle of the amphitheatre. There, on the withered branches, was the source of the tinkling. The tree was glittering with strange leaves—long glass tiles shaped like fingers, thumb-sized shards of stone and pottery hands. They dangled from every bough. 'Reece, don't!'

He halted, turning away from the spearman gesturing him closer to the glass-decked tree. 'What's wrong?'

'I have a bad feeling.' Holly held up her hands. 'A really bad feeling. This is not a good place.'

Couldn't agree more. He smiled at the spearman, before hurrying to clasp her hand. 'We don't have much choice.'

Holly looked down. 'Three shadows,' she said incongruously, gazing at his feet. 'You've got three shadows, little brother. There must be three suns in this world.'

Reece turned to see the small face of a faint red sun above the rim of the amphitheatre. He took a deep swallow and produced a slow wan smile as he looked back at Holly.

'I know we don't have a choice,' she said. 'I just wish we did.'

'Would you feel any better if I told this guy to get lost and we stuck with the giraffes?' he asked.

She nodded.

'Okay.' He'd humour her. 'I would, too. Just let me figure out how to do it.' He patted her shoulder. 'You stay here. I'll think of something.' Walking over to the tree, he felt the tinkling of the chimes become increasingly mournful and melancholy. The trunk of the tree was wizened and twisted, gnarled by bitter winds. It was a thorn tree.

Holly's absolutely right. He felt an oppression weighing down on him ever more heavily. *Something really bad has happened here.* He looked around the amphitheatre and could sense, as if time momentarily parted, crowds of people sitting there. Waiting. Watching. Passing judgment.

And then the impression was gone as he turned to look up at the tiles dangling on the tree. There were markings on each of them. None were the same. Each was as individual as the paper hands Holly had cut out for her Christmas tree.

That's what the leaves reminded him of. But these had an air of brooding malevolence that Holly's cut-outs never had. He examined the markings more closely as the leaves swayed to and fro. *Perhaps it's writing.* 'Now, look!' He turned to face the spearman. 'I…' He stopped as the warrior prodded him towards the tree with his spear. The point was barbed and sharp.

Reece automatically held up his hands and fell back a step. The spearman motioned him to sit beneath the tree. Reece, eyeing the spear-point, obeyed without a word of protest. With a curt gesture, the warrior signalled for Holly to do the same. With a shake of her head, she moved to sit down beside Reece.

'Etus Glyffy!' The spearman waved the giraffe away.

'Hmmm.' Glyffy stomped one foot down and then another. She glared at the warrior and, with a loud wump, dropped down onto the pavement. Then she wriggled her rump over the stones until she was next to Holly. 'Hmm,' she added, as she folded her forelegs awkwardly.

The spearman's face went through a half dozen expressions from amazement to apoplectic rage. 'Etus Caroon!' he bellowed.

Caroon frowned at the spearman and at Glyffy. He frowned at Reece and Holly, then at Glyffy again. Letting out a huge sigh, he took two long steps towards the tree and dropped, with an even louder wump, right beside Reece. 'Hmm,' he murmured when he'd finished crossing his legs.

The glass tiles chimed a slow forsaken lament.

'What's happening?' Reece asked.

'I think they've come to our defence,' Holly said. 'I think they're sticking up for us.'

'Well, they shouldn't have to.' Reece scrambled up. 'It's innocent until proven guilty.' *This is a judgment place. And we're in unimaginable trouble.* 'Hey, you!' He took a stride out from under the tree and called to the warrior.

A moment later, four huge spears thudded down right in front of his feet. They'd come from four different directions. Reece gulped. The spears were upright, angled into the very stones of the pavement—he didn't want to think how sharp they had to be to manage that. He took a step back, eyes wary as he scanned the terraces. He could see nothing.

His hand was suddenly tugged by something rough and wet. Looking down, he discovered his wrist was in Caroon's mouth. The giraffe was trying to drag him back towards the tree. 'Okay, okay, I get the message.' He sat down.

The spearman plucked the four spears from the ground and, hoisting them on his shoulder, began to prowl around the tree. Around he went, several times, in ever-widening circles, until at last he reached the terraces—and disappeared. Reece was astonished. He'd been watching the spearman intently, noting his movements—the way he'd stop to listen after each circuit, the way he'd pause every quarter-turn to look at the sky. As if waiting for a sign. Yet, to vanish: that was the last thing Reece had been expecting. *Now's my chance…*

'Don't even think about it,' Holly said, before he could make the slightest move. 'They've got sentries everywhere.'

Reece glanced around and realised she was right. Where moments ago he had seen nothing, a cloaked guard stood at every clockpoint. *Thirteen.* He did a quick count. *Don't like our chances.* 'Well, now what?' He looked up at the thorntree with its jangling glass leaf-fingers and pottery hands. *So how do we get judged?*

'What do they want?' Holly asked.

Reece decided to keep his suspicions to himself. 'Who knows?' He turned to inspect the thirteen guards. 'I've just thought of something.'

'What?'

'What if I want to go to the toilet?'

'Don't even think about it.' Holly crawled closer to Glyffy and pointed to herself. 'Holly,' she said. Then she pointed to Reece. 'Reece.' To Caroon. 'Caroon.' To Glyffy. 'Glyffy.' Then she pointed to the tree above them. And she waited.

'Ara koison toe-ry,' Glyffy said.

'Ara koison toe-ry bo-do,' Caroon amended.

'All that for 'tree'?' Reece asked.

'Maybe they were describing it.' Holly pointed to the glass tiles on the thorntree.

'Hmm.' Glyffy snorted and began an explanation so long, jumbled and incomprehensible, with constant injections from Caroon, that Reece couldn't pick up a single word.

'Forget that,' he said, when they'd finally finished. Raising his arm, he indicated a pale orange sun. 'Sun.' he said.

'Heimus,' Caroon translated.

Reece grinned. 'Houston, we have communication!' He pointed back to the sun. 'One heimus.' He turned his attention to the second sun: a golden yellow disk almost straight above them. 'Two heimus.'

'Three heimus.' Holly pointed to the small red sun above the rim of the amphitheatre.

The giraffes began giggling—they snorted and chortled and sniffed back tears of laughter.

Reece shrugged at Holly. 'I guess you said something funny in giraffe language.' He was startled when Caroon suddenly licked the side of his face, sweeping a long strand of hair up into a strange limp curl. 'Urgh!'

Over the next few hours, two of the suns set. The rosy twilight of the red dwarf sun cast inky shadows under the glass-leaved tree. A low moaning wind began to skirl around the stone terraces as the sky became darker.

All the while Reece and Holly gained more vocabulary. They learned how to count, they learned the spearmen were called 'Aerfren' and the green giraffe people were the 'Ettii'. One, by itself, was called an 'Etus'.

'Why couldn't it just be Etus and Etuses?' Reece asked, after one of his mistakes caused the giraffes to break into unrestrained laughter for at least the twentieth time. 'I'll never remember how they change their words when there's more than one thing.'

'Yes, you will.' Holly nodded at him. 'It's easy for someone of your scientific leanings.'

'It is?'

'Think of a circle,' Holly said.

'Uh huh?'

'One radius, two radii. Like one cactus, two cacti. So one Etus, two Ettii. One heimus, two heimi. Or rather i-heimus, zo-heimi. It's easy, really. I thought an alien language would be much harder.'

'Hol…' Reece decided that, if she found this so easy, he didn't want to know her definition of a difficult language. '…I take back what I said about you being an airhead.'

'When did you call me an airhead?'

'You don't want to know.'

As the shadows lengthened, the wind freshened and the day grew ever colder.

Their attention was drawn back to their guards. The spearmen still stood sentinel, watching their every move with hawk-like intensity. Reece wondered what would happen at nightfall. He felt sore and stiff from sitting so long on the cold pavement. However, he wasn't game to do much more than shift his legs every so often to avoid a cramp.

The sky was draped with violet as the last sun finally set. The pottery hands on the thorntree seemed to clap a welcome to the darkness. Reece shivered. He glanced around, trying to watch see the cloaked spearmen, but all he saw was the tips of their spears glowing with a ghostly blue light. *I wonder if they ever have a Changing of the Guard.*

An inky vapour rose out of the ground and obscured his vision. He felt the Ettii moving and realised they had positioned themselves so that their necks and bodies formed a circle, making a warm hollow for him and Holly to huddle into. 'Isn't this cosy?' she asked.

Reece wasn't sure whether she was being serious or sarcastic. 'Better than nothing. You think we should keep watch? We could do it in turns.'

'Would there be any point?'

Reece nodded in agreement, but realised he'd feel safer if one of them stayed on guard. Pretending to go to sleep, he curled up against Caroon. He watched Holly snuggle against Glyffy before turning his attention to the slow march-past of the stars. Their twinkling brilliance was like that of tiny burnished medallions. He spotted the Southern Cross. And one of the Pointers. But the other—Alpha Centauri—had vanished. The familiar constellations steadied his mind, connecting him with Earth and Dad and Mum. And home. *Home.* He found himself praying that somehow, someway, he and Holly would get home safely.

His eyelids drooped. In the distance he could hear a lullaby. The only word he could make out was 'faraway'. *Must be imagining it. Must be ... imag ... in*

Despite his resistance, he felt himself drifting into sleep.

The Tree
of
Plumage

Holly listened to Reece's snoring. It was comforting in its normality. The spearmen still hadn't moved. But one of the ghostly blue spearlights came towards them, bobbing up and down, as if on a wave of the sea. It rode across the inky drifts like a meandering mistlight.

She lost sight of it as it circled and, unable to continue the struggle against sleep, closed her eyes.

A minute later—at least it seemed that way—she jerked awake, her heart thudding. The sense of someone staring down at her had frightened her back into wakefulness. Looking up, she saw a dark shape against the starlit sky.

A hooded cloak, a face featureless in shadow. The dark silhouette raised a hand to its lips. Turning away, it reached out to the thorntree, its arm moving in and out between the glass tiles. Slow and silent, the figure passed its hand over every tile on three branches.

Searching.

Holly was sure of it. Right above her, a tile began to glow.

The figure turned and reached for it, plucking it effortlessly from the tree. The tile was glazed, and snow-white.

Holly stared. She couldn't remember seeing a white hand or leaf. Markings were etched on the tile, words shimmering in fluid silver. The cloaked figure stood motionless, as if transfixed. Finally it stooped, reaching out towards Reece. He stirred in his sleep, but didn't waken. Holly didn't know what to do. She saw the figure take Reece's water pistol from his pocket and hold it up, examining it in the starlight. Then the dark figure stooped over Reece again.

It was all she could do not to gasp as it held up the diamond-studded filigree necklace and studied it silently. The necklace was glowing. And changing. It was becoming a cuff bracelet again. She could see its light through the hand holding it, a hand whose long elegant bones were outlined like an x-ray. The bracelet shrank further. The figure turned it over, changing it from one hand to the other. It had become a ring—a radiant and resplendent ring, as shimmering and luminous as sunlit flowing water.

There was an intake of breath—a stifled expression of astonishment and wonder. She watched the figure raise both hands, one with the ring held between thumb and forefinger. She almost cried out, sure that the stranger was about to put the ring on and steal *her* property. But she stopped. *No need.*

The figure held the glowing ring poised above a hand without a ring finger. For several seconds, the figure stayed perfectly still, hesitating in apparent indecision.

Then it palmed the ring and stooped towards Reece. A moment later, it was standing tall again. Just as swiftly, it bent towards Holly. Closing her eyes, not wanting it to know she'd been watching, she held her breath as the stranger touched her brow with the white glazed tile.

Then the figure was gone.

Holly listened to the soft footfall as it departed. She expelled a long, soft breath. She waited and waited, but the figure didn't return. Finally, nestling so far down she was almost under Glyffy's legs, she fell asleep.

All too soon, it was morning. *The trouble in a world with three suns*, she thought, as she woke bleary-eyed and blinking at the lilac-robed sky, *is that night is so short*. She yawned, and stretched. And a cloak fell off her.

Cloak? Made entirely of tiny feathers, it was soft and warm and coloured in a graduation of greys: pale at the top to almost black at the hem, where a sprinkling of pure white down gave the effect of a snowflake border. *Am I dreaming this?*

Above her, the tiles on the thorntree clinked quietly, almost as if they were half-dreaming themselves.

The cloak must belong to one of the spearmen. She scanned their circle, realising their ranks had doubled during the night, when the giraffes began to stir.

Reece rolled over, winced and sat up.

'Don't know about you,' she said, 'but I need a wash.'

'You sure do.' Reece grimaced. 'You've got something on your forehead.'

'So do you.' There were fine silvery strokes on his brow that looked like a word.

She touched her own browline and found fine metallic particles adhering to her fingers. She remembered the dark figure of the previous night, pressing the white tile against her forehead. She didn't recall it touching Reece, though. Just looking at his water pistol. And staring at the mysterious necklace they'd found in the spacecraft. And before any of that, taking the glowing leaf from the thorntree. 'Reece, do I have something written on my forehead?'

Reece nodded. 'I have something on mine too, don't I? What's it say?'

'It's smudged.' Holly pointing at her own forehead. 'What's this say?'

Reece peered at her, his eyebrows creasing into a frown. 'There's an N…and a backwards kind of E…and a curvy arc going into a straight bit, sort of like an off-kilter Y… and then there's some bird droppings…'

'Reece! Try to be serious…' All at once, in her mind's eye, she could see the dark silhouette of the spearman with the shimmering moonsilver ring poised above his hand. That image, so sharp-etched, seemed to swing to and fro in her mind, as if it were the hinge of a doorway to something important.

'You know what?' Reece threw up his hands. 'I think it's the crime we're accused of.' He looked up at the glass tiles. 'Oops. Open mouth, insert foot. I wasn't going to tell you. I think this is a judgment place.'

'What crime do you think?'

'How would I know?' Reece asked.

'We've probably broken the law a dozen times here without realising it. Maybe if you plead guilty, they'll let us go.'

'Why should I? It's not as if I've done anything really and intentionally wrong.'

'You haven't done anything really and intentionally right, either.' Holly felt unwilling to humour him. 'Not since the moment you skipped out on the washing up.'

Reece ignored the jibe and pointed to the feather cloak. 'Where'd that come from?'

She didn't answer. Holding it up, she ran her hand across the soft feathers and marvelled at the muted beauty in the different tones of grey.

A sudden crunch behind her almost made her jump. Turning,

she saw that Caroon, pebbles dribbling from his mouth like crumbs, was munching on a rock.

Reece gaped at the sight. His face creased into a disbelieving frown, as Glyffy's huge neck curved around and both the Ettii proceeded, with obvious relish, to demolish several small piles of rocks. The rocks were sitting like miniature cairns on large bronze platters. 'I guess that's breakfast,' Holly said as the Ettii licked up the water pooled in the shallow bases of the plates and proceeded to look quite smug and satisfied.

'They must have diamonds for teeth.' Reece blew out his cheeks and smiled. 'Which I guess is good news and bad news.'

'How?'

Reece seemed fascinated by the Ettii gnawing away at the rocks. 'The good news is that I don't think we ever have to worry about the Ettii eating us.' He held up a finger. 'Especially good news since only yesterday we were being hoisted around in those mouths.'

'And the bad news?'

'The bad news is that I don't think we're getting any breakfast of our own.'

Caroon nudged Reece on the shoulder. It took several steady thumps before Holly caught on to what Caroon was trying to say. She laughed. 'They've left one rock for each of us.'

Reece shook his head at Caroon. 'Thanks, guys, but no thanks. You fellas go right ahead.'

'We should work on learning more of the local language.' Holly watched the Ettii finish off the rocks with gusto. One of the spearman came forward to collect the platters. He seemed to stare right through her before going away.

The morning passed. Holly distracted herself by accumulating new words. By the time the second sun had its own dawn, she had started to build sentences.

She tried to engage Reece but he was in one of his moods. Unanswerable question followed unanswerable question: 'What will happen if a 'copter flies overhead?' 'Don't you think it's really strange they haven't already come searching this way?' 'Unless the Ettii herd led them off, sis. Isn't that a depressing thought?' 'I like the giraffes much more than any of the humanoids on this planet, don't you, Hol?'

By midday—at least midday of the first sun—he was so morose, Holly wanted to strangle him. 'With three suns, you get three mornings, three middays, and three afternoons,' he explained. 'That means you should get nine meals a day—and we haven't even had one.' *Typical. Thinking about food must occupy at least ninety percent of Reece's brain all the time.* He was undoing all her efforts at distracting herself from hunger, thirst, cold and fear.

The ranks of the spearmen parted to allow a figure to approach them. The first thing Holly noticed different about him was that he didn't have a cloak. The second thing she noticed was that he had a pitcher in one hand and a bronze pot in the other. His spear was tucked under his arm.

'At least the pot's not big enough to boil us in,' Reece said.

Holly darted a shocked look at him.

'Not whole anyway,' he added.

'Please get the other foot out of your mouth, Reece.'

Half a dozen paces from the tree, the spearman stopped and put down the pitcher and pot. Then he drew a line across the stones with the tip of his spear. While Reece craned his neck towards the pot, Holly examined the face of the spearman, trying to gauge by his expression what the drawn line meant. 'Is this yours?' She held up the feather cloak.

The spearman's eyes were as iron-grey as the cloak's hem, his nimbus of hair as pale as the cloud-mist feathers on the yoke. He said nothing but his eyes gained a sudden wariness. Holly, staring at the hand curled around the shaft of the spear, saw he was missing a finger. So this was the black shape who had visited them the night before, taken the white tile from the tree and pressed it against their foreheads. This was the formless figure who had held the silver ring and almost put it on before giving it back.

Before giving it back? In the grip of a sudden dread, Holly realised she wasn't sure the ring had been given back—she hadn't seen it all day. *Does Reece still have it?*

'Tamizel.' Glyffy inclined her head in obvious respect.

'Etus Glyffy ri.' The spearman bowed his head in return. 'Etus Caroon ri. Avei?'

Glyffy began to speak, explaining what had occurred. Every so often, she would repeat something Holly had said, mimicking her words and tone with a curious lisp, while Caroon spoke Reece's replies as accurately as if they'd been recorded. Tamizel looked more and more troubled as the giraffes went on.

They'd make good spies. And maybe that's exactly what they are. I hope we haven't done anything to make them doubt us.

'Tamizel!' Reece attracted the spearman's attention. 'I'm Reece. And this is Holly.'

'Reece ri.' Tamizel looked sidelong at Holly, nodding with extreme courtesy. 'Olly ri.' He held out one hand, palm up. With the other, he pushed the pitcher over the spearline.

Even as Reece reached to grab it, he pulled it back swiftly, his outstretched hand jiggling up and down as if demanding payment.

'He wants something in exchange.' Holly handed the cloak to Reece. 'Give him this back.' But even before Reece could offer it, Tamizel shook his head and pulled the pitcher even further back.

'What do you want?' Reece sounded perplexed.

Holly couldn't think of a single thing they had the young

warrior could want. But Tamizel patted his chest near his shoulder, before pointing to the same spot on Reece's shirt.

'You want what's here?' Reece reached into his pocket and pulled out a toy gun. 'It's only a water pistol.' He slid it over to Tamizel. 'It's yours!'

Tamizel pushed the pitcher across the line. And this time, when Reece grasped at it, he made no move to stop him. Reece took one look at the contents, sniffed and obviously decided to take the risk. He drank a cupful, before handing the pitcher to Holly. 'Just have a bit. Save some for later.'

Tamizel was puzzling over the water pistol, just as Holly had seen him do the night before. He clearly knew what a gun was, because he held it correctly and pulled the trigger with slow deliberation, pointing it away from any live target. But when nothing happened he seemed unsettled.

Reece put out his hand. 'Here! Let me show you.'

Tamizel hesitated before handing the toy back. He watched intently as Reece undid the stopper at the back and poured water into the barrel. 'Holly…' Reece held up the gun. '…I'm not wasting this water. Not for anything. Open your mouth.'

She opened her mouth as wide as she could but his aim left a lot to be desired. '*Reece*!' Holly squealed. 'You did that deliberately!' Instead of squirting down her throat, the water had sprayed all over her neck and shoulders.

'Here!' Reece handed the water pistol to Tamizel. 'You try it!' He held his arms wide, making as big a target of himself as possible.

Tamizel aimed the gun and, grimacing, pulled the trigger. The last dribble of water shot out and made a dark wet splash on Reece's shirt. Tamizel blinked in disbelief. 'If you thought you were getting an alien weapon,' Reece said, 'I'll bet you regret this deal already.'

'Maybe it isn't a good idea for them to think we don't have any defence at all.' Holly glanced around the ring of spearmen. They had closed in and were observing with intense scrutiny.

Food. That will spur Reece to something useful. 'Lunch is getting cold in that pot of his. What else have you got to trade?'

'Haven't *you* got anything? Maybe I'll just trade *you* for something to eat.' Reece shrugged. 'No, they'd be soon be wise to that. They'd make me pay to take you back. With my head probably.' As Holly rolled her eyes, he reached into his pocket. 'Actually, I do have something to trade—*this!*' He pulled out the necklace. And it *was* a necklace, not a bracelet or a ring. It shimmered like stars floating on gossamer thread and entwined with droplets of light.

Holly stared. *I must've been dreaming last night. I could have sworn it shrank to a ring.* 'Do you think it's a good idea showing them it?'

'It's a whole lot better than starving to death.' Reece held the necklace out as an offering.

Tamizel seemed stunned for a moment. With a fierce jerk of his hand, he swept the necklace out of Reece's hand, flinging it to the pavement.

Holly stared up at the darkening expression on Tamizel's face, wondering how things could have gone so wrong so fast.

'I'm sorry about that.' Reece gulped as he scooped the necklace up and put it back in his pocket. 'I s'pose you've got something else in mind?'

If Tamizel did, he didn't answer.

A shout at the edge of the terraces caused the spearmen to hurry back to their original positions. Tamizel sighed and rose from the ground in one easy, elegant movement. He turned to face a warrior striding across the pavement. The newcomer was clad in fine black skins, with a cloak of snow-white feathers. Around his hair was a thong where long glinting jewels dangled.

As the warrior approached, Tamizel's stance became more

stone-like. Glyffy nosed her snout along the pavement, curved her neck around the bronze pot and slid it back towards Reece. Holly could see by his look of misgiving he didn't dare open the pot.

'Bobenny…' Caroon glared at the newcomer.

'Bobenny?' Reece asked. 'Is that like the chief of the tribe?'

'Bobenny ri.' Tamizel inclined his head as the warrior came to stand in front of him.

'I think Bobenny might just be his name. Look at those fangs round his neck!' Holly stared at a row of sharp white teeth interspersed with jet-black faceted gems.

Bobenny's face was quivering with anger as he thrust his spear into the pavement. He shouted at Tamizel, making sharp, furious gestures for over a minute. His dark eyes sparked like fire-raked coals. The tapering jewels dangling from the thong jumped and jangled until he finally took a long slow breath, as if to calm himself.

But as soon as Tamizel began to speak, he commenced bellowing again. Without warning, he slashed out at the thorntree, hitting a branch and causing the glass leaves and pottery hands to clink violently. He barked right in Tamizel's face before stabbing his finger towards Reece and Holly.

Turning to Caroon and Glyffy, his manner changed. He was loud, but firm—as if trying to explain a difficult concept to slow and ignorant children. Caroon and Glyffy both nodded their heads from time to time, let out a low sonorous 'hmmm' and, in general, made approving noises. They seemed to be totally on Bobenny's side of whatever the argument was. Totally. Until he tried to get them to move.

It became clear that, however much they agreed with him, they were staying put. Bobenny's anger gave way to frustration. Turning back to Tamizel, he began to yell once more. Tamizel's placid unyielding expression must have suddenly become too much for him because, without warning, he struck Tamizel's face. Tamizel's astonished look as he turned back from his instinctive flinch was entirely matched by Bobenny's own.

A moment later, Bobenny slewed around, advancing on Holly, his spear poised, ready to launch.

She froze.

Tamizel was even faster than Bobenny. He leapt in front of Holly and held up the white glazed tile from the thorntree. Bobenny's spear was aimed straight at him.

Bobenny sneered as he glanced at the tile. He was reaching out to dash it to the ground when Tamizel stepped back nimbly. His move shielded Holly even more closely. Bobenny, clearly frustrated, stood calculating his next move.

Caroon's head darted forward and, with one swift chomp of his diamond-hard teeth, bit through Bobenny's spear. The heavy tip clattered to the ground and Caroon thumped his jaw down on top of it before joining Glyffy in a sudden deep, dolorous groan.

Reece shook his head. 'I get the impression that Tamizel and Caroon just did a couple of very dumb things.'

'I think they just saved my life.' Holly felt queasy with fear.

Glyffy raised her head, swung her neck over to Tamizel and gave his face a long, slurpy lick.

'What was that for?' Reece asked. 'Being your protector?'

Bobenny glared. Grunting just one savage word to Tamizel, he turned away. Tamizel shrugged at his retreating back and extended his hand to Holly. With his help, she rose awkwardly to her feet. The feather cloak fell to the ground. She smiled at him. 'Thank you.'

He looked into her eyes. 'Tharnk…yuu…'

Reece picked up the feather cloak and got up. Beside him, the Ettii righted themselves in a quick scramble. Although they had given up groaning, their sighs were loud and heavy. 'What's wrong?' Reece asked Caroon.

The Etus sniffed.

Tamizel, his feather cloak draped over his spear-arm, took Holly by the hand and began to lead her across the pavement. Reece started after them and then stopped. 'Wait! Why aren't Glyffy and Caroon coming too?'

Holly pulled free of Tamizel's grasp and ran back to Glyffy. 'Why aren't you coming?'

'Remizay modan-di shiia ged.'

'Which means?' Reece asked.

'I haven't got a clue. But I think that wherever Tamizel's taking us, they can't go.'

'Why not?' Reece demanded.

'Who knows? But I think they want us to go with Tamizel. They trust him.' She thought of the slurpy kiss Glyffy had just bestowed on him.

'Maybe it's because we can't eat their food.'

'Shall I tell them then that your stomach thanks them?' Holly wrapped her arms around Glyffy's neck. 'Don't go too far away. I'm going to miss you.'

Reece nodded. 'Same here,' he said to Caroon. 'I've only known you a day, but I already feel about you like I do about Retro. I know you don't understand a word I'm saying but I feel like you're a part of my life I'd rather not be without.' He patted Caroon's neck. 'You take care of yourself, boy.'

Tamizel was again wearing his feather cloak. Holding his spear erect, he waved away the Ettii and gestured to Holly and Reece to follow him.

The circle of warriors standing sentinel around the terraces broke ranks and fell in behind them. Bobenny stalked to the front, right next to Tamizel. His chin was high, his look disdainful and blistering with restrained anger. He refused to look at Tamizel. The silence between them was taut, almost electric.

Tamizel's face was set in a determined glower. As they came up to the terraces, Holly expected they'd go back into the tunnel. She glanced along the flat plates of coal-dark rock layered in sloping tiers looking for it.

Bobenny, with a single word of demand, wrenched Tamizel's spear from him and plunged it into a small cavity in the wall of the first and highest terrace. He twisted the shaft, and like a key opening a door, there was a click and the sound of a lock being released.

Holly looked around. The rock cavity looked no different to a hundred other small rock cavities she could see: it was necessary to know its exact position to be able to find it. Bobenny put his hand to the rock face and pushed. A section of wall moved back and slid to one side. Bobenny turned to Tamizel, looking him straight in the eye.

Holly caught the glance that passed between them. Bobenny's expression seemed to say: 'Last chance to change your mind.'

Bobenny averted his gaze and preceded Tamizel into the doorway. Reece was close on their heels, Holly just behind him. She was ready for another dark tunnel, lit only by the blue halo-tips of spears. She was surprised to find they had emerged on a high balcony. Overhead, the rock ceiling was so close she could almost touch it. Far, far below, she saw—with amazement—an entire city, carved out of the glittering heart of the mountain.

Crystalline stalactites and gold-veined marble columns held up wide walkways and serpentine terraces. Dense forests grew beside glittering lakes, linked by high waterfalls and zigzag mazeways. Spiralling pillars with steps carved into them led from one level of the city to the next.

'It's a TARDIS.' Reece inspected the scene and nodded. 'Much bigger inside than out.'

'What do you mean?' Holly was awed by the vast grotto

below her, with its sparkling fairytale appearance. Warm, fragrant air brushed against her face; orange-gold pennons of light were reflected through intricate shafts from the rock ceiling above them.

'The mountain.' Reece nodded again. 'It's much bigger inside than out.'

Tamizel led them from the balcony down a steep stairwell carved into the inverted mountainside.

Reece muttered to himself, clearly re-assessing the situation. 'These aren't savage tribesmen, sis. This is a very advanced society. What's going on here? Are they hiding away from those black guys in the 'copters?'

'Maybe they thought we were with them!'

'Or that we're part of a trap. I guess that'd explain why they were watching us so carefully at the thorntree. It was a test of some kind.'

Holly realised she liked the situation even less than before. 'I'm not sure we passed the test. I think Tamizel just called it off. That would explain why Bobenny is so angry.'

'Maybe we should've gone with the giraffes.' Reece paused. 'I sure hope these guys feed us. And soon. What happened to the pot?'

'Don't know.'

They trudged on. And on. They passed levels where water trickled over rocks, where profusions of vines made green bowers over their downward path, where doorways could be seen in the rockface by the edge of their trail. The steps came at last to a broad gallery which swept down a curved stairway to a fountain in the middle of a paved courtyard. Holly was transported by delight. 'It's just like a fairytale…' The sound of her own voice, low with pleasure, gave her pause. 'Just like.' With a sudden brilliant smile, she turned to Reece. 'It's gorgeous, isn't it?'

'Incredible,' he confirmed.

'Keep smiling.' Holly turned up the wattage on her grin. 'I don't think any of this is real.'

For a moment, Reece lost his composure altogether. 'You mean it's an illusion?'

'One hundred percent. This is an exact replica of the fairy court in *Beyond the Morning Star*—the book Gran gave me last Christmas. They must be taking this out of my head.'

Reece swore and pointed to a nearby fountain decorated with mermaids and seahorses. 'How come if they're taking thoughts out of your head that they don't realise that you know that that's exactly what they're doing? And why don't they stop it if it's pointless? And why *you* anyway? Why not the stuff in *my* head?' His smile became wider. 'Okay—no need to answer that question. My thoughts, unlike yours, are entirely rational—they couldn't even think of trying to disorient us or deceive us with them.'

'Your thoughts are boring.' They passed to the left of the fountain. 'Imagine trying to navigate the pathways of a computer chip.'

'*Don't* give them ideas!'

They reached a pathway of light-saturated stones, bordered by a garden of midnight blue roses and garlands of tiny white sprays of jasmine. 'I seem to be the heroine of this fairytale.' Holly kept her smile on full beam. 'If it's holding true, we're about to arrive at an ivy-encrusted oaken door which can only be opened by my little finger.'

'You *are* joking.' Reece's upper lip twisted into a half-sneer. 'I think I'm gonna die laughing.' As he spoke, the ivy-encrusted door appeared at the end of the path.

Without a word, Holly went up to it and inserted the little finger of her left hand into the lock. With a snick, the door opened. Reece stared at Holly, an aghast expression on his face. He shivered as he followed her through the door.

Inside the building was a room magnificent beyond Holly's

imaginings. Its high vaulted ceilings was stippled with gold leaf; its immense fluted gold columns towered up through the roof.

Reece paused inside the threshold. 'This place is meant to make you feel insignificant.' He took a deep breath. 'It's working too.'

In the centre of the room was a golden pedestal. On that golden pedestal was a golden cage. In the golden cage was a golden falcon on a golden perch. Towering above the golden pedestal with its golden cage, housing its golden falcon on a golden perch, was a slender white-gold tree, its golden snowflake blossoms rustling with the melody of a slow lullaby. 'A colour consultant wouldn't have gone astray.' Reece sounded as intimidated as Holly felt by the grandeur and intensity of the gold. 'Or an interior decorator for that matter.'

'We're in trouble. This is the Esplumoir of the Green Giant's Castle.'

'Green?' Reece blinked. 'What's an esplumoir?'

Holly shook her head. 'Reece, what is it with you? You can't have blocked your ears that well. I've had to listen to Gran telling you stories of Emrys Merlin the magician since you were a baby—and you *still* don't know what an esplumoir is?' She sighed. 'It's a moulting room. See those feathers?' She pointed to the floor of the cage.

'Oh, you mean when Merlin's about to die and he says he's going to go into his esplumoir?' Reece's brows narrowed in a frown. 'I thought that was a tree…'

'It's a play on words, little brother. You, of all people, should know about those. Merlin's a man but a merlin is a bird—a falcon. And birds moult.'

'What's this got to do with the Green Giant?'

'See the feathers?' Holly pointed once more to the cage floor. 'They're pure gold. They fall off the poor bird because they're so heavy. The Green Giant is rich because of them. They've enabled him to build this golden palace.'

'Of course.' Reece nodded. But his expression said 'Huh?'

Which is probably good —because if he doesn't get it, what chance will Bobenny and Tamizel have? Holly reached out and took hold of Reece's arm. 'I know it's only an illusion. But let's be careful, just in case. That white-gold tree is the Tree of Protection. Don't be fooled by its enchantment. It'll lull you to sleep and then kill you, if you don't watch out. Especially if it thinks you're here to steal the golden bird with the golden plumage on the golden perch in the golden cage on the golden pedestal.'

Reece's mouth fell open. 'Holly…' His voice was thoughtful.

'Yes, Reece?'

'You read trash.'

She elbowed him with a sharp nudge, then tip-toed after Tamizel and Bobenny towards a door on the far side of the room. It opened onto a windy passage. Its walls were rough and damp and its high vaulted ceiling was chiselled out of rock. 'I don't recognise this.'

'So it could be real?' Reece ventured.

Holly nodded. 'Could be. On the other hand, maybe it's something I've forgotten.'

Tamizel led them through an archway. Out of the blustery gusts of wind, a silken banner hung in front of a doorway. The pale wooden door was lancet-shaped. A milky glass peephole was etched with a silvery design—a hand with an oval hole in the palm. Holly stared. It was exactly like Reece's silver hand, the one atop the Tree of Hands she'd been making. *Is this coincidence? Or are my thoughts being manipulated as they're plucked out of the recesses of my mind?*

Tamizel motioned to Bobenny to stay outside. Holly thought he'd argue but, despite a dark scowl, he stood aside and made a deferential bow to Tamizel. Reece just stared, obviously trying to figure out why Bobenny's status had suddenly diminished.

Holly yanked him through the doorway. Tamizel closed it

behind them and then pulled a long curtain across to cover it. In the dimness of the room, Holly's attention was drawn to the curtain. She liked its filmy design: it was a fine transparent gauze with velvet motifs of leaves and hands all over it.

Tamizel threw his cloak at the wall and it disappeared inside a wardrobe that opened and shut all by itself.

'Gulped down like a fly in a frog's mouth,' Reece said.

Holly knew what he was thinking. *Is it going to be us next?*

Tamizel clapped his hands. An immediate hiss straight above caught Holly's attention. Inside a ceiling shaft, shutters began moving. She caught a momentary glimpse of an angled mirror as light streamed into the room. Holly found herself standing in a dappled, dancing sunbeam.

'Do sit down,' Tamizel said, in perfect English, 'and make yourselves at home.' His smile was as fugitive as the sunbeam. 'Would you like a cup of tea?'

The Tree
of
Pledges

'You speak English!' Reece's expression was halfway between incredulous and scared.

'No.' Tamizel gently tapped the nearest wall. Deep brocaded armchairs began to form, like organic growths, out of the smooth surface. 'I can find enough words in Olly's thoughts for the purpose, though.'

'The purpose?' Reece demanded. *He's a telepath*, he mouthed to Holly. It took him a moment to realise how pointless it was to try to communicate privately when there was a mindreader in the room. 'He can look into our minds and see our thoughts.' He folded his arms. 'What purpose?'

Tamizel sat down and kicked his boots off. Reece stared as the boots thudded onto the carpet then seemed to slink off, of their own accord, into the dimness on the far side of the room.

'The purpose of communication, of course.' Tamizel divested himself of his jerkin and tossed it to the far side of the room. It too disappeared into the wardrobe that opened and shut in an eyeblink. 'That's better.' He shrugged and stretched as if he'd spent a hard day working. 'Do sit down please.' He gestured to the cream brocaded chairs. 'Food will be coming shortly—and in the meantime, we can talk.'

Sit down? Reece eyed the furniture dubiously. *On a chair that might be nothing more than an illusion?* 'Where are we?'

'You are in my ...' Tamizel hesitated. '...winter? No. Not quite the right word...' He shook his head, looking puzzled. He seemed unable to solve whatever riddle was troubling him. 'You are in my winter residence in the city of Finddias of the Farafolk. You are ...' Again, he stopped as if searching for the right word. '...under my protection.'

'*Protection.*' Holly's faint whisper lingered in the air as Reece eyed the brocaded chair again.

Tamizel's smile became disarmingly lopsided. 'Oh, sit down, Olly,' he said, 'and you, too, Reece. The chair's not going to eat you.' His eyes gleamed, as if he were relishing a thought new to him.

He got that right out of Holly's head, Reece decided. *I wonder if he can read two sets of thoughts at once or whether he has to concentrate on one of us at a time.*

'I'm *not* worried about the chair eating me.' Reece's eyes narrowed. 'I'm worried about the chair actually being there at all.'

Tamizel laughed. 'There's no illusion in this room. It's exactly as you see it.'

'It's real?'

'It's as real as any reality. 'Whatever, of course, 'reality' really is.' Tamizel grinned and shook his head. 'Your language is very amusing: *reality really is*!' He shrugged. 'As for illusion —surely you understand the need for just a little deception on the way here.'

'The thought crossed my mind that you don't trust us,' Reece said.

Tamizel held up his hands. 'Indeed, how could we let strangers know the secret way into Finddias? We could have blindfolded you, but you might still have memorised the path through the labyrinth. Illusion seemed the safest course.' His smile was thin and his grey eyes shuttered. 'It was a harmless trick, though we were well-chastised for it, nonetheless.'

'Oh?' Reece asked. 'How was that?'

'Olly's counter-illusion. A golden bird with golden plumage on a golden perch in a golden cage on a golden pedestal.' Tamizel raised his head and rolled his eyes. 'Gold, gold, and still more gold. My head was spinning—it was completely disorienting. I was lost—utterly lost—in my own city.' His gaze was cold as he turned to Holly. 'It was clever ploy to try to subdue us—gold fever is one of the swiftest and most crippling of all mental contagions.'

'I didn't do anything.' Holly held up her hands. 'I wasn't trying to subdue anyone. It was your own fault for picking up on that story and not something else.'

'You play the innocent well.' Tamizel's voice was soft as he peered closely at her face. 'It was the only story you allowed me access to.'

'I didn't.' Holly returned the gaze of his flint-flecked eyes with a steady frown.

'Serves you right.' Reece glared at Tamizel. A heartening thought occurred to him. 'You're not a true telepath then?'

Tamizel seemed disconcerted by the question. 'No,' he said, after a few seconds. 'At least not in the sense you mean. I am merely...' He paused, looking puzzled as he struggled to express himself. '...you do not seem to have a word for it... an alignment of like minds...a resonance of harmonies ... a tapestry of hearing... I do not know...' He broke off, apparently defeated by a lack of vocabulary. 'Sit down, Reece.'

Reece hesitated a moment more. He wasn't sure he believed a single word of Tamizel's assurance he had picked up English from a 'resonance of harmonies', but he felt that continued refusal would make him look stupid. The brocaded chair seemed to mould itself to his shape as he sat down. 'What's this place, Finddias? Why is it hidden? Why did you half-freeze us to death in that place under that thorntree?'

'What was written on the white tile?' Holly added.

'You ask too many questions…' Tamizel looked from Reece to her. '…for those who have given the Farafolk no reason to trust them.'

'But how do we prove we can be trusted?' Reece asked. 'Anyway—can't you see into our minds enough to know we can be trusted?'

Tamizel stared fixedly at him for several seconds. 'You can begin by telling me who you are and how you came to be in the Tree of Prophecy where the Ettii found you.'

'Well…' Reece folded his arms. 'If we're going to begin at the beginning, it was all Holly's fault. Just because I was a bit slow getting to the washing up.'

'*Slow?*' Holly objected. 'Slow! It would have been the end of the next century before you got to it at the rate you were going. Besides, Reece, you can't possibly believe in all seriousness that anything *I* did catapulted us to another planet.'

'Another planet?' Tamizel's face paled. He stared, his eyes narrowing. Reece could see him focussing his thoughts, trying to penetrate Holly's mind. *You mightn't be a telepath, but you're something not much different.*

'You come from a world with only one sun and only one moon,' Tamizel breathed. His voice was tinged with awe. 'Legend speaks of such.' He was silent for so long, staring so intently Reece began to feel nervous. 'It is said the Stardaughter will come from a world of Ones,' he said at last. 'She who is the Peaceweaver.' He seemed troubled. 'The tile said as much, but how can it be with a name like yours?'

'Name like mine?' Holly asked.

There was a tinkle at the door. Tamizel ignored it as he stared at Holly. And she was just as steady in her return gaze. There was another tinkle, more insistent. Tamizel, shaking himself free of distraction, turned to the door. 'Sjella,' he commanded.

With a flourish, the curtain pulled itself back, the door sprang open, and Bobenny entered. He was followed by a man and a woman bearing pitchers and platters, goblets and bowls. A table with a surface designed like the spreading petals of a flower emerged from the floor. Bobenny stood aside while the table was set.

'Mara tend da?' Bobenny's voice dripped with contempt.

'Mishruêl'la nyt kuuri.' Tamizel's tone was sharp.

Bobenny's laugh was short and derisive as he turned and left.

Reece noticed that, while the servants had glanced covertly at him, they'd all—including Bobenny—been very careful to keep their eyes from drifting anywhere in Holly's direction. The door closed automatically but, through its frosted peephole, the shadows of guards were clearly visible. Tamizel got up from his chair and yanked the curtain. 'I must get the automatics fixed.' Turning back, he smiled and his voice softened. 'And now for a long leisurely lunch. Long and leisurely, because if you eat too quickly after such a long time without food, you will be ill. And also, of course, because I enjoy talking to you so very much.'

As if anyone would believe that. Reece glanced at the door. Through the curtain, he could see shadows conferring together. He couldn't work out why one moment Bobenny was in charge and the next he was just a guard.

Holly must have wondered the same. 'Is Bobenny your boss or are you his?'

Tamizel poured a pale liquid from the pitcher into a goblet. 'Sometimes.'

'Sometimes? Sometimes which?'

'Bobenny is Master of the Hunt.' Tamizel sipped from the goblet before passing it to her. 'When I am hunting, he is my boss and I obey him implicitly. At other times, he is not my boss.'

Hunting? Reece frowned. *Is that what you were doing on the mountaintop? What precisely were you hunting?* 'Oh.' He paused. 'What'd you say to him?'

'When?'

'Just then.'

Tamizel hesitated. He finished pouring another goblet of drink. 'I said he has seen the truth for himself. Her thoughts are harps and angelwings, not crows or maggots.' He sipped from the goblet, then passed it to Holly.

She seemed stunned. 'Whose thoughts?'

'Your thoughts,' Tamizel said. 'They are heaven's thoughts: mysterious, wondrously strange.'

A sense of danger prickled Reece all over. *Quick, a diversion.* 'Strange, yes, locks that open with a little finger and…' He winked at Holly. '…green giants and esplumoirs and gold multiplying gold.'

'I don't understand.' Holly put the goblet down and folded her arms. Reece tried to signal as she glowered at Tamizel. 'One minute you're accusing me of tricking you with illusions and the next minute you say the same thoughts are divinely rare.'

Tamizel held up his hands. 'I am stumbling in trying to comprehend your alien world. I apologise if I have given offence, Lady Olly.'

Alien world? Reece was startled by Tamizel's perspective. *How strange that sounded—to think of Earth as alien, not this triple-sunned, double-mooned planet.*

'You haven't offended me.' Holly sniffed. 'I just don't understand how the two statements can both be true.'

Tamizel seemed relieved. His face cleared as he reached into his shirt. 'I will explain.' He held up Reece's water pistol. 'This weapon is an illusion like that we perpetrated on you. A deception, but harmless. Yet the difference is this: the Farafolk *meant* for you to see illusion as you came into Finddias, but this weapon is not meant as an illusion.' His smile was awkward. 'When I said your thoughts were illusions, this is what I meant: that the Farafolk were deceived, but not because you intended to do so.' His smile faded. 'Isn't that so?'

Reece pointed to the water pistol. 'It's just a toy.'

'Toy,' Tamizel repeated. 'Plaything.' He looked baffled. 'Such is unknown in Finddias.'

He held it out with a deferential smile. Reece pocketed it at once. *Let's try for diversion number two.* 'Well, I'm extremely grateful that food isn't unknown here. And I sure hope it's not an illusion. C'mon guys, can we eat?'

'You and your stomach.' Holly finally sat down next to him. He took up the goblet she'd been given and took a sip. At once his head became clearer. By the second sip, his thoughts were crystalline in their lucidity. He could sense a presence hovering, and realised it was Tamizel's thoughts listening to his own. *Had Holly sensed this too?* Behind Tamizel's thoughts, Reece could feel the mind: a stippling of light and dark, an evanescent blend of fear and dread and desperate, clutching faith.

Reece recognised the ache. *It's been with me since the moment Gran said that Dad was…* He flung the thought away. 'What's in this?' He held up the goblet.

'A kind of mead. An infusion of seventeen different herbs.' Tamizel took the cover off one of the platters to reveal baked meat and portions of vegetables. 'And this is a maevbeast roast. A trifle overcooked, just to be on the safe side.'

'Just to be on the safe side?'

'You're going to have to eat our food. But we will take what precautions we can.'

'I'm going to risk it. What about you, Hol?'

Holly's gaze met his. 'As Tamizel says, I don't think we've got a choice.'

Hunger makes a difference. Reece was soon convinced it was the best meal of his life. Half-way through the goblet of 'seventeen different herbs', he started laughing so much at the slightest provocation that he wondered about the alcoholic content.

He saw Holly push a second goblet to the furthest side of one of the petals that formed the top of the flowertable and shoot a forbidding glare at Tamizel.

Which just made Tamizel smile. He took Reece's goblet and drained it in one swallow. 'You still haven't told me how you came to be in the observation post.'

'Observation post?' Holly's scowl deepened.

Reece's thoughts had started to become fuzzy. Tamizel's unconcern at drinking from someone else's goblet bothered him. *Obviously bacteria and viruses aren't a big deal here. But maybe it's time they started worrying.* And then it occurred to him. *It's probably already too late.*

'The Cloud Tree,' Tamizel clarified, his serene smile directed at Holly. 'The Tree of Prophecy.'

Reece shook his head, trying to clear it. *Caroon and Glyffy must have been surprised to find their observation post occupied.*

'We were in Reece's cubby house…' Holly said. 'He calls it his workshop and he reckons he was building a time machine—but it's just a pretend game that he should have grown out of years ago. Anyway, there was this rainbow light, a kind of slither, which came from the sky. Then there was an explosion, and all these weird bubbles …'

She's got it all wrong. 'We somehow got caught up onto a spaceship.'

Reece pointed his finger at her. 'We floated for a while in zero gravity and then on re-entry, when the *g* forces kicked in, our weight increased probably a dozen times.' He took the necklace from his pocket. 'And then we found this.' The necklace shimmered, its silver glowing and its diamond facets dancing with light. 'We took it from the spaceship which was probably a pretty dumb thing to do but we had to avoid the wheeltrap.' *That disembodied voice—should I tell him?*

'Wheeltrap?' Tamizel seemed to close in on himself.

You know, now I come to think of it, that voice sounded a lot like Tamizel. He considered the possibility in silence. 'You were there,' he stated, growing more certain. '*You* warned us.'

'There?' Tamizel's face was suddenly ashen, his eyes like dragon slits. 'With the Invaders? On their ship? What are you accusing me of?'

'Nothing. Nothing. It just sounded like…' Reece faltered.

'I apologise for my brother,' Holly said. 'He's got a problem with words.'

'Foot-in-mouth disease,' Reece admitted.

'Foot *and* mou…' Holly began, before breaking off and clamping her lips shut.

Well, that's a first. She never usually misses a chance to rub it in. Reece turned to Tamizel.

'You need a doctor to rub something in your foot? Or mouth?' Tamizel looked perplexed.

'I'm fine.' *And you can be confused. Hol, we got a break here.* 'Back to the story. These guys in black were chasing us—Invaders, I guess—and just when we thought we were dead and gone, these trees zipped us away. When we woke up there were these green giraffes called Ettii talking to us in a language we didn't understand.'

Tamizel had turned his attention to the necklace in Reece's hands. 'What is it?'

Reece felt his suspicions rising once more. *You know what it is.* He recalled Tamizel's previous reaction back at the thorntree. *Or do you? Maybe you're testing my truthfulness.* 'It's a tachyon decelerator. Or so this voice that sounded like…' He broke off and amended his words. 'Or so we've been told.' *Wheeltrap. Tachyons travel backwards in time, so if we needed this to avoid the wheeltrap, then we must have come through some sort of portal in time.* He looked up and saw Tamizel staring at him, as if trying to read his mind. *Diversion number three.* 'It looks awfully like a crown, doesn't it? It fits my head just right!' He grinned. 'And don't listen to Holly tell you that it's just because it's swelled.'

'A crown?' Tamizel shook his head. 'It is far too small for that. Surely you would put it on your finger, not on your head.'

Reece glanced at the tachyon decelerator, then at Tamizel. 'Mighty big finger.'

'It looks like a necklace to me,' Holly said. 'Though it could be a bracelet.'

Tamizel blinked, before his eyes narrowed, concentrating on Holly and clearly skimming her thoughts. 'It looks completely different to me. It must have its own glamoure.'

'Glamoure?' Reece asked.

'It's a fairy power,' Holly said. 'An enchantment that makes you see things differently to what they really are.'

'This is a superior piece of technology.' Reece touched the necklace with his finger. 'Not some magical device with a spell on it.'

Holly folded her arms. 'Oh, of course, I forgot…' Her voice dripped sarcasm. 'You were the one who, when Gran read Ali Baba to us, insisted that the Forty Thieves had a voice-activated roller door.'

'It's time for dessert!' Tamizel clicked his fingers and the flowertable in front of them rolled up its inner petals and a tiny platform rose up out of the centre of the table.

Diversion number four and I didn't even have to try for it. Reece realised there was a small rectangular pot on the platform and in it was a miniature tree, as tiny and perfect as a bonsai. The tree was fruiting with what looked like wine-dark cherries. Its leaves were silver.

'Who eats of this, in harmony, shall be friends forever.' Tamizel gestured to Reece to take one of the cherries. 'But only if you wish.'

Reece found that the fruit was ripe and came away easily from the stalk. He put one in his mouth and took a bite. 'It tastes like an apple, not like a cherry at all.'

Holly took one of the tiny cherry apples from the tree and rubbed it against her arm. The wine-dark surface suddenly gleamed with silver threads. She handed the fruit to Tamizel. 'Yours,' she said.

He seemed momentarily taken aback. But, staring intently into Holly's eyes, he bit into the apple. 'Be careful never to do that again,' he said softly.

'Why?' Holly asked.

'It is an offer of marriage. A pledge of undying devotion.'

Holly gulped. 'I didn't mean anything like *that*.' Her voice was anxious.

It was a few seconds before Tamizel replied. 'I know.' His smile was slow and faint. 'And I didn't take it that way.'

Oh, we're in so much trouble. We need diversion number five. Now.

The Tree
of
Blood

A sudden snore came from Reece. The tachyon decelerator, still in his left hand, slipped to the floor. Holly was startled by the speed of his slip into unconsciousness and by the ringing chime of the necklace as it fell. She whirled on Tamizel.

'Before you ask, Olly, it is not my doing. It is undoubtedly a combination of many things: the herbs in the mead, hot food, exhaustion. Be suspicious of me, Olly. It's only natural.'

Holly stared, a thousand thoughts chasing each other through her head. Finally she decided that there was only one thing she really wanted. 'Do you have baths here?'

Tamizel burst out laughing.

'What's so funny?' Holly asked.

Tamizel rocked on his chair. 'It's difficult to explain…' He held his sides. 'But yes, if you want a bath, it can be arranged.'

'Arranged?' Holly wasn't sure she liked the sound of that. 'It's not a kind of public bath, is it? Like everyone together?' *Oops.* Roman baths, steamy Japanese baths, Swedish saunas. *I'm not going naked anywhere public. Not for anything.*

Tamizel must have caught the thought, for he made a new suggestion. 'I have something to suit you much better.'

'Like what?'

'Let me show you.' With a slow, almost languorous movement, he rose and stepped into the dimness on the far side of the room. A hidden door slid open at his approach allowing a shaft of cool, green light to enter. 'Come.' Tamizel extended his hand. He was a hazy shadow against a dancing emerald-hued sunbeam.

Holly went forward. She stopped as she reached the entrance. A tiny waterfall tumbled down a rockface into a pool. A profusion of purple-tufted grasses—*just*, she thought in surprise, *like the ones in Gran's garden*—moon-white flowers and trailing silver-edged leaves, glowed in a warm current of air.

'The waterfall is why I built my winter residence here,' Tamizel said.

Holly realised, for the first time, that his eyes were as dark and green as the shadowed glade of a forest.

He shrugged. 'The heat's piped in, of course, to make sure the flowers are always in bloom. After a hard day's hunting, there's nothing I like better than to just soak in the water and forget all my cares.'

Holly couldn't imagine anyone less like her idea of a hard-working hunter than Tamizel. *What kind of hunter has a bathroom like this anyway?* 'It's beautiful.' The scent of the flowers as they peeped out from between lustrous green leaves was heady, but strangely soothing. She looked up. Long glossy vines scaled the cathedral heights. She could just see the edge of a mirror tube which formed part of a light shaft.

'You can leave your clothes in the alcove.' Tamizel pointed to a rock seat set in the wall of the room. 'Call me when you've finished.' The door closed as he left.

Holly was as quick as she could be. It was tempting to lie on the rock shelf in the pool. Still she just washed herself and rubbed off the worst of the dirt before darting back, dripping, to where she'd left her clothes.

They were gone. Her shirt, her shorts—everything. In their place was a long gown in graduated shades of green. It was willow pale at the neck, deep velvety moss at the ankles and it flowed like a song. An embroidered border of tiny linked hands circled the hem. It was only when she realised it had hardly any back that her delight was transformed to anxiety. *I can't wear this.* She held it up in horror. *It's… it's… it's not all here!*

After a moment, she realised there was no choice. She was going to have to put it on so she could go out and demand her own clothes back. Slipping into the gown, she felt even more uneasy. The fabric almost slithered across her skin, arranging itself in shapely folds and soft clingy drapes. She looked down at her curves and suddenly wished them far away. She tried to pull up the back of the skirt closer to her waist. But no matter what she did, it slipped right down to the small of her back. Grabbing a fistful of fabric, she held it tightly behind her. *I want my clothes back right now*, she fretted. *I don't care how filthy they are. I want them now.*

She tip-toed to the door. It opened without a sound. She could hear voices in the outer room. One of them was Tamizel's. But the other wasn't Reece's.

With great caution, she poked her head outside. For a moment, she thought Tamizel was talking to the wall. Then she realised a face was flickering faintly and hanging in mid-air in front of him. *He's making a report.* She tried to pick up familiar words. Her name, and Reece's, were all she could make out.

She must have made a tiny sound, because Tamizel suddenly whirled around, cutting off his communication. 'You should have called me.' A smile sprang too quickly to his lips. Behind him, the face vanished smoothly into the wall.

'Where are my clothes?' Holly demanded. 'I want them back.'

'But you look so pretty in this.'

'But I don't feel comfortable in it at all.'

'That's strange,' Tamizel commented. 'The automatics are set to judge your mood and the occasion, and to select accordingly from the wardrobe.'

'Well, it got my tastes completely wrong. It must be my alien mind. Anyway I want my clothes back.'

'No doubt they're already at the laundry. I will organise their retrieval as soon as possible.'

'*Now!*' Holly snapped.

Reece woke up with a jerk. 'What'sh going on?' He rubbed his eyes and caught sight of Holly. 'Wow!' he gasped. 'Who's the gorgeous babe?'

Holly bared her teeth at him. '*Reece!*'

'*Holly?*' Reece shook his head and flushed a faint red. He gulped.

Tamizel tilted his head. 'You've both been invited to a reception. I was just about to tell Holly when you woke up, Reece.' His smile was at its most charming. 'Would you care to select some suitable attire from my wardrobe, Reece? It would be inexcusably rude to be late.'

'It's a party, is it?' Reece sounded far too cheerful for Holly's liking. 'Sounds like it could be fun. Where's the wardrobe?'

'Right here.' Tamizel pointed to the far wall.

'I can't go like this.' Holly felt panicky.

'Of course not,' Tamizel said. 'You need a cloak.'

Cloak. Holly breathed a huge sigh of relief. *I can wear the feather cloak.*

The wardrobe opened at Tamizel's approach. He was clearly startled as he viewed the contents. 'We seem to have a breakdown.'

His tone was disdainful as he picked at the chunky zip on the front of a black sleeveless shirt and eyed the leather pants and steel-toed boots.

'Whoa!' Reece looked in. 'This wardrobe is just fabulous!'

Tamizel's sneer disappeared and was replaced by the most polite and urbane of smiles. 'They appear to be your size, Reece.' He held up the clothes. 'You can change here.' He pointed towards an alcove. As Reece ducked into it, Holly stared at the recess of the wardrobe. There wasn't a feather cloak anywhere in sight.

'Now this…' Tamizel reached in to pull out a green velvet cloak. '…is the latest in court fashion. It's made so that it chimes musically as it swishes, not for any practicality.' He draped the cloak over Holly's shoulders and stood back to inspect it. 'Would you like a cloak pin?'

Holly pulled the soft folds of cloth around herself. 'It's lovely.' She snuggled into the cloak, feeling quite forgiving. She blinked—dazed. A moment ago, Tamizel had been dressed in grey, his feet bare. Now he was clad in black from head to foot, fully-shod in boots as dark as midnight. *How'd he do that? So quickly?* Tamizel presented such a stark and dramatic figure she felt intimidated.

Reece, coming out from the alcove, almost jumped as he noticed the transformation. 'I wouldn't want to meet you coming down a dark alleyway.'

'I didn't intend to be frightening.' Tamizel frowned. 'Merely understated.'

'That,' said Reece and Holly together, 'is not *under*stated.'

'Well, that certainly isn't either.' Tamizel indicated Reece's attire. He looked down at the steel-capped boots still in Reece's hands and shook his head in obvious disbelief. 'Put them on and hurry or we'll be late. The king is anxious to meet you.'

'King?' Reece asked. 'I don't have to bow, do I? I don't know how.

We don't have kings where we come from. Just prime ministers.'

'Follow my example. I will guide you.' Tamizel waited until Reece had managed to get the boots on before leading the way to the door. Just as he reached it, he stopped and turned to Holly, as if remembering something vital. 'Be very careful.' His voice was stern. 'Be suspicious. Do not offer anything, or receive anything. Remember the cherry tree. Do not become indebted to anyone, for anything at all, not even for something as simple as a drink.'

A cold tingle of misgiving shot up her spine.

'But we're indebted to you,' Reece said.

Tamizel pulled the curtain back from the entrance and, as the glass door slid open, he strode out past the guards. 'Hopelessly indebted,' he agreed.

'Come back, Green Giant,' Reece whispered as they entered the court. 'All is forgiven.'

Holly understood his feeling at once. The reception was so glittering and sumptuous the sensation of insignificance they'd felt in the gold esplumoir was multiplied many times over. The room, lit by thousands of glowlights embedded in the walls, was magnificent. The atmosphere was so dazzling she realised she would have been anxious and uncomfortable even without Tamizel's warning. The lords and ladies of the Farafolk were so regal and resplendent in their appearance they were intimidating.

Tamizel had been right—his clothing was exceedingly understated compared to the peacock opulence of the crowd. In fact, she and Reece were both very plain compared to the luxurious rainbow brocades and diamanté weaves milling about them. Even the velvet cloak which tinkled as she moved was unpretentious, almost subdued. She was just about to whisper a comment to

Tamizel when she noticed an astonished look on Reece's face. *What have you seen, little brother? What can be more bizarre than the ebony nest of birds fluttering and twittering inside that woman's twig crown?*

She turned her head to follow his line of sight. A woman with hair the colour of dancing flame was coming through the crowd towards them. She waved at Reece and Tamizel. She wore a skirt that moved and sparkled like a waterfall sweeping over a cataract. But that wasn't what was causing Reece to keep turning his head, trying to pretend he hadn't noticed her. Above her waist, she was wearing nothing. Nothing at all. The fiery hair tousled over her shoulders did little to hide her nakedness.

'Tamizel-ri.' Her voice was a bright warble. As she waved her hand, it tinkled with the sound of sapphires striking tiny crystal bells. Tamizel's groan was so faint it was only just audible. He took a step back. 'Reece-ri!' The woman kept coming. Smiling at Reece, she kept blowing kisses towards him.

Holly felt them as they ducked past her to land with an audible pop on Reece's cheek. 'Hol…Hol!… Sis, rescue me! Tell me what to do.' Reece was blubbering as the woman continued to wend her way to him.

It would serve you right if I left you to deal with her yourself. 'There's only one thing for it, Prince Charming.'

'What's that, Hol?'

'Look her straight in the eye, m'lord.'

Reece's response was lost as Tamizel tried to hold in a splutter of laughter. He failed. A moment later he was holding his sides. The woman with the twig cage of twittering birds on her head spoke to him and he gathered himself together sufficiently to say a few words to her. Then he broke into unrestrained laughter once more. The woman began to giggle herself.

Holly thought she was laughing more at the fact that Tamizel was laughing than because she found anything especially funny about the situation. A moment later, a group of Farafolk around them joined in, nudging each other and pointing at Tamizel. There was, however, a nervous edge to their laughter. Their faces darkened and all cheerfulness left them as they turned, as a single body, and inexplicably directed their attention at her.

Holly's glee at Reece's predicament dissipated. She felt uneasy and self-conscious once again. *I want to go home.* It was an instant before she remembered that home was impossibly far away on another planet in another star system entirely.

The bare-breasted woman touched Tamizel on the arm while smiling at her. Something about her glance told Holly the smile concealed a stiletto of murderous hatred. *I don't know how I've done it, but I've made an enemy.*

A ripple of delicate chimes sounded behind her and she felt a cold draught on her back. Her cloak was gone. Whirling, she saw it being whisked away through the crowd, its bells tinkling, carried off by some officious-looking person. 'Hey!' she called, raising her arm.

'Don't call the high chamberlain *that*,' Tamizel said at once. 'Even if he deserves the insult. Didn't I warn you to be careful? We don't need more attention than we've already got.'

'Don't blame me!' Holly grabbed at the back of her dress and bunched it together. 'It's you that brought us to everyone's attention. By laughing. What's so funny? And I didn't insult the chamberlain.' *All I said was 'hey!'*

'I don't mind you arguing with me.' Tamizel's voice low and calm, belying the expression in his eyes. 'Just don't do it in public. As we say here, a modicum of dignity would enhance your prospects all round.'

'A modicum of dignity?' Reece was staring. 'That's just what the voice said on the spaceship.'

'It's a common saying here.' Tamizel waved a dismissive hand.

'I want my cloak back.' Holly could feel a hundred eyes focused intently on her back and all at once she felt sick with nerves. 'Tamizel, can you *please* find something… any…?'

She was cut off by the stentorian voice of the herald. 'Tamizel-ri, Reece-ri, Olly-ria.'

'Follow my lead, and do exactly as I say.' Tamizel put his hand under Holly's elbow and escorted her across the room and down a long sweeping stairway. Reece was right behind them, ducking out of the way of the woman with the cage of birds on her head, as they made their way through the heart of the crowd—a crowd that parted in haste at their approach. 'This is the throne-room.' They made their way into a new and lofty hall. The splendour of the ante-room paled into insignificance. Light itself seemed to hang in the air and sparkle with elusive, floating brilliance. It was like walking through shining snowflakes. The draperies were airy shimmers of white gold weave and the throne was surrounded by a profusion of leaves and flowers, with tiny birds darting in and out amongst the foliage. Their song was liquid and dream-quiet and, when they perched on the branches and peered out between the leaves, their eyes were as bright and gem-like as jet. Holly stared at the King sitting at ease on his throne.

As Tamizel bowed, the pressure of his hand on Holly's elbow and his nod at Reece indicated they should follow his example. Then the King beckoned Tamizel forward.

'Don't move.' Tamizel set his foot on the dais and approached the throne. He raised his right hand in a salute, his palm open, his missing finger very conspicuous. Standing there, he made a stark contrast to the King. Tamizel's eyes were like grey-blue smoke, his skin pale and translucent, his hair as black as frozen, ice-embedded grass.

The King, on the other hand, was a study in gold: golden hair, sun-dusky skin, tawny eyes, a sunny smile. When he spoke, his voice was firm. He sounded kind. He was cordial to Tamizel who answered his questions defensively and in an increasingly unhappy tone.

Soon it became obvious there was considerable discord between them. The King would say something in his amiable way and Tamizel would retort sharply. The names 'Olly' and 'Reece' were the only recognisable words in the quarrel. At last Tamizel came away from the dais, bowing before he stepped back to where Holly and Reece were standing. 'It's time to dance,' he announced.

'What?' Reece stared at Tamizel. 'But what was that all about?' When there was no answer, he lifted one of his steel-toed boots. 'I can't dance.' His smile was one of obvious relief. 'Didn't bring my dancing shoes, so I guess I'll just have to sit this one out…' Before he could say another word, he was grabbed by the woman with the cage of birds singing in her hair.

Holly felt a hand on her forearm. Expecting to see Tamizel, she turned to find she was being led into the dance by the King himself. *Oh no*, she thought. *I can't dance. Unless you count the Chicken Dance. Where's Tamizel?* She wanted to back out, but she was too scared to say anything. *Keep your mouth shut, Holly Polly. Just zip those lips and lift your chin in a grin.* She managed to produce a passable smile and bobbed down in a curtsey to the King. He gave a signal and the dance began.

She noticed Reece was in a mess straight away. He hadn't taken more than two steps before he stumbled over his own feet and knocked against his dancing partner. In a flailing attempt to catch her before she fell, he broke the cage of birds on top of her head. His steel-capped boots crunched the twigs to splinters as escaping finches darted away in seemingly endless procession.

The birds circled the dancers in a soaring ribbon of flight, curved back, then executed a wild twittering loop of gratitude around Reece's head. They nipped the woman who'd been wearing them on her head, and at last fled to the foliage around the King's throne.

Holly tried to concentrate on the rollicking dance steps as she was propelled around the room. She knew her smile was slipping dangerously and that she was beginning to look as panicky as she felt. She could see Reece picking up twigs and handing them to his dancing partner. His apologies were abject and profuse, but he only seemed to be creating more embarrassment for himself. His dancing partner scowled at him as he pressed broken twigs with reckless frenzy into her hands.

As the dance ended, she threw the pieces at him and flounced off. *We need help, Tamizel.* Reece was standing alone and wretched in the middle of the dance floor. She'd never once wanted to comfort him before in her life but, for the first time, it was a serious temptation. However, fearful of giving offence, she didn't dare leave the King's side. Her smile re-asserted itself. Out of the corner of her eye, she searched the room for Tamizel. *Help! I know you can hear me, Tamizel. Alignment of minds, resonance of harmonies and all that. Where are you?*

She froze as she felt a touch at her back. She turned. A brightly-dressed man was behind her, bending over with an intent look on his face as his finger poked her spine. She glared at him. The man screwed up his face in a dour pout. An instant later, Holly felt a cold, clammy hand slide down her back. She jumped and spun around.

The King was gone, but there was the woman with the flaming hair and the waterfall skirt, hand outstretched, smiling inscrutably. Something prodded Holly's shoulder-blade from behind. She whirled again.

And there was another man, trying to poke her with a broken twig. Glowering at him, she felt her back pinched again. She slewed around, starting to breathe heavily, only to feel another hand stroke her. Turning wildly, she realised she was surrounded.

Tense faces loomed over her. *Tamizel!* She screamed silently as she felt her back pinched again. She was sweating, panting and frantic with fear as she looked into the eyes of the Farafolk and saw only unfathomable hostility. They were swarming bees, stinging with a cold and implacable purpose. She could see that they knew they were hurting her, but they didn't care.

Her back was nipped and pressed, tweaked and twanged, twisted, prodded and pummelled. She tried to slap their hands away but they only hemmed her in more closely. Dizzy and shocked, she thought the ordeal would never end.

It was only a minute before Tamizel appeared, but it seemed like forever. She threw herself against him and he swept her through the crowd, up the staircase, and out of the palace.

The chamberlain who had taken Holly's cloak came running after them, calling plaintively, her cloak tinkling and chiming in his hand. She glanced back and saw Reece whisking it away from him as he hurried after them. The guards who had accompanied them to the reception, fell in behind them, keeping pace.

Holly felt a sob escape her. *No, don't break down.* She saw people lined up along the streets, staring as they rushed past. Tamizel guided her off the road, into a series of arched hallways that offered an occasional glimpse of the terraced city through the overhead spans.

By the time they reached Tamizel's residence, Reece caught up with them. 'Holly, calm down. Holly, relax...'

She whirled on him, ready to give vent to the hysterical scream she'd been holding in. He pushed Tamizel aside as the door opened and glared at her. 'Calm. Down. Sis.' His voice was stern as he emphasised each word. 'She's always hated people touching her,' he said to Tamizel. 'Just go inside while...'

Before he could say another word, she tore the cloak out of his hands, bundled it into a tiny ball and threw it as hard as she could at Tamizel. Then, stalking past him into the room with the flowertable, she picked up the tiny potted tree and hurled it at him as well. It smashed against the wall as he ducked.

'Holly! Stop being an idiot.' Reece was becoming angry. She didn't care. He probably thought the last thing they needed was to lose their one friend because of a fit of hysteria. She snarled at Tamizel and looked for something else to throw.

'Hol*ly*!' Reece grabbed her arm and twisted it behind her back. 'Listen to me.' She tried to wrench herself out of his grasp. 'Listen to me! Calm down. Stop being an idiot.'

'Let go of me!'

'Only if you promise to calm down. Stop being an idiot.'

'Stop saying that!'

Reece increased the pressure on her arm. 'Oh, I'm sorry, I didn't realise you wanted to keep it a secret.' He sucked in a deep breath. 'Holly, we're safe here. I'll let you go if you promise me not to do anything you'll regret.'

'*Safe*?!' Holly spat. 'Safe?' She glared at Tamizel. 'He set us up!'

'Olly, I'm sorry.' Tamizel came forward, his eyes pleading, his voice a whisper.

'Sorry?' Holly shoved him back with her free arm. 'You lied to me! That wardrobe didn't choose this for me.' She plucked savagely at the side of the green dress. 'You did! Didn't you?'

'It was necessary.' Tamizel's face was subdued and solemn.

'And you got that … that… chamberlain… to take my cloak.' She tried to hold back the tears but it was impossible.

'That, too, was necessary, Olly.'

'I hate you,' Holly stormed. 'I *hate* you. You pretended you were our friend, but you lied. You said we were under your protection, but that's another lie. We should have stayed with the Ettii. All you want to do is humiliate us.'

'I *am* protecting you, Olly,' Tamizel insisted.

'Holly.' She screamed her name at him, tormented by his calm deferential tone. 'Holly, Holly, *Holly*. My name's Holly, damn you. You speak perfect English, so stop pretending you can't say it.'

Tamizel looked aside. He seemed to shrink inside himself before turning back to face her accusations. His eyes closed for the briefest of moments. 'Holly.' The word was almost inaudible.

'Everything you are, everything you say is a deception.' Holly felt her face quivering as she glanced at Reece for support. 'I want to go back to the Ettii.'

Reece let go of her arm. He looked appalled. 'Let's talk about this.'

'What for? We can't trust anyone here—how can we stay?'

Reece went to retrieve the cloak she'd been given. 'Here put this on.' He turned to Tamizel and adopted an authoritative tone. 'My sister and I would like to discuss something in private, if you don't mind. If you could leave for a few minutes, I'm sure we can sort this out.'

'There's nothing to sort out, Reece.' Holly folded her arms. 'We're leaving.'

Tamizel's face was inscrutable. 'I have an offer.' He took a long, slow breath. 'Holly is tired, and that's why she's irritable. I have a place where she can rest—and you can still together in private...'

'I'm not irritable because I'm tired,' Holly snapped. 'I'm irritable because I've been attacked by a pack of wolves! And because you tried to trick us.'

'Where's this private place?' Reece asked.

'This way.' Tamizel walked towards the far side of the wardrobe. As he neared the wall, an archway materialised. He gestured to the room beyond.

'C'mon.' Reece grabbed Holly's hand and pulled her forward. She began to struggle but he implored her, 'Please, Holly,' in such abject unhappy tones that she gave in.

As soon as they were through the archway, the wall closed up behind them. Holly slewed around, wrenching herself from Reece's grasp. 'We're trapped.'

'Holly!' Reece snapped. 'Stop it! Just stop it! You're alienating the one person we can communicate with here—the one person we desperately need. Can't you see that?'

Holly stared at him. Hot tears began to stream down her face. 'I'm scared.' Her voice caught on a sob. 'I want to go home, Reece. I want Mum and I want Dad. And I want them *now*.'

'So do I.' Reece was silent as he turned to inspect the room.

It was changing before their eyes. A circular canopy of dark star-strewn silk was descending from the ceiling, the sinuous bough-like posts of a four-poster bed were emerging from the floor and a brocade chair was making its way out of the wall.

Reece flung himself into the chair. 'I'm frightened too, Holly, and I want to go home too.' He took a deep breath. 'But there's no way.'

Holly, dejected, sat down on the edge of the bed, her lower lip quivering.

'No way,' Reece repeated, 'unless we get help from someone like Tamizel. And maybe not even then.'

Holly threw her arms out and fell back onto the bed. She stared up at the canopy. 'We can't trust him.'

'We don't know that.'

'*What!*' Holly bolted upright. 'How on earth can you possibly say that?'

'Because, stupid,' Reece almost sneered, 'the one thing you should have done is the one thing you haven't done.' He glared at her. 'Did you think to ask Tamizel for an explanation before you started blaming him for what happened?' He held up his hands. 'Holly, who got you out of there? Me? Or Tamizel?'

'I'm not apologising to him.' She dropped back down onto the bed. 'He set us up.'

'So?' Reece held up his hands. 'For crying out loud, Hol, we're aliens! At least from the Farafolk point of view. We could be spies. You saw those hornet 'copters. I don't know what's happening on this planet, but it sure ain't one big happy family here. Of course the Farafolk tested us! They'd be fools if they didn't.'

There was a knock on the wall.

Reece called out, 'What is it?'

'May I enter?' Tamizel's voice asked.

'No,' Holly snapped, but Reece's loud 'Yes, of course,' drowned her out. The archway opened, the wall appearing to melt fluidly aside to create it. Tamizel came into the room. His smile was tremulous as he held a board in his hands.

'Holly has something to ask you,' Reece said.

Holly's hands balled into tight fists and she shot a mutinous grimace at Reece.

'Yes, Olly?' Tamizel corrected himself almost instantly. 'Yes, Holly?'

There was a momentary hush. No one spoke. Reece stared pointedly at Holly. But she couldn't bring herself to ask for an explanation.

The silence was becoming awkward. 'When I was very small…' Tamizel lowered his eyes. '…and something made me sad, my nurse would play this game with me.' He tilted the board so they could see it. 'It always made me feel happier. Would you like to play?'

'Yes.' Reece spoke far too quickly, and Holly realised he wasn't giving her a chance to reject Tamizel's overture. 'We'd love to.'

She bared her teeth at him.

Please, he mouthed at her. 'It looks a bit like chess.' Reece eyed the squared gameboard as Tamizel put it down on the bed. It was covered in alternating white and green squares.

'It's called fletch.' Tamizel took some playing pieces from out of his pocket. 'I'll play for winter and you play for summer.'

Reece's expression was quizzical. 'What are the rules?'

'That depends on how seriously we are playing.' Tamizel placed the playing pieces on the board. 'Fletch is played to determine the winner in all sorts of contests. It may decide the fates of princes or kingdoms. Prisoners have gained their freedom through it. And lost their lives, too, of course. Fletch may be as momentous as a duel to the death, or there may be nothing more to it than the pleasure and honour of winning at a game of skill.'

'Oh.' Reece was good at strategy games but Holly could tell from the sound of his voice that he didn't like the prospect of this at all.

'Since you've accepted my challenge,' Tamizel said, 'I am the one to choose the stakes.'

That's not fair. Another trick. Why didn't you say so from the start? You've been playing this game since childhood, so what chance has Reece got?

'I think,' Tamizel went on, 'that we should play for the greatest prize of all, don't you?'

'And what's that?' Holly demanded.

'Truth.' Tamizel stared straight into her eyes. 'The winner may ask any question at all—and the loser must answer with perfect truth.' His gaze didn't move. 'Do you agree to the stakes?'

Holly felt relieved. 'Yes, I think we can agree to that.' A thought struck her: *he's sure to win, so why would he be doing this unless he believes there's some truth we haven't told him, and he can't think of any other way to get it from us? Why doesn't he just ask his question and read our minds?*

She frowned as she looked down at the alternating squares, winter-white and summer-green. Nothing made sense anymore.

'Okay. So how do you play?'

Tamizel tapped the side of the board and the tiny playing pieces seemed to come to life. Holly stared as a dozen black ravens, all on white squares, cawed and flapped their wings. A dozen blue wrens flitted around, exchanging places on the green squares at the far end of the board.

'The object of the game is to have an undivided land. To restore the proper season. Let me show you.' He clicked his fingers and one of the ravens hopped forward onto a green square. 'If you can...' He clicked his fingers again. '...make a defensible diamond where one of your pieces is surrounded...' *Click!* A raven hopped forward. '...on all sides...' *Click!* went his fingers again and another raven hopped beside the first. '...by its own allies, then that diamond of territory becomes yours...' *Click!* With squawks of victory, the ravens rose from the playing board and all the green squares beneath them turned, beneath Holly's fascinated gaze, to white.

There seemed to be a faint malevolent glint in the triumphant gleams of the raven's eyes as they fluttered back down to the board and settled in place. Holly took an instant dislike to them.

'Lucky we aren't playing for anything much,' Reece said. 'Just truth.'

Holly watched as Tamizel cleared the board and re-set the playing pieces. The tiniest of green stalks suddenly protruded through the white of several squares, unfurled their miniature bell-shaped heads and momentarily became clusters of snowdrops before the whole of four white squares mossed over and turned back to their original green. She blinked in disbelief.

'Guests may have the advantage of the first move.' The faintest of smiles appeared on Tamizel's lips. 'Show the wrens where you'd like them to move. They'll understand if you point.'

Understand? Are they alive?

'Right then.' Reece's forehead was wrinkling in thought. He indicated for the middle wren to move forward one place.

I guess the pieces are like pawns in chess. Reece can't possibly win, but one thing's for sure about my little brother—he's not going let anyone walk all over him.

Tamizel glanced at her as he clicked, countering with a similar move of his central raven. Reece responded by pulling up a flanking wren. Tamizel's reply was a mirror move of Reece's.

'Can I move diagonally?' Reece dropped his chin into his hand.

Tamizel nodded.

The game progressed in studied silence. It was when Tamizel's brow began to pucker that Holly began to feel better. *Thought you'd take him down easy, did you?*

She lounged on the bed by Reece's side. He was the first to make a diamond. The tiny wrens went into a riot of warbling, several of them somersaulting in the air as the diamond turned green.

'First blood to summer.' Tamizel tilted his head in acknowledgement. 'And to think I was intending to go lightly on you, it being your first game.'

Reece grinned. Stretching out on the bed, his face a picture of concentration as he watched Tamizel's next move. It wasn't long before a white diamond appeared on the board and the ravens cawed in victory.

I'd like to core you lot! Oh please no, don't let me become like Reece. Holly shrank inside as she watched him deliberately allow one particular wren to become surrounded by ravens. He obviously thought he understood the rules of the game and was trying a strategy to thwart Tamizel's efforts to make another diamond. As the last raven hopped into place, the wren made a desperate attempt to flee.

It was too late. The ravens turned on it in a savage frenzy and, a moment later, the tiniest of blue feathers floated up out of the mêlée. The square turned red.

Holly, shaking, hid her face in the coverlet.

'You didn't tell me that could happen.' Reece's voice sounded torn between horror at the sight of the blood-stained beaks of the ravens and a kind of detached curiosity. 'This *is* just a game, isn't it? The birds aren't real?'

'Just a game,' Tamizel agreed smoothly.

Holly wasn't so sure. She looked up. The red square heaved suddenly and, from it, a tiny trunk sprouted. Soon a tree emerged from the square, its leaves turning russet and blood-coloured with the hues of autumn. The ravens flew up to roost momentarily in the tree, before tumbling down to resume their places again.

Tamizel looked disconcerted by the appearance of the tree. 'This is a rare happening. Now you've given me a dilemma.'

'Why?' Reece asked.

'If I take the tree, I will have to defend it—and that will tie up my ravens while you're marauding over my land and conquering it. But if I don't take the tree at this point, I've brought my ravens here to no avail. If you then make it yours, you'll have a launch point into my territory. From a tree branch, you can drop to any square along its length.'

'Tough choice.' Reece shrugged.

They played on. Tamizel chose to take the tree, withered and wizened as it became. He left it with some defenders before moving on. But his ravens seemed to have lost their formation, while Reece kept his wrens in a tightly-disciplined pack. Diamond after diamond fell to the green. Finally the wrens led an attack on the raven-held tree itself.

'You've won.' Tamizel's voice was tinged with astonishment. The ravens had fled the tree and now the wrens ascended it.

Blossoms peeped out along its boughs as the board became a carpet of flowers. Petals fell from the tree, dropping down to form thick scented drifts. The tree fruited. And the fruits fell. Seeds from the fruit sprouted and new trees grew.

A wood appeared: a wild wood.

A miniature white stag appeared from out of the shadows of the trees, stepping warily from the edge of the wood. And still the birds carolled and the green grew deep and lush and thick. 'But the game's over,' Tamizel breathed, shaking his head. He looked up at Reece, obviously caught between wonder and puzzlement. 'It can't do this.'

'Well, it is doing it.' Reece folded his arms, as the wrens began another paean of song and the trees of the wood stretched their limbs to the light. 'You let me win.'

Tamizel couldn't take his eyes off the board as the reign of summer went on and on. The white stag bounded forward, leaping effortlessly towards the boundary before halting at the edge of the table. 'I admit that was my intention to start with. However you were too good an opponent. My mistake was to underrate you.' He looked up and scrutinised Reece's face. 'But I doubt if I'm the first to make that error. Nor, I suspect, will I be the last.'

Reece pulled himself upright. He glanced at Holly. 'We get the prize, sis.' He took a deep breath. 'Well, if truth's our prize, I'd better make our question a good one.' His face screwed up as he looked at Tamizel. Then at the board of summer with its singing birds. 'Shh!' he admonished the finches.

The instant quiet startled Holly.

'The truth, the whole truth and nothing but the truth.' In the silence, Reece's voice sounded booming and portentous. 'Why are you so afraid of us? So afraid that you won't even say Holly's name correctly?'

Tamizel closed his eyes. 'Hollë,' he whispered, almost in a rasp, 'is the name, in our language, of Lady Death. As yours Reece, is that of the Lord of Mortality.'

Death? Mortality? Like we were gods? Alien gods? Holly realised Tamizel had worked very hard to conceal his fear.

Reece was incredulous. 'Lady Death? Lord of Mortality?' He shook his head. 'No, you've got it completely wrong. My real name is from Welsh and it's Emrys, like in Emrys Merlin, the great enchanter of King Arthur's Court. It means "*im*mortality".'

Tamizel's eyes flicked open. 'Then why shorten it with its opposite?'

'Reece is only a nickname. It doesn't signify anything.'

'Only a nickname?' Tamizel's cobalt eyes went wide. 'You expect me to believe that?' He stared, meeting Reece's open gaze. 'You do, don't you? And a name doesn't signify anything? The sky will fall before that's the case. But why, why if names means nothing to you, why do you conceal the truth of your name with a lie?' His face was draining of colour, becoming ashen. 'I trusted the counsel of the Ettii and defended you both. I have pledged my honour to the King that you are lost and harmless travellers—children almost. I trusted the word on the Tree of Judgment and Blessing. How can your glamoure be so strong? Yet… no one has ever defeated me at fletch before. And you accomplished it so easily. You cannot be as young as you seem…' He fell to his knees in front of Holly. 'Spare us, Lady Death,' he begged.

The Tree *of* Stars

Reece grabbed Tamizel by the shoulder and tried to pull him up. 'You've got it wrong. Holly's a *lot* of things—believe me, I know 'em all—but Lady Death sure isn't one of them.' He shook his head. 'As for beating you at fletch, it's like you said: you underrated me. You couldn't know I've played lots of computer games and chess, and even though they're not fletch, strategy is strategy, when all's said and done.'

He was so grateful when Holly backed him up. 'Yes, strategy *is* strategy. Oh please get up, Tamizel. You're scaring me. I'm not Lady Death, I promise.'

Tamizel raised his eyes to meet her gaze. If he was still unsure about her real identity, he gave no sign of it, taking refuge in polite apology. 'Then you forgive me for thinking it?'

'Oh yes.' Holly was clearly flustered and confused. 'Oh please*please***PLEASE** get up.'

Tamizel rose from his knees. Reece heaved a huge sigh of relief. 'But wait a minute—if you Farafolk thought Holly was Lady

Death, why did the court treat her like that? Why did they keep on pinching her?'

Tamizel paused before answering. 'Hollë is the dark devourer. Whenever she walks amongst mortals, she disguises her form. She may appear as a bent old crone of kindly countenance, or she may come as a lovely young girl.' He nodded at Holly. 'Either way, you can tell it is Hollë the devourer because she has no back.'

'No back?' Reece asked.

'No back,' Tamizel repeated. 'Some say she is hollow, others say that the flesh of her back is rotting and putrescent, crawling with maggots.'

'Couldn't you tell straight away from this pathetic excuse for a dress...' Holly flounced one of the front panels of the skirt in the air. '...that I'm completely ordinary front *and* back?'

Tamizel looked down at the floor. 'I tried to tell the King and the court that I could detect no sign of glamoure, but...' He hesitated, almost as if he were unwilling to commit himself to his next words. '...but the more I insisted your thoughts were innocent and guileless, the more they felt that I was being swayed by my feelings. They decided I simply wasn't qualified to judge the matter and they insisted on being sure for themselves as soon as possible.' He held up his hands. 'Please believe that I did not anticipate the attack. I thought the Farafolk would trust the testimony of their own eyes. But it seems that fear can take away the ability to think clearly. Everyone thought they had nothing to lose. Because Death and her Consort had come to visit.'

'Consort?' Reece couldn't help his yelp of distaste. '*Me*?' He watched Holly visibly shrink from him.

'You bickered together just like an old married couple,' Tamizel said.

Reece shuddered.

'What happens now?' Holly sounded more mollified than Reece expected.

Tamizel smiled, almost diffidently. 'First, we should get the wardrobe to choose another dress for you.'

Reece knew she'd meant what would happen when the Farafolk knew she was just an ordinary girl. *Is Tamizel evading the real question?*

Holly clutched the cloak around herself more tightly. 'I don't trust that wardrobe.'

'Nevertheless, perhaps we should try.' Tamizel inclined his head. 'It wants to make amends as much as I do.'

He left the room. Less than a minute later he was back, his face half-hidden by a billow of bright orange taffeta bundled in his arms. 'How about this?' He held up the dress for inspection. It had a black bodice bordered with jewelled flowers. Puffs of marigold sleeve encased a satin undergown.

Reece watched Holly's expression. She was smiling. The dress was elegant—and most importantly, there was lots of it. Lots and lots of it. Skimpy, it most certainly was not. 'Or this?' Tamizel laid the first dress aside on the bed and held up another. Like the first, it had a black bodice, but this dress floated where the other had billowed. It had a long-sleeved beaded overlay and layer upon layer of dark chiffon in a trailing skirt.

Reece could tell it was the dress of her dreams. She fingered it, her lips compressed as she held back her unalloyed delight. *She doesn't want him to know she likes it.*

'It's a bit formal.' Her tone was dubious. 'Doesn't the wardrobe do anything casual?'

Perhaps you're right to be suspicious, sis. What if Tamizel's effort to make amends is not an apology but just a change of tactics? He's accepted our word Holly isn't Lady Death far too easily. He hasn't even asked for evidence. Not that we could have given him any.

'Too formal?' Tamizel inquired. 'One moment.' He left the room, but was barely gone long enough for Reece to exchange a questioning glance with Holly. He returned holding a very plain long-sleeved blue gown of the finest cashmere. Just looking at it showed how soft it was to touch.

'That's some wardrobe.' Reece watched Holly wrinkle her nose and pretend disdain as she took the cashmere gown. *I know everyone has their price. But who'd have thought Holly's was a couple of dresses?*

A flurry and a bustle sounded outside. As Tamizel turned, frowning, a tiny woman came through the door, carrying a tray.

'Jaizee!' Tamizel exclaimed.

'Tamizel-ri, couven'meir!' Jaizee's rosy, wrinkled face puckered in disapproval as she tutted and shook her head.

Reece stared. Her hair was standing on end and blue fire was sparking around her throat. She was wearing a necklace: darts of white fur alternating with amber beads. *Static electricity! Her teeth must be permanently on edge.* 'What did she say?' He was so fascinated he couldn't take his eyes off her.

'She said that I'm an idiot,' Tamizel replied. 'A statement with which I could hardly agree more.' He nodded. 'Reece, Olly, this is Jaizee. My nurse. Of long ago.'

Reece noticed that Holly was 'Olly' again. He knew he should make a stand on her correct name. Between the wild hair, the sparking necklace, and the thought that this was the person who'd taught Tamizel fletch, he was insatiably curious. He held out his hand. 'Hello, Jaizee.' He desperately wanted to feel a jolt and find out if she held an electric charge.

Jaizee ignored Reece's hand, put down her tray and went up to Holly. Poking her scowling face just in front of Holly's nose, she kissed her boldly on the forehead. 'Iý Tammiz g'gena.'

'What'd she say?' Reece was still half-mesmerised by her necklace.

'I said,' Jaizee announced, articulating her words precisely, 'that that was for making my little lamb laugh.'

'Oh.' Reece glanced at Tamizel. 'Doesn't the little lamb laugh much?'

Jaizee shook her head. 'Never until you two came.'

He's not that gloomy.

'How come you speak English?' Holly rubbed her forehead.

'I brought Tammiz up,' Jaizee answered.

'Tami*zel*,' came the terse correction.

Jaizee ignored him. 'His thoughts were once the rhythm of my day and even though he has turned against the Music, there is enough melody still bubbling in his heart for me to understand him. My thoughts are attuned to his as his are to yours.'

Turned against the Music? What's that mean? Reece was wondering if she'd been sent to protect Tamizel, to make sure he didn't fall for the tricks of Lady Death and her Consort—*urgh! consort!?* He shivered with distaste—when she turned to Tamizel. 'Your brother-king desires to see you.'

Tamizel looked irritated. 'My brother, the king, wants to see me,' he corrected. 'Why?'

He's a prince? Of course!

'You're the king's brother?' Holly asked.

'To the great misfortune of Lord Tammiz.' Jaizee was as free with information as Tamizel was secretive. 'And to Varyien's immense advantage.' She inclined her head towards Tamizel. 'Your brother-king bids you make haste.'

Brother-king? That doesn't sound like the brother of a king. Maybe he's not a prince. It sounds like a shared kingship. Reece frowned. *Oh, what have we got ourselves into? Holly's right—we're being used. Used*

Tamizel seemed furious at his nurse's remark. 'I suppose you've been sent to make quite sure nothing happens to my visitors while I'm away?' His voice was like splinters of ice. 'Jaizee, they're under my protection. Remember this—whatever orders you may have, you owe your first loyalty to me.'

'Even though you have turned against the Music?' Jaizee was unmoved by Tamizel's anger. 'My first loyalty is not to you, my allegiance is to the Music.'

'I hear a different melody now, Jaizee. It is not that I have turned against the Music—I have found the true song.' His voice dropped and his gaze met hers squarely. 'Be careful what you believe. And who you believe. For Olly is not Hollë. And it may be she is the Stardaughter.'

And why is this all being said in a language we can understand? Reece's misgivings increased with every word.

Jaizee's smile turned more than a little scornful. 'The Stardaughter? The Peaceweaver? Ah, see what delusions take hold when we deny the Music. Is this what you will tell Varyien? He will laugh at you.' Her gaze was tender as she took hold of Tamizel's hand and traced lines across his palm towards the gap where his finger was missing. 'I had hoped that you were just going through a phase in which you'd simply mistaken rebellion for independence. But now I'm not so sure. In the end you will never find joy without the Music.'

'I've made my choice, Jaizee.' Tamizel shook off her touch. 'I'm not turning back, whatever you think of me, whatever anyone thinks of me. And I don't regret a thing.'

'Ah, you fill me with such sadness, my Tammiz, my lambling. But have no fear for these children. You can depend upon me. I will not violate your trust.' Jaizee's smile faded. 'Mi'tem probat ku'uras?'

'Ebbet ail'n h'jurt.' Tamizel hurried out, looking both harassed and worried.

'What did he say?' Holly asked Jaizee.

The old nurse looked at her with a curious expression. Reece didn't really expect her to reply, but she didn't hesitate. 'He said that he felt his doom sidling up to him on little cat feet.' Jaizee sidled up to Holly and put an arm around her. Holly instantly disengaged herself and moved to Reece's side.

Tamizel's not the only one who feels doom approaching. Except it's not a cat. Doom's a spider spinning a sticky web around us.

'But you, of course, are not Hollë.' Jaizee's smile was back. 'So how could his doom be so early?'

Reece stared at her. *If you only know English because you read Tamizel's mind as he reads ours, how do you manage this fluent conversation, Jaizee? How many lies are we being told?*

'Tamizel's the king's brother?' Holly folded her arms in a self-protecting way.

'True.' Jaizee was willing to talk. 'And king himself, had he not turned against the Music.' Suddenly, clapping her hand over her mouth in a dramatic gesture that nearly caused Reece to laugh out loud, she affected to recollect her position. 'Here am I prattling on when you, no doubt, would like to change into this lovely gown.' She stroked the cashmere dress in Holly's hands, momentarily causing the woollen fibres to stand on end and the blue fire spinning around her neck to leap and faintly crackle. Then she turned to the tray she had brought in. 'I have some lovely milk and cookies here, just for you both.'

Reece flung up his hands. 'Okay, okay! Quit with the games, whoever you are. *Milk and cookies!?* Yeah, sure, you do the same things here as we do back on Earth. Next you'll be telling me that every planet in the universe has milk and cookies!'

'Earth?' Jaizee's brows came together in a faint crease.

Reece wasn't deceived. He just caught the gleam of triumph in her eyes, before it was extinguished by a look of kindly concern. *So that's what she's here for. To pump us for information. Tamizel mustn't have been getting it fast enough.*

He glowered at her before stooping to take a cup of milk from the tray. 'This is so thoughtful of you.' The milk tasted very strange but he endured it to the last drop. Then he yawned. 'Milk always makes me so sleepy, you know.' He lay down on the bed, yawned again, and closed his eyes. Soon he began to snore.

He hoped Holly would know he was shamming it. He hoped she'd take the hint. She did. He heard her sipping the second glass of milk. He heard her kick off her shoes. 'What a delicious nightcap.'

Reece wondered how long they'd have to wait before Jaizee left the room and they'd be able to abandon the game. It seemed like it might take forever.

Holly had just lain down at the end of the bed. She'd tried not to gag at Reece's stinky feet but to listen intently for the sound of Jaizee leaving. She waited and waited to hear footsteps heading for the door but there was nothing until one of her shoulders was shaken urgently.

'C'mon, sis, rise and shine.' It was Reece's voice. He sounded irritated. 'Or are you going to sleep through *another* whole day?'

Holly opened her eyes. 'I wasn't asleep. I was just dozing off…'

'Not asleep? You've been out like a light for a night, a morning and most of this afternoon.' Reece raised his eyebrows. 'Though how anybody could have slept through Tamizel's rampage beats me.'

'Tamizel's *rampage?*' Holly pushed herself up on her elbows.

She realised she was tucked beneath the coverlet—and had no idea how she had got there. She looked around: all the furnishings had disappeared and the walls were blank.

'While Tamizel was with the king and I was pretending to be out to it, Jaizee brought in interior decorators and completely re-styled the place.' Reece held up his hands. 'When Tamizel got back, he went off his brain. Berserk. I thought I was at ground zero during a thermonuclear explosion.' He gave a low whistle. 'After he threw Jaizee and her design crew out, he was just as nice as could be. He didn't really want to explain anything, but I guess he felt he had to. Hol, I'm not sure he's keeping secrets from us, so much as he's an especially private person. But honestly I don't have a clue what upset him—all I know is it was about the bees.'

'Bees?'

'Bees. There were bees embroidered over everything, and that, apparently, was why they had to go.' Reece shrugged. 'Don't ask me the reason—I wasn't game to risk having Tamizel froth at the mouth by asking any more questions.'

'You've been stuck with Tamizel for a whole day? Oh, I'm sorry, Reece.'

'It's okay. He wasn't mad at *me*.' He stared at her. 'But I tell you, sis, I've seen enough now to know I'm very glad it wasn't me he was angry at.'

'Maybe it was an act.' Holly threw aside the coverlet. 'Reece, what kind of nurse turns up and redecorates the apartment of the king's brother without permission?'

'It sounds suspicious, I know, but I don't think Tamizel was acting. You had to be there, Hol.' He smiled. 'C'mon, you must be starving. Let's go find him.' He turned towards the door and his voice dropped to a thrilled whisper. 'Sis, you should see my Wild Wood now. The white stag's almost ready to eat from my hand.'

My Wild Wood? What's this 'my' bit? Holly followed Reece through the door into—a ruin.

The room was a mess. There were drapes strewn across the floor, chairs upturned, the table was on its side. Holly stared at the chaos. Tamizel was on a ladder, surrounded by loops of dangling wires and conduit. His head was inside a hole in the ceiling. 'The core programming's been altered.' He sounded livid.

'Can't you set a manual override?' Reece called up at him.

'What does that mean?' Holly asked.

'Lady Holly!' Tamizel ducked down to smile at her. 'You're awake!' His smile became diffident. 'It means I will end up with a perfectly bland and featureless residence, but that is infinitely preferable to the present situation.' His smile vanished. 'Are you hungry?'

'Yes.'

'Then let's go out.' Tamizel jumped down from the ladder.

'Can we go to the Field of Fountains again?' Reece asked.

Holly frowned. *Reece went out with Tamizel while I was asleep? Why didn't they wake me? They left me alone!* Her mouth twisted, her eyes narrowed.

'Let's go to the Star Pool,' Tamizel said. 'It's very calming. Just what I need right now.'

'The Star Pool it is then.' Reece fell in so quickly with the suggestion that Holly was almost alarmed. *What's happened between them while I was asleep?*

'We'll need cloaks.' Tamizel strode to the wardrobe. It didn't open at his approach: he had to push part of the wall aside to reveal its contents. The selection within was plain and durable, not stylish. Tamizel handed out a green plaid mantle to Reece and a dusky grey one to Holly. He swung a long black cloak over his own shoulders before reaching down and picking up an empty scabbard and swordbelt from the very depths of the wardrobe. He buckled them on.

Leading the way to the door, he pushed it open. Holly, fastening her cloak with an ornate gold pin she found on the neckline, was surprised. 'Aren't the automatics working?'

'I had to turn everything off.' Tamizel's voice was cold and surly. 'The default repair had been changed to replicate bees as the main design motif.'

'What's wrong with bees?' Holly asked. 'They're so cute.'

'*Cute*?!' There was a pained and dark softness to Tamizel's voice as he turned away and pushed through the door.

Holly, unsettled by his mood, was happy to see that the guard had gone. Then she wondered just how far they *had* gone. She watched for them as they set off, Tamizel and Reece walking on either side of her, like an escort. The city seemed eerie and deserted. It was several minutes before Holly noticed some people strolling in an enclosed tree-lined park.

The people stopped, turned, and stared at them in silence. Holly, despite her misgivings about Tamizel, found herself shrinking closer towards him.

The only other sign of life was several lean dogs, like whippets, scurrying out of their way. *What a strange place. What do the people do all day?* Their path wound uphill, following a long cobbled curve. They came to a carved stone stairwell with sides constructed of hexagonal pillars. It spiralled quickly out of sight behind a stand of white barked trees like autumn birches with tawny-yellow leaves. Tamizel mounted the steps and began to lead them out of the city. Soon they were climbing a hill on a rough track, through a glade dappled with topaz and emerald light. It was strange to look up and see rock high above them: a cavern roof instead of a sky. Holly couldn't make out where the light was coming from.

'Look!' Reece pointed back through the green shadows of the trees. 'I can see the Field of Fountains—and the king's palace.'

Holly turned her head. Far below, there was a wide shallow lake, with concentric rings of fountains shooting high in the air. The heights of the fountains varied according to a timed pattern. It looked like the water was dancing. The edge of the lake sparkled like diamonds.

'The trees around the Field of Fountains are really amazing,' Reece said. 'They're metal sculptures with mirror leaves.'

Holly tried to appear disinterested. She watched Tamizel covertly, wondering why he was wearing a scabbard without a sword. 'I didn't realise we were up so high.' *We haven't climbed far. Are distances deceptive here—or is Tamizel still using illusion on us?*

They went up a gently-graded path that wound in and out amongst the trees and soon lost sight of the palace and the fountains below. *I wish I'd been as smart as Hansel and Gretel and brought something to make a trail back.*

'*Snow!*' Reece rushed ahead to where a white drift formed a sparkling bank overhanging the path. 'It's *snow*, Holly!' Scooping up a mound of crackling ice in his hands, he dashed back to her. 'Look—it's real!'

'Have you never seen snow before?' Tamizel asked.

'Not for real.' Reece pressed the sparkling white coldness into Holly's hands. 'Feel it, sis.'

Holly cradled the snow in her palms. *So cold*, she thought. *Cold enough to bite. Like Tamizel.*

'There's more up ahead,' Tamizel said.

The snow began to melt in her hands. Flicking it off, she turned and realised Tamizel was gone. He had forged ahead without waiting, Reece on his heels. Holly stood there still, debating whether or not she would follow them. *They make such a great pair together. I wish I could just leave them and go find Glyffy.* Climbing the path, she came to the top of a small rise and saw a still dark pool in a broad natural cup of rock. She felt a sudden desire to turn and run. *This planet certainly goes out of its way to give you the creeps. If this is Tamizel's idea of beautiful and calming, I don't want to know what his idea of disturbing is.*

Tamizel was already half-way down the slope, with Reece only a few steps behind. She followed them, dragging her pace with every step. By the time she reached the pool, Tamizel and Reece were sitting on a large flat stone, peering into the water. Next to them was a cloth laid out with fruit, pastries and cheeses. *This trip isn't spontaneous. It's been planned well in advance. And as meticulously as a military campaign.* She was amazed Reece had ignored the demands of his stomach long enough to actually look into the pool.

'It's like a huge wishing well.'

Holly stared at the reflections of stars in the still dark water. Looking upward she saw, not at a sky, but solid rock. *Just another illusion.*

But when she looked back down into the water, she saw a new reflection—the stars were still there, but now they were netted in the branches of a vast tree. It was tall and stately, ancient, mysterious, majestic.

'Wow!' Reece had seen it too. She was surprised by his reaction. He rarely felt enthusiasm for anything other than a new piece of electronic hardware.

As she stared, she heard a whisper. It was the Tree. It was calling. Calling Reece's name—insistently—over and over.

'What's that?' Reece jumped back.

Holly wasn't surprised. The Tree was frightening. A wild impossible thought occurred to her. *It's like, just like, those stories Gran used to tell us about Emrys Merlin. How he never died but was trapped in a rowan tree and how he's called over and over through the ages to be set free.*

'Who's that?' Reece sounded fearful.

'What do you mean?' Tamizel seemed puzzled. 'The stars you see are merely real-time images of the sky outside the mountain.'

'Yeah,' Reece said slowly. 'But what about the tree?'

Tamizel looked at him, eyes widening. 'You can see a tree?'

'Yes.' Holly peered at him. 'A tree with stars in it.'

'A tree of stars?' Tamizel's look was wondering and full of respect as Reece nodded at her. '*I've* never seen it. Hardly anyone ever does.' He swallowed and his expression turned fearful. 'Who are you?' he breathed. 'What do you want with me?'

Reece ignored the question. 'What is It?' He turned to Holly. 'Did you hear it say anything?'

She nodded. 'A name.'

'It's The Tree of Time.' Tamizel eyed them both. 'The Stormtree of Ruēl. It grows in the space between time and eternity as they flow endlessly through each other.' His expression changed and his eyes lit up in a way Holly hadn't seen before. 'The stars that glow on its branches are its first fruits, as we, perhaps, are its last.' It was the way Tamizel spoke as much as what he said.

'Trees are important here, aren't they?' Holly asked.

'They are important to *me*.' Tamizel smiled and changed the subject almost awkwardly. He turned to Reece. 'You said "wishing well" when you first looked into the pool. Does this mean that stars are wish objects in your world?'

'Only when they're falling stars.' Reece sounded grateful for the change of topic. 'Meteorites, that is.' He smiled. ''Course it's just a silly superstition really. Holly might believe it, not me.'

'I wouldn't wish on the stars in this pool if you paid me a trillion dollars every week for the rest of my life.' Holly stood on the edge of the pool and peered into its dark depths. The reflected stars winked up at her like icy eyes. But there was no tree any longer. *It's another trick.* 'There is something *wrong* here.' She rounded on

Tamizel, feeling unsettled by everything about the place. 'Why did you bring us here?'

'Oh *Holly*!' Reece snapped. 'What's wrong with you? Stop it—stop suspecting everything and everybody.' He jumped up and stood on the rock, facing her. 'Just to prove to you there's nothing wrong, I'm going into the water.' He began to take off his boots.

Tamizel jumped up and gripped his arm. 'No!'

'What?' Reece started to shiver.

'You can't go in.'

'But why not? What's wrong?'

'You can't go in without an invitation.'

'Is that all?' Reece rolled up the legs of his trousers. 'Give me an invitation then…'

'I can't. I'm not a woman.'

Reece stared at him, open-mouthed. 'What's that got to do with it?'

'This is a sanctified place. Only women may enter the water uninvited.'

Reece shook his head. 'I don't believe this.' He glowered at Tamizel. 'Can Holly give me an invitation?'

'Yes.'

'Terrific.' Reece turned to her. 'C'mon, Hol. Invitation, please.'

That's it. That's just what I felt. This place is restricted—it excludes, it doesn't include. It divides us, when it should be a healing place.

Without a word she slipped off her shoes and stepped into the stars. She had to stop herself from yelping. The water was bracing and cold. *The pool must be snowmelt. My feet are blocks of ice.* Perversely, she felt happier, and no longer wanted to leave or get out of the freezing water. Taking off her cloak, she threw it on the rock at Reece's feet before paddling along the shore line. She hoisted up her skirt and ventured into deeper water. In the distance, she could see an icy mountain stream tumbling down a cliff face to feed the pool. There was a cave high on the cliff and shadows passing across its mouth. She moved slowly, wondering if the shadows were birds. Turning her face to catch a better look, a glint of light angled into her eye. She stopped, attracted by the light, to stare at a long silver sliver just under the water's surface. 'Reece. Come and see this.'

Reece was off the side of the rock in an instant, splashing towards her and howling as he cursed the cold. He turned, looking back at Tamizel. 'C'mon,' he said, visibly shivering.

'I don't have an invitation.'

'Hol,' Reece yelled, 'invite Tamizel too, willya?'

Holly looked back at them both, knowing reluctance was showing on her face. 'Oh, come on, Tamizel.' She pointed just in front of her. 'I don't know what to make of this.' She paused, adding under her breath, 'But somehow I'm sure you will.'

Tamizel jumped off the rock into the chill dark water, soaking his long black boots right up to the knee. He waded over to Holly in long, even strides. 'What is it?'

'I think it's a sword.' Holly was still pointing as Reece arrived.

There, just below the surface of the water on a raised platform, was a long gleaming blade. The centre seemed to writhe with a whirling mist, but the edges were sharp and dark. There were faint markings along its entire length. 'Pick it up.' Tamizel folded his arms.

Holly turned to look into his eyes, but his expression was inscrutable. She bent down and laid her hand on the hilt. As she lifted the sword clear of the pool, shimmering runnels of water fled down its sides. 'You take it.' She handed it to Tamizel.

He grasped the hilt and held it up in front of him, his eyes seeming to lose focus as he gazed at the intricate runes along the blade. Both the darker edges and the cloudy centre seemed to have merged now into a pale even steel. 'Mistblade.'

Before he reached towards the empty sheath hanging at his side, Holly knew why he'd worn the scabbard and sword belt. And she was equally aware that he could not have claimed the Mistblade without her. He couldn't have entered the pool. *So what are you going to do with us, Tamizel, when you've quite finished using us both? Throw us wherever it is you dump your garbage?* She looked up at him, finding his eyes and staring fixedly into them. They were as black and cold as the pool itself. For the first time, it dawned on her that whenever she looked at him his eyes were a different colour. *Chameleon. I know as much about you as I do about the true colour of your eyes.*

Reece's expression was dark and forbidding as he watched Tamizel slip the sword into its sheath. His voice dripped sarcasm as he turned to Holly. 'I guess, dear sister, this makes you the Lady of the Lake.'

The Tree of Webs

A month passed. Holly's growing fluency in the language of the Farafolk more often than not made up for Reece's verbal blunders. They shared a room in Tamizel's residence—Holly took the bed while Reece commandeered a spot just in front of the door. It was his single concession to their shared fear. 'I'll sleep here and if anyone tries to sneak in, I'll try and stop them. But if they get me anyway, your job is to brain 'em, Hol.'

Holly had moved a huge ornate candlestick to the bedside so she could reach it quickly and, if necessary, 'brain 'em'. But who was to be brained, she didn't know. When it came to Tamizel, she was torn. In one sense, she had to trust him utterly—there was no choice. In another sense, she was sure there was something unspeakably wrong in the world of the Farafolk.

The day at the Star Pool had ended dismally. The picnic had been spoiled by the indelible impression that they'd been used. Despite Tamizel's efforts to cheer them with amusing stories, they had both sat like glum, miserable lumps, staring at the fruit and cheeses and delicate pastries as if they were sick. Reece—who, in Holly's memory, had *never* ever turned down food—ate a single berry before announcing he didn't feel particularly hungry.

At last, defeated by their despondent gloom, Tamizel packed up the uneaten picnic. No one said a word as they went back down the track. Reece told her later that he'd watched the sword swinging at Tamizel's side and felt betrayed. Holly thought he was trying to comfort her with the admission but it only made her feel more stupid not to have seen Tamizel's hidden agenda.

Before long she began to have bad dreams. Gigantic insects began to haunt her sleep. Sometimes there was a voracious ant and sometimes a tumescent spider. Other times it was an enormous hornet, or a bee or a mantis. Once Holly found a napkin with an embroidered golden bee that had escaped Tamizel's purge of Jaizee's re-decoration. Her nerves were so frayed it was too much. She shook in fright.

The monster in her nightmares settled into a terrifying combination of spider, bee and mantis. It had a masked face and a voice like Tamizel's. Sometimes the immobilising stings of the spider stabbed at her before she was lashed up in cobwebs; sometimes the gigantic mandibles of the mantis grabbed her throat and slavering jaws crunched at her head. One night, when the mask fell off the monstrous harpy she finally saw its face. It was her own. She woke up thrashing and sweating, in a lather of fright.

She realised Reece was trying to compensate for her constant tiredness by being particularly alert. He never left her side. Their days were spent attending an endless round of parties, receptions and amusements especially designed for their entertainment. Everything, it seemed, that could be done to make amends for the attack on her back was being done. She was invited to banquets and balls, galas and revelries, dances and concerts.

Everything was laid on, in fact, except an apology. Very soon, that lack began to trouble Reece. 'Tamizel had least to do with what happened to you at the reception,' he confided in Holly. 'And he's the only one to have said "sorry". So why don't we trust him?'

Soon other things began to weigh on Reece's mind. He was a practical person who liked to know how all things worked. Everything: things mechanical, things not-so-mechanical. And he couldn't figure out how the society of the Farafolk operated. 'How come, sis, no one works around here? How come it's party, party, party all the time? Who cooks, who cleans, who sweeps and vacuums, who dusts, who takes out the rubbish? Who repairs the broken automatics?' He stared at Holly. 'Much as I hate to bring it to your attention, sis: who does the washing up?'

Occasionally they would capture a glimpse of Bobenny at one of the galas they attended. This would remind them of the Hunt and the Ettii and the black troopers in the 'copters. Despite an avid curiosity, he never acquired enough words to frame a decent question about any of them. Holly's own efforts were always brushed aside. And they both had enough experience to know that asking Tamizel would get nowhere.

Their schedule was booked for weeks in advance. The sheer number of invitations pouring into Tamizel's residence for them both was stupendous. Not even the undiminished hostility of the lady who'd worn the bird-cage on her head and who made a point of insulting Reece whenever their paths crossed, made any difference to their volume. Holly, bereft of sleep, was so exhausted the individual feasts, high teas, luncheons, brunches, dances, performances, concerts and diversions all ran together in a dream-like miasma.

Until one supper at the king's palace. After dancing with her, Varyien claimed he was charmed by her manners and invited her to sit with him at the high table. Wine flowed freely and even though Holly had barely a sip, she felt her mind fogging over. She couldn't understand all the conversation around her, but she could make out enough to know that wit and spite laced the laughter, not any enjoyment of each other's company. Tiny potted apple trees like Tamizel's silver-leafed bonsai appeared at several places on the table, but these were golden-branched with plump, rosy fruit.

Holly thought back to the quiet ceremony when Tamizel had presented the tree as a symbol of enduring friendship, making it seem such an important, almost solemn, occasion. *It's nothing more than after-dinner mints.* She watched Varyien's courtiers snatching at the apples and eating gluttonous handfuls. Reflecting on Tamizel's subtle and crafty ways, she was hardly paying attention to Varyien as he reached for the largest, ripest fruit on the golden tree in front of him. Instead of eating it himself, he turned and held it out to her.

Holly's brain cleared in an instant. The fog vanished as an abrupt silence fell over the table. She froze and stared at the king's hand, the apple nestling in his gold-dusted palm. Transfixed by the fruit's shiny, immaculate skin, she could smell its freshness and perfection, its sweet lusciousness, its desirability.

'This can only be meant for you, Stardaughter.' Varyien's voice dropped to a whisper. 'Grant honour to me as I grant honour to you.'

No. No. What am I going to do? Panic threatened to overcome her. *Stardaughter!* Her hands were shaking. *That was just Tamizel playing one of his games. Who could be stupid enough to believe it…?* She was trying desperately to frame a polite refusal when she saw her hand rise of its own volition and reach out… *He's forcing me.* Her mind went blank with disbelief and terror as her fingers touched the fruit.

Then Reece was there. Tipsy and unsteady on his feet, he stumbled against her and sloshed an entire goblet of wine down the front of her dress. 'Whoopsha-daishee, Holly Spholly.' His voice was slurred as he peered over her shoulder at the spreading purple stain. A wide drunken swing pushed Varyien's arm away. The apple fell out of Holly's nerveless hand. 'Aww, sis, whatsh a messh of your dressh! We'd better go get it wasshed up righssht now, afore it getshh ruined.' Ignoring Varyien's angry protests, he pulled her up. 'Sssorry, mate, don't unnnerstand a word.' He peered at Holly's dress. 'Itsh ruined!' He dragged her towards the staircase. 'Rooned!' He waved at the court. 'We'll be righsht back! Save our sheats, folks.' He wove an unsteady path around the chamberlain barring their way. 'Rooned!' he crooned in the chamberlain's face, 'We'll all be rooned, said Hanrahan, if thish rain doeshn't shtop.' He hiccoughed at the chamberlain. 'Thatsh a famous Aurstrahlian poem.'

'You're drunk, Reece.' Holly was so grateful for his intervention she could almost have kissed him. 'I'd better get you home right now.'

'There'll be bushfiresh, for shure, no doubt. We'll all be rooned, shhaid Hanrahan, before the year ish out.' Despite Reece's weaving and swaying, he managed such a swift pace through the city streets that the guard had to run to keep pace with them. They reached Tamizel's residence with Reece singing at the top of his voice. 'The Jabberwock …'

As soon as the door had shut behind them, all signs of intoxication disappeared. 'What on earth happened?' he asked Holly.

She stared, astonished by the transformation. 'Don't you know?'

'All I know is that the whole room went dead quiet and everyone was looking at you.' Reece scrutinised her face too closely. *Did he know how sleep-deprived she was?*

Holly caught him up in a fervent hug. 'Thank you.'

His head jerked in surprise. A moment later, as he eased his way out of the embrace, Tamizel walked in.

His eyes held a quizzical look. It took him a moment to realise Reece was completely sober. 'Good save.'

Holly fled into the bathroom. She didn't come out for hours. When she finally did re-appear, her hair wet and her skin red and raw from scrubbing, she approached Tamizel. 'It was a misunderstanding, wasn't it?' Her voice was far more timid than she thought wise. 'It wasn't like I thought. I got it all wrong, didn't I? He's already got a wife, hasn't he?'

Tamizel was clipping his nails. 'Several.' He didn't look up. 'You'd certainly make an exotic addition to the royal harem.'

'Why?' Holly sat down next to Tamizel and searched his face as he blew across his fingertips, inspecting them carefully for chips and nicks. *What's wrong? He's never acted like this before—he seems vain and almost spiteful.* 'But why does Varyien want *me*? I've nothing to offer.'

Tamizel didn't look at her. The state of his manicure seemed to be holding his entire attention. 'You are Holly. That is enough.'

'That's no answer. Would it be *enough* for you?'

Tamizel paused, his hands momentarily motionless in mid-air, before he rose and left without a word. It was hours before he returned and, by that time, Holly and Reece had eaten. Then they'd watched the white stag bound in and out of the trees and the shadows deepen in the Wild Wood as if time ran a different course there.

'I'll get to the bottom of it,' Reece promised her. 'If it's the last thing I do.'

But as soon as Tamizel came in and they caught a glimpse of his face, all their carefully planned questions evaporated. 'What's happened?' Holly stared at the gaping wound across Tamizel's forehead.

'You need a doctor?' Reece lurched forward to help Tamizel.

His face was a terrible mask of dripping, slowly-crusting blood.

'It does not concern you.' Tamizel headed across the room, trailing drops of blood all the way. 'I need to spend some time alone, that's all.' The door to the room with the pool and the waterfall opened at his approach. 'I will see you in the morning.' It was a crisp dismissal. 'Sleep well, Holly. Sleep well, Reece.' The door closed.

They stared after him. After staying up another hour and making several futile speculations about what had happened, they went to their bedroom. 'I won't get a wink of sleep,' Reece said.

Holly agreed but, despite her anxiety, lost consciousness almost at once. She awoke with a start late the next morning. Stepping over Reece's body, snoring in the doorway, she ventured outside, determined to confront Tamizel. But he wasn't there. The waterroom door was still locked.

This worried Holly. *What if he's bled to death in the bath?*

She was just wondering what to do when Reece sauntered over and pounded on the door. 'You okay in there?'

'Won't be long.'

I don't like the way he sounds.

Three hours later, they were both beginning to wonder whether 'won't be long' had a different meaning to what it did on Earth. They'd eaten, slammed the door on an escort that had come to take them to a luncheon engagement and got rid of Jaizee as soon as they realised her inquiries about her little lambkin's health didn't extend to answering any questions about how Tamizel came to be wounded in the first place.

Reece prowled around, fiddling with small switches belonging to the automatic systems that Tamizel was still in the process of repairing. At lunchtime, he pounded on the door again. 'You hungry in there? I'll make you up a plate of something nice.'

'Thank you, Reece. But please don't bother. I'll be with you shortly.'

Another three hours passed but there was still no sign of Tamizel. Holly tried to remove the bloodstains on the floor. They reminded her of the red square that had appeared on the fletch board. *Sacrifice*. She cornered Reece. 'Are you sure he's all right?'

'No. But what can we do? Break the door down?' His mouth twisted. 'I don't s'pose you've spotted a store while we've been here which sells battering rams?'

'I haven't spotted a store for anything.' Holly stared at him. 'What're we going to do, Reece?'

'Make dinner,' Reece answered, with an emphatic nod.

'No, I mean, what're we going to do about being here and finding out what's going on and most importantly, about getting home?'

'We're going to make dinner.'

'Do you ever think of anything other than food?'

'Quite often.'

'Then what are we going to do?'

'We're going to do the next thing.' Reece sighed and nodded. 'We're going to go on one step at a time. I can't answer how, or even if, we're going to get home. You understand this place better than I do, and you speak the language much better, so if you don't know what we're going to do about being here, how can I know? All I do know is this—that we do the next thing, whatever it is, and we carefully consider each step as we take it. Now—having given some thought to the pros and cons of making dinner, I still think it's probably the very best thing we can do next.'

I've never before realised the benefits of having such a practical, unimaginative brother. 'I'm so scared, Reece.'

'At least we've got each other.' Reece stared her straight in the eye. 'I'm *really* sorry about the washing up, you know. This is all my fault. If I hadn't been trying to get out of it, we wouldn't be here.'

'Do you ever wonder about what's happening to Mum and Dad?'

'All the time. I worry that Gran was right and that Dad's been arrested for our murder.'

I'd forgotten that prediction. 'Did Gran ever say anything to you? Strange, I mean? About Dad?'

Reece was silent a moment. 'What's it matter here?' He changed the subject abruptly. 'I've still got the tachyon decelerator, you know.' He patted the pocket of his jacket. 'Right here. Next to my water pistol.' He smiled. 'It's the key to getting home, I think.'

'The water pistol?' Holly returned his smile.

'No, dopey.' Reece delved into his pocket and brought out a dangling chain of silver filigree. 'Here.' He pressed the glittering mesh into her hand.

Holly held it up for a moment against her neck and then looked at Reece. 'Let's make dinner.' She slipped it into her pocket.

They made dinner and ate dinner and Reece pounded on the bathroom door again and Tamizel said he was almost finished. But hours later, when Holly and Reece decided to turn in for the night, he still hadn't emerged.

Reece tried hard to be reassuring. 'If he really needed our help, he'd ask for it, I'm sure. Probably he was out with the Hunt and got hurt. If it was really serious, Bobenny would've known and I'm sure we'd have had more visitors by now.'

'Who are you trying to convince?' Holly watched Reece curl up by the door. By common agreement, they left it open so they could listen for any sound in the next room. Until just as she was drifting off, she thought she heard the slide of the waterroom door opening. But she was too far gone into the realms of sleep to be able to pull herself back into wakefulness.

Moments later, she was jolted into full consciousness by a scream.

There was an instant of disorientation as she leapt up and grabbed the candlestick. She heard Reece call 'dalla' for lights and realised the scream hadn't been his.

As dazzling brightness flooded the room, a shadow flitted past him, careening across the wall and over the ceiling high above him. It was gone so fast, Holly wouldn't have been able to swear she'd seen anything at all.

Holly followed Reece as he hurried into the next room. 'Was it you that screamed?'

Tamizel didn't answer. He was sitting in a chair, pale and shaking.

Holly, still holding the huge candlestick, came stand beside Reece. 'Is everything okay?'

'A bad dream.' A thin smile curved Tamizel's lips. 'I'm sorry to disturb you.'

Holly stared at him. There was very little sign of a head wound—the skin was still healing and newly pink, but the blood and the gaping injury were both gone.

'You sure you're right?' Reece asked. 'You don't really look it.'

'It was just a bad dream,' Tamizel repeated steadily.

Holly looked at Tamizel's face, trying to see behind the mask. Her belief he was constantly hiding the truth from them led her to a ghastly suspicion. 'Are dreams real here?' Her voice was unable to hold back the sudden dread she felt at the mere possibility.

Tamizel burst out laughing. 'Are you having nightmares?' His mouth had a wry twist.

Holly said nothing, stung by Tamizel's sudden mockery. She took her candlestick and marched back to the bedroom. She was about to order the door closed when she heard Tamizel's whisper to Reece. 'Find out what she is dreaming.'

'Dreams *are* real?' Reece's return whisper sounded aghast.

'Dreams are the viewpoint from the inside. Often they are nearer the truth than any exterior perspective.'

'Is that supposed to mean "yes" or "no"?'

'It means please don't frighten Holly. Just find out what invades her sleep.'

'Don't frighten her? She's already frightened. She's terrified, in fact.' He paused. 'Of this place. Of you. Of the king. How can she refuse to marry Varyien if he insists? What if he won't take "no" for an answer?'

'He won't ask again.' Tamizel's voice was cold and flat. 'The matter is settled for once and ever.'

'How can it be settled?' Reece's voice changed as if he'd realised something of significance. 'You fought him…? You fought the king? You had a duel? Didn't you? Over Holly?'

'It's not a matter for public debate. Please don't refer to it again.'

He won. Holly felt as if her heart had stopped beating. *Tamizel was badly wounded, but he won.* She wondered if Varyien were dead. *But he couldn't be. We'd have heard.*

'So does she have to marry *you* then?' Reece asked.

'Of course not. Even if I desired to, I am not free to marry her. My betrothal has just been announced.'

'Now that *is* a surprise.' Reece sounded taken aback. 'Anyone we know?'

'You ask too many questions especially for this time of the night. I'm tired—and you must be, too. Go to bed, Reece. *Please.*'

Why does Tamizel's betrothal mean he can't marry me? If the king has a harem, why can't he? She was standing just inside the doorway when Reece came in. One look, and she knew he realised she overheard what they said.

She poked her head out and caught a glimpse of Tamizel in an unguarded moment. His head was bowed, his face lined with anguish, his eyes were bleak and hollow.

But when she woke up the next morning he was unrelenting in his cheerfulness. She came out to find him brooming away furiously at some gauzy milk-white filaments hanging from the ceiling, all the while humming a bright, skipping tune to himself. 'I hope you don't mind…' He swiped at a long strand of gossamer. '…but I've cancelled all your engagements for the day.'

'More than fine by me.'

Reece came to stand beside her. He watched as Tamizel wound the filaments into a sticky ball and threw them into a wastebin. 'Tell me, do you do all your house-keeping yourself?'

'When I have to.' Tamizel whistled briefly and, a moment later, a small stepladder scooted into the room and settled itself next to his feet. Climbing onto it, Tamizel reached up and pulled aside one of the ceiling panels. A cascade of fine net-like filaments tumbled down out of the cavity, falling as long strands towards the floor. Tamizel attacked the sticky mass with his broom.

'I don't understand,' Reece said.

'What don't you understand?'

'Well, you're the king's brother and I guess if anyone could have servants, you could. But there are none. Which is fine. I s'pose that's your choice. But I've been wondering for a while if there are ordinary people here. We've been here a month and we've met no one but royalty and aristocrats.' Reece looked up, his expression quizzical. 'Correct me if I'm wrong. But even the court seems to be divided—there's a kind of High Court, composed of you and the king and a couple of other courtiers. Then there's the women and sometimes I get the idea that they're the real rulers, but they're not. I'm not sure who is, but Varyien isn't, is he?'

'You'd like to meet the ordinary people?' Tamizel swiped at a cluster of white sticky strands.

It was so evasive Holly's breath was almost taken away.

Reece's eyes narrowed. 'Yes.'

'I'll ask then…' Tamizel paused. '…if they want to meet you.' He stopped his cleaning long enough to look them both up and down. 'They're much more fussy than the court about who they associate with.' Turning his attention back to cleaning the ceiling cavity, he poked his broom higher into the recess, accidentally dislodging some wires. They fell down, sparking, and as they dangled Tamizel slowly reached out with his maimed hand.

'No!' Reece said.

The look of longing on Tamizel's face as his palm curled to enclose the jumping sparks so frightened Holly that she screamed. *'Tamizel. No!'*

It was over so quickly that as Tamizel nonchalantly stepped off the ladder and immediately suggested breakfast, Holly wasn't even sure what had happened. She'd seen a desire in Tamizel's eyes that was so incomprehensible and scared her so much, she'd have done almost anything to get him away from those wires in the ceiling.

Breakfast took hours—Tamizel made them something very like pancakes, but in doing so, he described every step of the process and taught them a great treasure trove of words. Words, not just for the ingredients, but for each of the actions involved in the cooking. Then he told a story about how he'd once upset Jaizee when she'd been making him pancakes for a special treat. He'd been eating the mixture straight from the blending bowl and got shirt after shirt covered in paste. Exasperated, she'd told him that, if he messed himself one more time, he'd be wearing the pancakes themselves, because there'd be nothing left clean in his wardrobe. Which was exactly what had happened. He'd had to go to court, wearing pancakes. 'She did it deliberately. To teach me a lesson.' He rolled his eyes. 'It was *soooo* embarrassing.'

Reece laughed at Tamizel's mortified expression. 'Didn't your mother stop her?'

Tamizel froze, just for a moment. Then he recovered and a

smile tacked itself to his face. 'You don't know Jaizee, if you think she'd be influenced by anyone.' And with that, he launched into a whole series of funny stories about different people they'd met in the past few weeks. The day passed swiftly.

Holly found it hard to find an opportunity to slip away for several minutes. When she finally did, she discovered Reece fixing the wires in the ceiling. With a strange look, he closed the cavity and took the stepladder to the bedroom where he hid it under Holly's bed. She watched him tie it as securely as he could to one of the bedposts. 'Just let him try whistling for that!'

At that moment, Holly realised she hadn't been mistaken. Reece had seen the look in Tamizel's eyes too. Hours later, when they finally retired for the night, his last action was to check on the ladder under her bed. It was still tied securely to the bedpost.

'Even if he can whistle the knots undone,' Holly said to him, 'it won't be able hop over you and out the door.'

Reece rolled his eyes. 'Are we sure of that?' He sighed. 'Sleep tight, sis.'

Reece had been shocked by the look on Tamizel's face when he'd reached out for the electrical wires. The intensity of the longing had been startling. As he'd shouted, he realised he actually did like Tamizel and would hate to see him hurt. The probability was that the prince was genuinely trying to guide them through a very difficult transition. Maybe his help wasn't entirely without self-interest, but he was undeniably kind and sympathetic. The rest of the court—with a few exceptions—were glitteringly self-centred and diamond-cruel.

He put his head down on his pillow on the floor when he thought he heard a soft noise outside. The gentlest of thumps, followed by what almost sounded like a quickly-stifled scream. 'Everything okay out there?'

There was no answer.

Reece got up and opened the door. He noticed a pale luminous sheen floating through the room. It was as if a ghostly patch hung in the air. 'Tamizel? Are you all right?'

'Go to sleep, Reece.' The familiar voice coming out of the strangely lucent darkness didn't reassure him. He closed the door, leaving just a slit open into the next room. Dropping back down to his place on the floor, he decided to keep watch. All was going well when the ladder slid out from under the bed and shimmied over to him. As it extended through a hole that appeared in the roof, he realised it was capable of reaching heaven itself. So he climbed the ladder and was just about to press the entry bell on heaven's door when he jolted awake. It had been a dream.

He got up and found the door was stuck. He had to put his shoulder to it in order to force it even partly open. He sidled out into the main room, only to be stopped by the sight in front of him. Everywhere fine shimmering strings of white hung from the ceiling. There was a strange cloying smell in the room. 'Tamizel?' No answer. Reece pushed his way through the gauzy strands, trying to brush them aside but finding the more he flung them away, the closer they adhered to him. 'Tamizel?' The clinging musky smell had a faint death-like putrescence to it. He was beginning to feel a frantic, sickening anxiety. 'Answer me, Tamizel!'

The faintest of sounds came from the side wall. Reece made his way towards it, looking for the source of the noise. Then, near one end of a shrouded lump adhering to the wall, Reece spotted a dark pair of glade-green eyes trapped in the whiteness. They blinked. 'Tamizel!?' Reece felt faint. '*Tamizel?*' Nausea threatened to overcome him, but he scrambled forward through the sticky filaments. Reaching the encased white form, he tried to pull the shroud away from the wall—but it was like sticky rubber and the edges sprang back with a sound like a wet slap. Then realising that Tamizel's eyes and nose were both free, he plucked and pulled carefully and, a minute later, managed to rip open a hole for the mouth.

'Thank you, Reece,' were Tamizel's first breathless words.

'What's happened?'

'If you could find a sharp knife…'

Reece instantly had a better idea. 'The sword. The sword from the Star Pool.'

'A knife, Reece…'

'Where's the sword, Tamizel?'

'I gave it to the king.' Tamizel sounded exasperated. 'Did you think I wanted it for myself? I withdrew all claim to the sovereignty it symbolises long ago.'

'Withdrew? You mean, abdicated?'

'Reece, please get a knife…'

There was a loud gasp at the bedroom door.

'It's okay, Hol,' Reece called over his shoulder. 'We've just got to find a way to get Tamizel out of the predicament he's got himself into.' He pointed to the sticky webs of white netting. 'See what comes of trying to fix the automatics yourself? What a mess! I think you should get a technician in.'

'Technician?' Holly pushed the pale filaments aside. 'Are you kidding? This isn't a breakdown of the automatics, Reece. This isn't anything normal.' She stared at Tamizel trapped in the shroud. 'Maybe we should just leave him there until he makes us a solemn promise.'

'What sort of promise?' Reece watched Tamizel staring at Holly, his expression completely unreadable, his eyes cloistered and dark.

'To tell us the whole truth. About everything.'

The Tree
of
Lightning

Holly wasn't even angry when Reece point blank refused to extract the promise she wanted. She couldn't muster any emotion. A curious detachment seized her as Reece ran for a knife and carefully cut Tamizel out of the webbing.

'I'm having nothing to do with that kind of thinking.' He scowled at her as he hacked away at the white shroud. 'It only leads to trouble. If Tamizel wants to tell us what's going on, that's fine, and if he doesn't, that's fine, too. Who do we think we are to be demanding anything? We owe him our lives. Maybe we should try to act a bit more grateful every now and again.'

After a moment of silence, Tamizel spoke. 'Reece, you melt me. Your sincerity is a sun so hot the walls of secrecy I've built about me cannot withstand it.'

Reece halted, taken aback for a moment by the earnestness of Tamizel's gratitude. Tamizel closed his eyes, as if meditating. His voice was soft and low as he began to intone:

As he finished the song, Reece succeeded in freeing his legs. Tamizel struggled—bending, twisting and contorting himself until his feet were able to reach the floor. Reece continued to cut at the sticky webbing binding Tamizel's arms and torso to the wall. Finally, as the last of shroud was torn aside by Tamizel himself, Reece smiled and asked, 'Breakfast?'

Tamizel appeared to have a second skin of grey fine-spun gauze. 'Holly's right, you know, Reece.' He sighed and shook his head. 'There are more important things than food. I need to tell you the truth about Finddias.' He looked around as if the walls had ears and eyes. 'But not here. Somewhere private, somewhere safe.' Without even stopping to wash off the sticky webbing still adhering to his skin, he led them out, through the city, past verdant gardens and light-drenched waterways, into narrow labyrinthine passages where houses jostled each other and the streets were filled with noise and bustle and laughter.

So these are the common people. Holly gazed around without surprise as Tamizel escorted them down a crowded laneway. *Somehow they're just like I imagined them to be.*

The ordinary people were scruffy, dirty and smelly. They

were as shabby and simply-dressed as the Court was bright, gorgeously-apparelled and sophisticated. But it was easy to see there was no deception about them. And there no doubt either how they felt about Tamizel: they kissed his shadow as he passed, they reached out to touch his swirling cloak, they tried to stroke his arm as he put his hands up to command a passage, they wept at his approach and cried even more bitterly as he disappeared from sight.

Holly had to hurry to stay close to his side as he swept along. The common people whispered insistently to Tamizel, asking—as far as Holly could tell—the same thing over and over and over again. She didn't know what it was, but she realised that Tamizel's repeated answer had the words 'little cat feet' in it. *Doom. That's what he said came on little cat feet.*

She hurried along passages as cramped, sooty and oppressive as the caverns of the Farafolk Court were vast, light-filled and airy. Reece stayed right beside her. She was sure they'd finally lost the discreet guard that had shadowed their movements for weeks. She was even surer, without being told, that Varyien did not receive the same response as Tamizel from the common people.

They stopped at last at a pale yellow door with a plaque inset in the wall next to it. The plaque was a pottery slab with the impression of a hand and, as Tamizel put his own hand to it, the door slid open. Reece and Holly followed him into the darkness beyond. As the door slid shut behind them, silence fell. The bustling crowds of common people could no longer be heard, only a faint plip-plop of falling water.

The darkness was so complete Holly couldn't make out any shapes at all, not even Reece standing next to her.

'We're almost there.' Tamizel's hand reached out to take hers in the darkness. She felt his fingers slowly entwine hers, all but the missing ring finger. It was like being held by a velvet vice. 'Now we climb the secret stair.'

'Secret!?' Reece sounded dubious. '*Secret?* It may have escaped your notice, Tamizel, but a lot of people saw us come in here.'

'The best kind of secret is the one that's so open, no one thinks it's a secret.' Tamizel chuckled. 'Come on. Three steps and you'll find a stairway. I'll guide you.' He led Holly forward. 'One, two, three, stop. We're at the stair. Now just put one foot after another and up you go.'

'How far is it?' Reece asked.

'A thousand steps,' Tamizel said.

Holly heard Reece's faint gasp. She was glad the darkness covered her expression of dismay. Barely a hundred steps later, she was sure she was going to die before the top. She was huffing, but the air on the staircase was so chilly she could feel the sweat turning to cold droplets on her face. *All that partying hasn't made a climb like this any easier.*

'Rest stop,' Reece called, to Holly's undying gratitude. She groped her way down onto the steps and gasped for breath. Reece knocked against her as he sat down.

Tamizel leaned against the wall. 'I want to bind myself with power, to sing the uncreated song; I want to ring, to wind the tower with gardens measureless miles long…'

'Gardens full of trees?' Reece interrupted, between ragged, uneven pants.

'Oh yes, full of trees,' Tamizel confirmed, his voice almost dreamy. 'Fruit trees, spice trees, trees that give sweet syrup, trees for shade, trees that simply delight the eye.'

'So, is it a magic song?' Reece asked. 'That one you keep singing?'

'Magic?' Tamizel asked. 'In that it is a song of heart's desire, it may be so—but no, I haven't deliberately put any magic into it.'

You may not need to do anything deliberately. Maybe, like Merlin, you're just so magical that it spills out of you wherever you go. And then it hit her. *I'm starting to think of this place in terms of magic, not science. I'd better watch myself.*

'I think we're right to go on now.' Reece got up. Tamizel found Holly's hand and stood her up as he linked elbows with Reece. They set off again. The staircase became steeper and they had to rest four more times on the way to the top. 'All I can say is,' Reece said in short heaving breaths at their last stop, 'thank heavens it's downhill on the way back.'

Tamizel said nothing. He simply linked arms once more and led them on. Soon the darkness began to grey and Holly could see Tamizel's shadowy form.

'There's light ahead,' Reece rasped. 'We're near the top.'

They came out, not on the rocky blustery shelf Holly had been expecting, but on the inside of a spiralling sandstone chimney. It was like the interior of a chambered shell. A waft of air, so slight it was little more than a wavering touch, disturbed the stillness of the heights.

'No!' Holly despaired at seeing the curved upward slope. 'It's too much.'

'We're just going around the corner.' Tamizel took her by the hand once more and, guiding her up part of the sandstone spiral, helped her step across onto a small platform with an archway leading to a parapet of rock.

Below them was a sweeping vista of the cavern. As Reece followed them onto the parapet, he gawped. 'There's the Star Pool.' He pointed to a lozenge of scintillating darkness far beneath them. 'And the city.' The tall spires and high, sturdy turrets of the king's palace had thinned to threads, the cobbled lanes of the city were narrow ribbons and the Farafolk mansions had become mere flecks on the landscape. 'How high up are we?'

'Not very,' Tamizel said. 'The roots of this mountain are twice as deep as we are high.' He took a step back, gesturing for Reece to stand beside him. 'Follow me.'

'That's no answer.' Reece whistled at the view. 'Do you know you're absolutely the most evasive person I've ever…?' He turned and broke off.

Holly followed his gaze. There was no sign of Tamizel. A rock wall stood where Tamizel had been a moment ago.

'Wha…?' Reece turned to Holly, then back to the rock wall. 'He did say "follow me". I suppose he thought we were watching. Okay, we stand with our backs against the wall just like he was.'

Holly did as he suggested. Reece stood next to her. Nothing happened. They turned to each other. 'Let's try leaning back.' Reece didn't sound confident. 'Together now, on the count of three.' He gripped her hand, tightly and unexpectedly. 'One, two, lean.' They felt the wall give way, just as the rock floor slid them backwards and plunged them straight down. Holly squealed.

The drop was very short. A moment later, they were in a passageway. Tamizel, hands on his hips, was glaring at them. 'Quiet! What took you so long?' He didn't wait for an answer. 'Shh!' His finger was on his lips. 'We're in the Cave of the Sarazen.'

'And what's the Cave of the Sarazen?' Reece whispered.

'A place where we can be alone to talk. Where we won't be overheard.'

He beckoned them towards the end of the passage. Holly realised they were on a balcony. It was like a minstrel's gallery overlooking a banqueting hall. *Always overlooking things.* Holly peered down. *I wish that meant we were being overlooked.*

Not far from the edge of the balcony was a floor littered with downy feathers in soft, earthy colours and shades of blue, lavender and lilac. It was as if a vast feathery forest had shed its plumes at the approach of winter. There were hundreds of mounds dimpling the floor and just beneath the balcony, where the covering of feathers was sparse, Holly could see that the mound was transparent and there was a child inside. She almost cried out.

Tamizel clapped a hand over her mouth. 'I don't want the Guardians to know we're here. It's not long until the Unfolding, so we're fortunate—they'll be busy with preparations for the First Flight.'

'Are they dead?' Holly whispered.

'No. They're waiting to be born.'

Holly stared. The silence enveloped her. She felt her mind quiet itself and begin to listen, intently, expectantly, to the hush of the room—and beyond. She thought of the times when she'd walked by herself and listened to the empty silence of the farm, with only the lonely screeching of the crows for company, but that sort of deserted silence was nothing like this. This was a silence that waited—it was filled, not empty.

'Tell us about this world.' Reece locked gazes with Tamizel. 'Not just what you think we need to know—tell us everything.'

'That's too much. Where would I begin?'

'At the beginning,' Holly said.

'The beginning…' Tamizel sighed. 'The beginning is shrouded in legend. It was so long ago—and on another world entirely. That beginning world was a mist-filled garden—the Bright World, we call it. It was not harsh and merciless like this world is with its long decades of sun-time and ice-time. But then a great catastrophe came to the Bright World out of its sapphire skies. Before the disaster, one of our ancestors who could see a little into the future warned us to flee. A place, she said, had been prepared for us in deep heaven. Dreamfall, she said, is its name—and it will be for us a dream or a nightmare. A dream if we were to cast off all the evil in our midst, or else a nightmare, if we remained shackled to the Dark.' Tamizel sighed again. 'There was dissension. Some believed, some did not. Those who did not believe her called those who did the Fearing Folk, but those who left that Bright World in their grand moonships called themselves instead the Farafolk—the folk of the far journey, the pilgrims. They pledged themselves to a new beginning. And for a long time after they reached Dreamfall, all went well. They built citadels and storehouses on the surface, bridges and waterways. They prospered. But then, as one ice-time approached, mysterious disappearances became more and more frequent, and it became apparent that evil had manifested itself amongst them, unawares. No one knows how, but we had summoned the Death Queen—the Dark Mother—from the Bright World to Dreamfall.'

'Hollë?' Reece asked. Holly could see by the look in his eyes that he thought this sounded all too much like a fairytale.

'Hollë,' Tamizel confirmed. 'But the Farafolk foolishly made a bargain with Hollë, to keep her from devouring them. In return for some concessions, she would leave the Farafolk in peace.'

'Concessions?' Reece asked.

'She wanted a husband.'

'What does Hollë look like?' Holly asked him. 'Does she really have no back?'

Tamizel was silent a moment. 'Her true face is masked—except to those whose dreams can penetrate deception.' He turned to look Holly squarely in the eyes, reaching for her mind in a way he hadn't done for more than a month. 'You've seen her, haven't you? Does she have a back or not?'

Holly shook her head. 'I haven't seen anything in my dreams except...' She broke off as she felt Tamizel retreat from the edge of her thoughts. *That's why the monster had my face. Because it's got my name.* She watched as violent shudder passed through Tamizel.

'I see,' Reece said, after several seconds' silence. 'The Court's afraid Hollë's come back to demand a new husband.'

Tamizel, taking a deep breath, seemed to recover his poise. 'Not exactly—Hollë, you see, demands a new husband at the start of every ice-time and every sun-time.' As Reece looked startled, he went on, 'That was one of the concessions. She changes her husband with the seasons. So one of her children will always be heir to the throne of Dreamfall.'

'But that means that Varyien is a child of Death…' Reece began, before interrupting himself. 'And *you?*' he asked, appalled.

Tamizel nodded. 'Hollë is my mother. As a dutiful son, I was supposed to fight Varyien for the throne—but I never thought terribly much of that idea. It's an ancient custom brought from the Bright World. Hollë has several sons after each mating—of course, not all of them can rule. So they fight until there's only one survivor.'

'You mean a duel to the death?' Reece asked.

Tamizel nodded.

You should be either king or dead. There don't seem to be any other options here. 'How come you're still alive when Varyien's the king?'

'Because I won the fight against all my brothers. But I didn't kill them. Then I relinquished the kingship.'

'You could take the throne easily,' Holly said. 'The common people love you.'

'The common people love me simply because I avoided a civil war. There were factions and allies, fanatical followers of Hollë, who would take the throne for me, whether I wanted it or not. They didn't want to be ruled by Varyien or the others. I said I wouldn't have bloodshed, I wouldn't have brother fighting brother and sister slaying sister. And to make sure everyone knew I meant what I said, I did this…' He held up his hand with the finger missing.

'Why's that mean you can't be king?' Reece stared at the

maimed hand.

'Because no one can ascend the throne who is not physically perfect. This small blemish disbars me—but it also serves to continually remind everyone that I do not serve Hollë. I have turned my back on her Music and I serve Ruēl of the Wounded Hand.' Tamizel took a deep breath. 'That's why I was so angry with Jaizee—she thinks it's a phase I'm going through—and she keeps trying to replace the symbols of Ruēl's hand around me with symbols of Hollë. She's just like most of my other sisters—and the common people, for that matter. They're terrified of Hollë's return, and of her anger when she realises what I have done. We are, after all, just mortal and Hollë is so strong. But I have always trusted that Ruēl would somehow rescue us. But now the time is almost gone, and still there is no sign from him.'

'Jaizee is your sister?' Holly thought she had misheard.

But Tamizel nodded.

'What are Hollë's symbols?' Reece sounded perplexed. 'You mean the bees?'

'What else but the bees? The High Court are all Hollë's sons—the drones of her queendom. Varyien, Bobenny, Karuveh and Midíork. Haimirel too, but you haven't met him. A pity, since he's the only one of us worth meeting. Like you, Reece, he's seen the Tree of Stars. And there's me. Do you know what makes a drone so different?'

Reece shook his head.

'We have no father—we have only one set of genes, that of our mother.'

'It's called "haploid". That's the scientific word.' Reece sucked in a ragged breath. His gaze met Holly's. 'Merlin had no father, only a mother.'

That's right. Holly felt a tingle up her spine as she stared at Tamizel. *You're Merlin, son-of-the-mother. I wonder what*

'Tamizel' means?

Tamizel was speaking again, whispering so softly now that Holly had to strain to hear him. 'So you see I am not really of the Farafolk at all. I have only Hollë's genes.' His voice was full of pain and fear. 'Don't you understand? I *am* Hollë.'

Reece threw up his hands. 'No, you're not!' He pointed to Holly. 'Any more than I'm her! And we're twins! Not that we've got exactly the same genes, but…' He broke off. 'But you know what I mean.'

It sounded lame but Tamizel was thoughtful. 'Perhaps there's something in what you say, for I do not feel like her at all…' He took a deep breath. 'I sang you my song of Heart's Desire, but my true desire—the one I yearn for above all others—I cannot even speak of.'

But he didn't have to say. Holly knew. *You want a father.* Her mind fled back to Gran's words the night everything began. *Ask your mother who your real father is.* Holly felt the icy splinter in her heart push deeper. 'And who are these?' She swept her hand to indicate the gel-covered mounds below.

'They are the Sarazen. This generation of Hollë's children.' Tamizel sighed. 'I would like to break the cycle and not bring up any drones, but that would mean killing some Sarazen here. Pointless, since Hollë could immediately replace them. She doesn't even need to mate to produce sons. But if I could break down the barriers between the Court and the true Farafolk, there might be a chance. The Court are my part-sisters, and are, like me, descended from Hollë, but the difference for them is that they have a drone for a father. It's the ordinary Farafolk from whom my sisters take husbands who are the descendants of the original pilgrims.'

She's taking over. Making a new species. I wonder how many pure Farafolk are left, uncontaminated by Hollë's genes? Holly gave Tamizel a searching look. *You're right, you* are *Hollë. So how come you're okay? How come you're not hideous and evil?*

'I don't get this.' Reece shook his head. 'I reckon the Farafolk could rise up out of their slavery any time. So why don't they?'

Tamizel's smile was thin and twisted. 'You haven't been listening, Reece. If you'd seen what Holly's seen in her dreams, you'd know. The Farafolk have made an accommodation with Death in order to protect themselves and their children. They have no options—and servitude is the price they pay.' He looked around, gesturing at the mounds in the floor. His tone changed to that of a lecture. 'The Sarazen begin life as blind, worm-like embryos crawling up the spirals of the chimney from deep below in the birthing place— until they reach here. Some instinct draws them to this cave where the temperature is just right for their final incubation. They burrow into the floor and secrete the gel that protects them until the Unfolding. They are vulnerable now, but once ready for the First Flight, they are strong—strong enough to work almost straight away. The Guardians here watch over them as they sleep.'

'Before your last rapid change of subject,' Reece butted in, 'I was just about to ask something. What does all this have to do with Varyien wanting to marry Holly?'

Tamizel took a deep breath. 'There is a legend of the Stardaughter: when she comes, Hollë's time is at an end. The Stardaughter will reign as the new Queen, the Peaceweaver. The fact you both have a similar name was a matter for great fear at first, but now a cause for great hope.'

'Is that why you gave Varyien the Mistblade? To buy him off so he wouldn't think any more about marrying Holly?'

'*That's* why you gave it to him?' Holly, incredulous, turned to Tamizel. 'Oh, you darling!' Her smile was so radiant Tamizel glowed in response. 'Thank you.'

Reece kicked her. *Huh?* Then she saw the light in Tamizel's face, the kindling happiness in his eyes. *Careful, girl.*

'About the sword!' Reece exclaimed brightly. 'Don't even try to change the subject, Tamizel. You still haven't explained the Star Pool.'

'It's simple. The Sword of Invincibility is one of the Hallows of Sovereignty. After I defeated my brothers in combat, and the Mistblade came into my possession, I had a thought. Without it no one could rule. We'd be forced to find another way to govern ourselves.'

'That doesn't explain why it was in the pool—or why Varyien is king.'

'The sword is indestructible, so I decided to hide it. One day when I was very young, I'd explored far from the Snow Citadel and found, here in the mountain, a vast and labyrinthine cave system. I'd followed the underground streams through the darkness and discovered a pool. When I was pondering the problem of the sword, I remembered the pool and I thought to myself that there, under rock and water, was a perfect hiding place. So I took the sword to the cave and to be totally sure it would never fall into the wrong hands, I spoke words of binding over it—so that not even I could retrieve it. I transformed the pool into a Star Pool, accessible to none but the Stardaughter.' Tamizel laughed. 'In whom I did not believe.' He shook his head. 'But it was naïve to think that the mere absence of a sword could topple kingship. Legends are deceptive.'

It was suddenly clear to Holly. 'So that's why you took us there. You wanted to find out if I was the Stardaughter.' She folded her arms. 'But I'm not.'

'Of course,' Tamizel went on, ignoring her denial, 'the Sword of Invincibility was the very thing we needed when the Invaders came. I deprived us of it, never thinking there would come a time when we needed it. And that's why I gave it to Varyien—not to buy him off—but because it might be needed. It's only nine years since Dreamfall was conquered. The Invaders stormed down from the stars in their space-ships. The Snow Citadel was taken before we knew it in a surprise attack. The slaughter was beyond comprehension. Mariffea, my brother, who was king before Varyien, forced me to lead the survivors to safety while he covered our retreat. All I could think of, by way of sanctuary, was the caves inside this mountain.'

'You've built Finddias in nine years?' Holly asked, astonished. 'But… but…' And there were so many buts in her mind that it became nearly impossible to choose one. 'But how did the Sarazen get here? You gave me the impression this is where the Sarazen have always unfolded.'

'That's so. We couldn't escape Hollë. Perhaps there is something built into us that doesn't wish to escape. I don't know otherwise how I didn't realise I had made my Star Pool and hidden the sword in the heart of Hollë's domain. The glamoure is so strong here I should have sensed it. I've no excuse. My cavern of sanctuary is straight below the ancient amphitheatre—the place of judgment and trial by ordeal, the arena of death where I fought my brothers, and where for centuries before us, drones have died in countless numbers. I should have felt the blood.'

Holly thought of the amphitheatre with its black pool and its thorntree decked with judgment tiles. *I felt the blood.* She recalled the Ettii and the observation post in the Cloudtree. 'Why are the Invaders here? This is not just a new world to conquer, is it?'

'They came to find the secret of the Eye of Ruēl and to use it to arm a machine they were building. They had heard that the Eye held limitless power and they wished to harness it.'

'The Eye of Ruēl?' Reece asked. 'What is it? Does it really have limitless power? And who is Ruēl anyway? You talk about his—or is it *her?*—hand a lot.'

'The Eye, like the sword, is one of the Hallows of Kingship. A coronation isn't legitimate without it. It's a crystalline lens, larger than a grown man's hand. Whoever possesses it is rightful ruler of the Farafolk. Another reason, Reece, why the Common People haven't risen up to throw off the chains of their slavery. Perhaps you see them as superstitious, but the fact is that Hollë's Children possess the Hallows of Kingship—and some of the Hallows being of Hollë and some of them being Ruēl's, hasn't made the matter any less complex.'

'Surely they've figured out by now that if they can do without the sword, they can do without the Eye,' Reece said. 'And anyway I doubt if it has limitless power. Or else Hollë would have taken it long ago. To stop you using it against her.'

'Reece, you think in such simplistic terms,' Tamizel chided. 'Perhaps Hollë has perverted the Eye for her own uses. Or perhaps it tickles her fancy that we have a source of power we do nothing but look at. From a distance. Only the king may look into the Eye of Ruēl. Perhaps…'

'Have you looked in it?' Reece interrupted.

'I'm not the king.' And before Reece could challenge his blatant evasion, Tamizel went on, 'There is a saying: it is perilous to possess the Eye of Ruēl, for it may possess the possessor. There are many legends about it—some say that the Eye is a store of power, which the right key or word will unleash. Others that it is merely a channel for the boundless might of Ruēl. Only one thing is agreed by all those who've looked into it: within it you can see an evil so powerful in its potential that if it is unleashed, the existence of every living thing is threatened.'

'You don't really believe that, do you?' Reece asked. He paused and glanced at Holly.

She was unsettled by Tamizel's silence. 'How could the Invaders have known about it?'

Tamizel shrugged. 'No one knows. We have no contact off

Dreamfall. But then maybe we've advertised our presence somehow.' He paused, reflecting a moment. 'After all, Hollë with her sticky webs found us here soon enough, across the void of interstellar space.'

Reece frowned. 'Sticky webs? Like that stuff you were wrapped up in?'

There was a long silence before Tamizel spoke. 'I have been chosen by lot from among my brothers as Hollë's next husband. Normally, it is the king's duty to be so. His *final* duty.'

Holly gasped and spluttered. 'Sounds like the election was rigged to me.'

Tamizel didn't look at her. His face was set like flint. 'That's why the Common People pity me and weep in public. But the truth is, of course, that they're as much relieved for themselves as sorry for me. Hollë has never once risen to our defence against the Invaders, as many had hoped she would. Some believe she is now making us all suffer for my rebellion. They are secretly hoping that this will restore them to her goodwill.'

Reece began stammering. 'B..b...but she she's your...' He couldn't bring himself to say the last word. 'You can't m..m..marry your...your... your...own...'

'It's not uncommon here, Reece.' Tamizel's tone was matter-of-fact. 'My brothers' wives are their sisters also. It would be beneath them to marry the Common People. Besides, Hollë says she's not displeased I've been selected—in fact, she tells me she's relishing the opportunity to show the Farafolk exactly what will happen to those, like me, who turn away from her Music.' His head dropped briefly to his maimed hand. 'I don't know how much longer I can hope that Ruēl will save me.'

'She told you?' Reece was obviously still scandalised by the thought of Tamizel marrying his mother. 'I mean, *herself*? So you have seen her?'

Tamizel's face was hot with apparent humiliation. He turned away, unable to look either of them in the face. 'She has appeared to me in the night.' His voice was a whisper. 'And when she does, she looks exactly like the one I love. Her innocence intoxicates me and that's why in the shroud-trap, I cannot resist her. I have betrayed my love, I have betrayed myself, I have betrayed Ruēl. He will not save me now.'

'No.' Holly slapped her hands on her hips. 'That's not true. She only wants to make you think that.'

'That stuff was like a web, not a …' Reece began. 'What's she going to do to you?'

'What do you think?' Tamizel said, still staring elsewhere. 'Surely you know what happens to the drone after the mating flight. But don't worry. There's no need for concern about your own future. I've made arrangements with Haimirel and his wife for both of you to be taken care of.'

'No need for concern about our own future?' Reece jumped up. 'We've got to do something, Hol. This is an absolute emergency.'

A shuffling sound came from the far side of the floor below. 'We have attracted the attention of the Guardians. We must go before we're seen.' Tamizel rose, with his usual elegance, and led them back along the passage.

'Why did you bring us here?' Reece asked, as they reached the trick doorway that led to the outside. 'Really? Surely you could have told us this story somewhere else.'

Tamizel gestured them into position before pressing a hidden lever. 'I wanted to see with my own eyes how long it is until the Unfolding.' They were hoisted up back to the parapet above the city. 'On the day of the Unfolding, I must wed Hollë.' Without waiting, he stepped back onto the small platform that led through the archway towards the spiral chimney.

Holly stared at the back of Tamizel's cloak. She was only just beginning to feel the full shock of his revelations. Looking up for a moment as they reached chimney, she was so dazed by his disclosures it took her a second to realise the significance of what she was seeing. 'Look!' She pointed to several black dots, moving high above them, and clambering down the chambered spirals of stone.

'Invaders!' Tamizel stared, momentarily frozen, before turning to Reece. 'You and Holly go back down the stairway as fast as you can. Warn the city!'

'What are you going to do?' Holly asked.

'Stop them, of course. Have you got any weapon?'

'No.' Reece sounded flustered. 'Only my water pistol.'

'Give it to me then,' Tamizel said. 'It might be just what I need for the perfect illusion.'

Reece stared. 'You're kidding me.' When he saw that Tamizel was being perfectly serious, he reached into his pocket and handed the water pistol over.

'Go quickly!' Tamizel pushed Reece towards the entrance to the stair. 'If I fail, the survival of the city depends on you.'

'I'm coming with you,' Holly said firmly to Tamizel. 'I can help.'

'No,' Tamizel said, his voice soft and torn. 'No, Holly.' The last word was almost a caress.

In that moment, seeing the unguarded expression on Tamizel's face and the tenderness in his eyes, her suspicion became certainty. *I'll bet I'm the last to know. Tamizel wouldn't fight his brothers to the death for the kingship, but he nearly got himself killed fighting Varyien over me.*

'Go with your brother,' Tamizel pleaded with her. 'Please.'

Holly glared at him mutinously, but she followed his orders. However, as soon as she got inside the door, she turned to Reece. 'You go to the Sarazen Cave, and tell those Guardians whoever they are, what's happened. They should be able to warn the city. I'm going after Tamizel.'

'Hol,' he protested, 'I don't speak the language.'

Holly left him and sprinted out the door after Tamizel.

The black dots moving down the spiral had drawn closer—and, as soon as one was within firing range of Tamizel, a lance of light hurtled across the chimney, just missing him. It shattered the stone above his position. He squeezed back against the wall as the explosion spat fragments across the chimney.

Holly watched him pull out Reece's water pistol. Holding it up, he squeezed the trigger. A bolt of light speared out of it, cracking into the wall just between two of the troopers. Stunned by an illusion of blinding light, and disoriented by the magnified echo, they lost their balance and fell, hurtling into the darkness at the base of the chimney.

Holly clung to the wall as they flailed past, screaming, looking down only when they'd passed from view. *Hollë's realm. They've gone down to her. Maybe she won't want Tamizel now. Maybe he's safe from her. Maybe she'll be satisfied.* She looked up. The Invaders were retreating. *Too easy. They must be going for reinforcements.*

Tamizel was following them, so she kept going breathlessly. Up and up. The Invaders disappeared over the edge of the chimney. Tamizel vanished too. Still Holly went up. Finally, she crawled exhausted over the lip of the chimney, only to find Tamizel sitting there, near the edge, his hair and clothes juddering wildly as he watched a flight of a dozen hornet 'copters rising in the air. Behind them a dark rolling bank of cloud almost camouflaged their ascent. She heaved deeply. 'They'll be back. You must evacuate the city.'

Tamizel's attitude was strange—he was ignoring her. 'What's that?' He pointed at the green-black cloud roiling across the sky in the direction the 'copters were heading.

'It's a storm.' Holly looked at him, wary with doubt. 'Isn't it?'

'A storm,' he repeated.

Holly could feel him skirting the edges of her mind looking for images of what 'storm' might mean. This surprised her— not only because he reached into her thoughts so rarely now, but because when he did so it was only to discover the meaning of concepts alien to him. How could a storm be alien? 'Yes!' His voice was tinged with wonder. 'It *is* a storm—the Tears of Ruēl.'

'Don't you have storms here?'

'Only duststorms and great winds—but not water that spills from the sky.'

'But doesn't it ever rain?'

'Our water is a garment that rises from the earth in mists and springs—it does not descend in power.' Tamizel's face was shining. 'Ruēl *is* coming. Beyond all hope, he is coming.'

Holly wasn't sure about Tamizel's eagerness. *This Ruēl has an evil Eye. We don't need any more trouble than we've already got.*

Tamizel stood up and raised his hands towards the skirling clouds. A rush of wind caught his cloak and lashed it back into a twist of black. 'You should not have come.' He raised his voice above the rising shrill of the wind. 'But I'm glad you did.'

Holly shook her head. 'It looks bad. I don't think those 'copters were wise to come out with a storm like this brewing. And that means we're not wise either. We need to find shelter.'

'A tree?' Tamizel asked.

'Yes,' Holly said, before immediately retracting her assent. 'No. Trees attract lightning.'

'Lightning?'

Holly could feel the riffling fingers of his thoughts as he sought the image in her mind. And when he got it, he smiled. He smiled as she'd never seen him smile before. 'Oh, yes.' He seemed alive with delight. 'I know just the tree.' He took her hand and, as the winds whipped in a frenzy around them, stepped off the cap of the chimney and down onto the flat ledge of rock where the hornet 'copters had been. 'Where are the sentries?' he shouted, above the keening of the wind. 'We should have been warned long before the Invaders ever made it into the chimney.'

With Tamizel's arm around her, Holly scurried across the rock ledge to a huge tree leaning at an angle over a wide crevasse. Its leaves were battered against the wall behind it.

Swift inky shadows raced towards them down the far side of the chasm and across its deeps—Holly looked up and saw that they were formed by the low ragged wisps of a cloud front, speeding in front of the main bulk of the storm. 'We've got to go back.'

They reached the tree and huddled out of the full force of the wind on its leeside. Listening to the roar of the wind, Holly tried to make Tamizel understand. 'It's not safe here.'

Tamizel seemed perplexed. 'This is a sentry post,' he yelled. 'I don't know why there's no…' And then, as he looked up and she followed his line of sight, she saw the sticky white threads of a shroud-trap. He put his arm around her and turned her face aside. 'It cannot be. Hollë would not betray us to the Invaders.' His eyes narrowed. 'What purpose would it serve…?' He broke off.

She had to make him understand the dangers of trees and lightning. *If only Reece was here! He could explain the science of getting killed by electricity.* 'We've got to go, Tamizel.'

'I think it's too late.'

'Of course it's not too late. What on earth do you mean? *Please* Tamizel, please let's go…'

But Tamizel continued to ignore her and together, they watched through the leaves of the tree, as the storm drew closer. The wind died and an eerie silence fell—one sun was still behind them, dappling the trunk of the tree with gashes of light, the sky luminously red. Ahead, the sky was black, the bulk of the storm still stampeding towards them, its rain sheeting down in wild curtains of water. Lightning forked from earth to sky, thunder caused the leaves to tremble. And the wind was shrieking again. 'The Tears of Ruēl…' Tamizel held up an arm towards the sky.

The intensity of his gaze frightened Holly even more than the storm did. She renewed her efforts to persuade him to leave. 'It's dangerous, Tamizel. Let's go. Please.' She grasped his wrist and tried to pull him away from the tree. 'Oh, please, *please*, Tamizel, let's go.'

'But look——!' Tamizel's attention was entirely focussed on the storm. 'Look how Ruēl's sorrow is so turbulent and passionate, not gentle at all.' His face was radiant as lightning slashed the darkness once again.

Oh why are we here? It can't just be curiosity. Sudden panic overwhelmed her. 'Tamizel…' she cried, her voice pleading. 'This is just a storm—but storms are dangerous—we have to get out of it.'

Tamizel pressed Holly's hand. His smile of reassurance was maddening. The first hard icy droplets of rain hit the leaves, wetting both their faces and causing him to laugh out loud. 'Cold!' He raised his face in delight. 'Then he is not angry with me.'

'What?' Holly felt a sense of imminent disaster threatening to overpower her.

'I was so afraid he was angry,' Tamizel said. 'But then his tears would be hot, hot with rage.' He took Holly's hand and turned it so the palm was upwards. Then he placed Reece's water pistol in it. 'I understand now. Thank you, Stardaughter.' His voice softened. 'And please thank your brother for me too. You came in time, both of you. Too long unfulfilled a hope makes a stone of the heart. But more than my heart was threatened—I was in danger of becoming the spirit of stone itself.' He stared at her, as if committing her face to memory. 'I'm so sorry for what's happened, Holly. I never wanted to hurt you. I've got to go now. Goodbye.'

'Go?!' Holly asked incredulously. 'But *where*?' *Ohpleasepleaseplease what's happening?*

Tamizel took off his cloak and draped it around Holly's shoulders. 'The ring.'

'The ring? What ring?' she cried.

'The necklace. Your necklace. Give me your necklace.'

Holly shook her head, terrified by the helpless feelings flooding over her. 'No!' She was wild with anger, afraid she was being deceived again. *Was what you told us a pack of lies, Tamizel, just to get us to trust you again?*

'Oh please trust me, Stardaughter,' Tamizel pleaded.

Holly stared at him, tears beginning to well in her eyes. 'Don't do this to me.' A groan escaped her.

'Trust me, just this once.' Tamizel put his hand out.

Holly, with a whimper, reached into her pocket and took out the necklace. As she dropped it into his hand, it became a ring.

'Thank you.' Tamizel palmed it. Reaching up, he grabbed hold of a branch of the tree and swung himself into it. Rain pummelled him fiercely, but he hardly seemed to notice. He clambered easily from branch to swaying branch, climbing higher and higher.

'Tamizel, come down.' Holly's voice was a frantic sob. 'Come down.' The terrifying sense of foreboding seemed to melt her bones. 'Pleaseohpleaseoh*please*, come down.' She found herself screaming. Her tears were dashed away by the stinging rain.

Tamizel turned momentarily, his face vibrant with hope. He looked at her. 'I love you,' he shouted. 'I loved you from the first. From the moment you said, "Look her straight in the eye."' The lightning struck.

The Tree
of
Iron

Reece scrambled out of the stone chimney into the freezing, lashing rain. The low clouds scudding across the mountaintop were green-dark and eerie. A howling wind buffeted against him in wild, tumultuous gusts; a flash of lightning, so bright it was almost unbearable, tore the sky apart. For a moment, he felt as if time itself was a canvas that had been ripped apart for an instant. He was sure he had been dazzled by the light of heaven itself. He screwed up his eyes. After several seconds he opened them again and raised a hand to shield his face from the rain, desperate to see if there was any trace of Holly or Tamizel. But all he could see was a bright white afterflash.

He waited as the rain beat furiously down on him. His vision cleared a little. Half blind and off-balance, he slipped and slid across the ledge of rock. *Where are you idiots?* He almost fell but managed to right himself before hitting something. Peering into the rain-soaked gloom, he looked for any sign of shelter. *Nothing.* There was nothing he could see.

Then the lightning flashed again—bright, but not as

incandescently brilliant as the last bolt—and he saw it. A tree. *Always a tree.* Battling the bludgeoning fury of the storm, he struggled toward it. Then he heard a muffled voice. Making his way quickly towards the indistinct sound, he stumbled on the uneven ground. The torrents of water sweeping over it and the rain stinging his face impeded his progress so much he fell several times. At last, he discovered it was much easier to crawl forward on his hands and knees. As he neared the tree, with its demented swaying branches, he realised with relief that the sound was coming from Holly. She was calling—calling the same thing, the same name, over and over. 'Tamizel!' she was crying. 'Tamizel!' Just as he reached her, lightning flashed in the distance and Holly's figure, holding to the trunk of the tree and leaning out far over the edge of the cliff, was silhouetted against a dazzling curtain of light. Like the instant of photographic exposure, it was a scene he felt would be imprinted forever on his mind. 'Holly!' he screamed, trying to make himself heard above the rain. 'What's wrong?'

'Tamizel's …' Holly hesitated. 'I don't know. Fallen. I don't know…' A sob caught in her throat. 'He was up in the tree and he…' She couldn't finish.

With a sense of dread, Reece clambered up onto the closest swaying branch. Although the wind was abating, the slippery wet leaves slapped at his face. Holding tightly on to the branch above him, he gingerly worked his way along its length. To his profound relief, by the time he was nearing the end of it, the wind and the rain both began to ease. The sky was paling to a luminous, almost pearlescent grey. By the time he was peering over the edge of the precipice itself, the rain had stopped altogether. He could see a ledge not far below where the roots of the tree coiled and divided, but there was no sign of a body there. 'I think we'd better get help.' Reece inched backward, his grip still tight on the upper branch. After a few cautious steps, he realised it was getting harder and harder to move his hands—they seemed to be adhering to the branch above. He stood for a moment, one hand firmly grasping the branch, while he examined the other. It was sticky with white glue-like strands. 'Urghh!' He couldn't help his expression of disgust. 'It's *her*!'

He wiped his palm on his sodden shirt, but it made no difference to his hands. He decided to worry about removing the sticky gum once he'd got back on the ground. He reached up to grab hold of the upper branch once again. 'Oww!' He'd put his hand on something hard and sharp. Pulling the offending object out of the white webbing, Reece realised at once what it was—it was the tachyon decelerator and it was shaped like a ring. *Ring? But it only looks like a ring for Tamizel.* Already it was changing shape. It grew larger and thicker, becoming more crown-like. Reece called to Holly. 'Here!' He threw it with extreme care. It flew into her hands, shimmering into necklace form as it sped through the air.

Holly was staring at it. 'Reece, the lightning hit and he fell. He can't be dead. He can't. He wanted this for—for… what? He's gone, he's really gone, and now it's here. I don't want it, I want him. I want Tamizel.' She raised the necklace and Reece could see she intended to fling it into the crevasse.

'No!' He clambered out of the tree. 'Stop, sis! We might need it…'

Holly froze, her hand upraised behind her.

'*Please,* Holly,' Reece begged. 'It might be our last hope—we might need it to bargain or something.'

Without a word, Holly put the tachyon decelerator into her pocket.

Reece didn't bother to disguise his relief. 'I think we've got to go for help straight away. I can't see a way down the cliff, and Tamizel's certainly not up here.' He realised how thoroughly wet his clothes were. And how sticky and uncomfortable he felt. Especially his hands. 'How did he fall?' He guided Holly away from the tree. 'What was he doing up the tree in a storm anyway?'

Holly shook her head, feeling helpless. 'He wanted to see it—the storm, I mean,' she whispered. 'The Tears of Ruēl, he called it.' Her voice sounded like it was threatening to break. 'I'm not sure he did fall, Reece. For a moment I thought he jumped. The lightning… the lightning… he seemed fascinated by the whole idea of it.'

Fascinated by the whole idea of it. The immediate image that sprang to Reece's mind was a vivid memory of Tamizel's hands, cupped around two sparking wires dangling from the ceiling and Tamizel's face, full of awe and curiosity. *He hasn't fallen. But what's he done? And why wasn't I here to stop him?* A devastating realisation hit him. *Tamizel's gone—he's deliberately gone and left us.* A sense of deep aloneness swept over him. Even his thoughts felt alone. A surge of anger pulsed through him. *Tamizel, you were my only friend here. How could you do this to me? Without you, I'll be totally reliant on Holly. I can't manage the language like she can.*

As they headed back to the rock chimney, Reece felt more and more morose. Holly's eyes were so blinded by tears he had to support her most of the way to stop her from slipping on the wet rocky ground. 'We'd better hurry. I don't know if Tamizel is hurt or not, but we have to get search parties out before the Invaders come back.' He pulled Holly up the side of the rock chimney and over the lip. Soon they were inside, heading downward on the spiral track. *Thank heavens, downhill all the way.* What had taken them both hours to ascend now took only minutes to descend. In no time at all, it seemed, they were back at the thousand steps.

Holly's voice echoed in the darkness. 'You got to the Guardians and warned them, didn't you?' she asked as they pounded down the stairs.

'Of course I did. I told them that there were Invaders. I don't know if they understood, but I did the best I could.'

'*Reece!*' Holly stopped. 'What if your warning was useless? What if we've betrayed the Farafolk? No wonder no help has arrived. You didn't get through to them.'

Reece kept moving. 'I tried.' The dark stairway ended so abruptly he almost hurtled into the door. It sprang open at the force of the collision and he stumbled into a dimly lit passage. It was deserted.

'Where is everyone?' Holly came up behind him.

He looked around for the crowds that had been present when they'd been here with Tamizel. 'Doom,' she whispered. 'Doom coming on little cat feet. Oh, you were wrong, Tamizel. You were so wrong. It was coming for you in a bolt of lightning.'

'Stop it!' Reece snapped. *I don't want to think about Tamizel. It's too hard. I refuse to believe he was gone.* 'Maybe they're making dinner. The Court kitchens must be down here somewhere.'

Holly just rolled her eyes. He was surprised she didn't make a comment that he was eternally pre-occupied with eating. Instead she looked for directions. 'Do you remember which way we came?'

Reece glanced around. 'This way...' He pointed in the direction that had a marginal uphill slope. 'I think.' Even as they threaded their way along the gloomy passages, back towards the realms of the upper court, they met no one.

Reece could feel Holly's increasing anxiety. She wanted someone in authority—anyone—so that the search for Tamizel could begin. He wanted Bobenny. He felt sure that the leader of the Hunt was the right person to approach with the news of the Invaders. *Unless...* A terrible thought occurred to him. Perhaps the Farafolk had left Finddias for a new hiding place, as once they had left the Snow Citadel. Perhaps there was no one left here—no one but himself and Holly. *But that's stupid.* Relief flooded through him. *They simply haven't had enough time.*

Even as he was thinking this, black-garbed shapes glided in from the shadows. With the poise and soundless step of panthers readying themselves to pounce, troopers barred the laneway both in front of them and behind.

Without a word, Reece raised his hands in surrender. Holly followed suit.

Minutes later, having been dragged through the passages and then through the wider corridors which led to the upper dwellings of the Farafolk Court, they found themselves at the Field of Fountains. There a terrible sight met Reece's eyes. The common folk, thousands of them, were herded like sheep into dazed, silent groups. High above them, on slowly spinning anti-gravity platforms were armed sentinels. Below the platforms, silver-clawed robots patrolled the pens.

The members of the Court were chained together, their glittering clothes looking out of place, their haughty mannerisms gone. They were crowded near the fountains where the mirror-leaves of the sculptures glinted in the sunshine. As Reece was paraded forward past the metal trees, he noticed how cowed and frightened the Court looked.

There's something odd about this world. Which I should've noticed long ago. There are trees everywhere—even when there aren't any trees. All different kinds—but not like those Tamizel wanted in his garden, the garden he'll never have now, if he's really dead. These trees are like watchers, strange watchers, waiting for battle.

He and Holly were escorted around the metal tree and brought to a halt right in front of it. It was only when they stopped that they realised someone was bound to it with heavy fetters. It was Varyien—the king.

One of the Invaders seemed to be taunting him—but Reece couldn't make out a single word the man was saying. The Invader turned from Varyien as they approached. Reece could see him quite clearly. His complexion was oily and greenish-grey, almost cadaver-like, his face seemed much too thin for his heavy frame, and his eyes were golden slits under his bulging brows. He spoke peremptorily, questioning Holly and Reece's captors. Then he waved them away with a dismissive gesture, indicating they were to place their prisoners with the common people.

One of the guards began to move them on. He was vicious in his repeated shoves at them both. They were just passing a small group of courtiers, when one of his thrusts sent Holly tumbling. The tachyon decelerator, glittering brightly, fell out of her pocket. She made a grab for it.

'Aghin!' the leader yelled.

Even Reece could figure what that meant by the reaction of the guards. One of them stomped on Holly's hand. Another picked up the necklace. He and Holly were dragged back and searched. He stared as his water pistol was taken from Holly. The necklace was handed to the leader, who examined both it and the water pistol for fully a minute. When he pulled the pistol's trigger and a limp arc of water dribbled from the barrel, his face took on an expression of incredulity. Then he laughed as he peered at the barrel.

Reece thought at first that he was barking. 'Made in China,' he said, still barking as he turned and strode toward them.

'You speak English!' Reece was startled into speech. 'Are you from Earth?' As soon as the last word was out of his mouth, he realised how stupid he'd been.

Tamizel had spoken English, but he hadn't come from Earth. *You idiot. How could you have fallen for it? This brute didn't even play Jaizee's trick and you've already told him where we come from. That could be fatal. Most things are around here.*

The man ignored him. Taking Holly's face in his hand, he

scrutinised it from every angle. She shuddered at his greasy touch. Finally he spoke again. 'You are not of the company of those who inhabit this world.' His English was perfect, if stilted. He turned to Reece. 'No, I am not from Earth.' His mouth curved into a broad smile, showing fanged teeth. 'But still from the neighbourhood.' His smile thinned. 'May I introduce myself? I am Aanundus. And you are?'

From the neighbourhood? Reece felt queasy. *You speak English far too well for an alien. And obviously read it as well, if you knew what the brand on the water pistol said.* However, he decided there wasn't much point in concealment. 'I'm Reece. And this is my sister, Holly.'

'You are from Offworld?' Aanundus asked.

Reece nodded. There was nothing to be gained in denying what he'd already virtually admitted. Aanundus held up the water pistol. 'This has no weaponry capacity. What purpose does it serve?'

'It's a toy.'

Aanundus stared at him through narrowed eyes, bright and cold and yellow as a wolf's. 'But this is not.' He held up Holly's necklace—and now it looked like a heavy silver armband, decorated with serpentine scrollwork. 'This is a tachyon decelerator mesh which seems to have acquired a camouflage function. What are you doing with it?'

'We picked it up by mistake.' Reece frowned, trying to look as young and innocent as possible. 'Tachyon?' *Would it be possible to put Aanundus off the scent?* 'Really? Would that be like particles that travel backwards in time?'

Aanundus' mouth curved in a thin lupine smile. 'That is so. You are young indeed to be aware of the tachyon clustering theory. Are you responsible for the camouflage function?'

Reece didn't have a clue what tachyon clustering theory was, nor the slightest idea of why the decelerator mutated between a ring, a necklace, a crown and a bracelet. But he could sense trouble coming whatever answer he gave. He had the feeling Aanundus wouldn't believe the truth. Not that he knew the truth anyway. So he decided on an attempt to turn the question back on the questioner. 'You wouldn't be interested in creating a time machine, would you?' He smiled brightly. And then without thinking, he added a careless afterthought, 'I've done some experiments myself.'

Holly glared at him.

He realised too late he'd been caught in his own trap. *Are you out of your mind? You're digging your own grave.*

Aanundus' eyes glittered and his smile twisted a little. 'And the price of your insights?'

Reece took a moment to size up the opportunity presenting itself. 'I'm sure…' He took a deep breath and hoping he wasn't volunteering for the biggest mistake of his life. 'I could re-create the results of my research, if only you'd let the king down and set all the Farafolk free.' He pointed to Varyien on the frame. 'There's nothing he can give someone like you. Nothing at all.'

'Information,' Aanundus said. 'He can give me information.'

'So what information do you want?'

'The same that you do. The same you have obviously come to this benighted world to obtain. The secret of the Great Eye of the Farafolk.' Aanundus pointed to Varyien on the metal frame. 'The king is being most uncooperative. I was just explaining to him, as you arrived, that a thousand of his people will die for every minute he hesitates in handing over the required information.' He sighed, raising his hands as if the whole matter of an imminent massacre were beyond his control and entirely Varyien's fault and responsibility. Then the wolfish smile returned. 'But now I do not need him.'

'You don't?'

'The crystal, as you undoubtedly know, does not easily yield its secrets. I have examined it with a full spectrum of radiation, cast a shadowscan and an ultraprobe, subjected it to a bombardment of every known particle ray, shed a magnetic inversion—all to discover that it's nothing more than a perfect converging lens.'

All in the last half hour or so? 'It's been a big disappointment.' Reece nodded, trying to look knowledgeable. 'Any cheap trashy magnifying glass could be substituted and no one would ever know it.' He shrugged. 'But I guess it's natural that legend has exaggerated the properties of the Eye out of all proportion to the simplicity of its true nature.'

'Good try.' Aanundus chuckled and barked to himself. 'Almost, I believe you. Your disguise is perfect, Lord Tamizel, and, had I not been informed of your facility with illusion, I would certainly be deceived.' With a curt gesture, he indicated for one of the guards to restrain Reece. 'But who else would bargain for the life of a coward like Varyien? Who else is renowned for a willingness to sacrifice both himself and his honour for that which no one else believes in? Who else is so familiar with the art of illusion that he could readily adapt it to a device like this?' Aanundus held up his arm where the tachyon decelerator gleamed brightly on his wrist, its silver scrollwork rippling like the flow of a swift-moving river. 'Who, but you, Lord Tamizel?'

'Tamizel?' Reece was dumbfounded as the trooper wrenched his arms behind his back. 'This is ridiculous. I'm not Tamizel.'

Aanundus snorted. 'Oh, yes, of course you are not Tamizel. On the contrary, you are Reece—a young man from a planet still limited to chemical propulsion rockets. With Earth's current technology, it would take thousands of years for you to get here.' His barking laughter had a coarse edge to it. 'If you are not Tamizel, where is he then?'

'Well right now, he's probably at the bottom of a cliff.' Reece didn't want to admit it but there was nothing else to do. 'And if he's still alive, he's probably broken every bone in his body.'

'A cliff?' Aanundus inquired, still amused. 'Where would this cliff be?'

'On top of the mountain, where the rock chimney is.'

Aanundus turned and began speaking in his own guttural language to the guards who had captured Holly and Reece. A moment later, one of the troopers raised his weapon, pointed it at Holly's head and forced her to march off. Accompanied by three other guards, they began to make their way back towards the underground passages where Reece and Holly had been first captured.

Reece was horrified—the last thing that he'd intended was to get himself separated from Holly. But he didn't quite understand how or why it had happened. 'Where's she going? What're you going to do to her?'

'She will merely identify the cliff you spoke of. If Tamizel is there and is still alive, they will bring him back.'

'But you said I was Tamizel!' Reece exclaimed.

'And so you almost certainly are. There is, however, still the remotest possibility you might actually be telling the truth. It would be foolish of me to come away empty-handed because I did not consider that option, however unlikely it might be.' He nodded to the guard holding Reece. 'Mal-a!' he growled. An instant later, Reece felt as if his arms were being wrenched out of their sockets. He began to struggle, and as he did so, he watched in surprise as Varyien was released from the metal tree.

Seconds later, his surprise turned to alarm as he was propelled forward and thrust against it in Varyien's place. 'But I'm not Tamizel and I don't know anything.' His voice was edged with fear as restraining cuffs were snapped onto his wrists, elbows, knees and ankles.

'Then we shall see who you really are and just what you do know.' Aanundus was almost cheerful. 'Pain, I understand, interferes greatly with the ability to sustain an illusion. Pain loosens tongues and unlocks secrets. Shall we see what your pain has to offer me?'

'But I'm *not* Tamizel,' Reece exclaimed. 'Ask anyone.'

'Do you take me for a fool?' Aanundus pulled back his lips in a feral grin. 'Why would they answer the truth?' He laughed. 'Of course, perhaps their concern for their own skins may prompt them to dispense with lies once they see what happens to you.' His mouth twisted into a mocking derisive curve as he glanced at Varyien, Bobenny and the small group beside them.

It's the High Court. Reece stared at them. *Varyien, Bobenny, Karuveh and Midíork. That grim-faced man I don't know must be— what did Tamizel say?—Haimirel? No wonder Aanundus thinks I'm Tamizel—he's the only one missing. How can I convince him?*

Aanundus turned again. 'Now I wouldn't want you, Lord Tamizel, in the midst the conflict of emotions you are obviously experiencing at this moment, to miss appreciating the finer points of my exquisite bouquet of irony. And so I will point out that I am using the Eye itself to pry out its own secret.'

'I can't give you the secret…' Reece gritted his teeth. '…because I'm *not* Tamizel.'

'Ahh, but then I don't necessarily expect to get it from you.' Aanundus gestured towards the king and the High Court. 'One of those cowards is bound to crack—and it's just a matter of determining which one.' He reached up with one hand, pulling down, almost effortlessly, one of the protruding branches of the tree.

Reece stared, striving to believe the evidence of his own eyes. The strength required to bend the branch as Aanundus had just done was unthinkable. 'I am sure an appropriate demonstration will expose the weakest link.' Aanundus strode over to a large squat box at the feet of one of the guards. Opening it, he took out a large crystal lens. 'The Eye of Ruēl.' He raised the curved glass above his head. He turned the lens around so that it caught the light and all the Farafolk could see it. 'As I said before, it is an excellent converging lens.' He took hold of the metal branch and, after examining it for a moment, placed the lens in a position half-way along its length. Then he fastened it securely in place, before turning his attention to the mirror leaves and twisting them around one by one until they aligned with the Eye.

I can't believe this is happening to me. Reece watched Aanundus re-position the mirrors. His insides felt as if they were turning to water. *Maybe, if I close my eyes, I'll wake up and find it's only a nightmare.* Incongruously, another thought flitted into his consciousness, banging about like a clumsy moth. *If only I'd done the washing up, none of this would have happened.* His eyes followed every movement of Aanundus. Despite the chilly air, he was sweating. Aanundus pushed the branch of the metal tree slowly upwards, bending it around until it was just in the position he wanted. Reece's heart palpitated with increasing wildness.

'Now what's it to be?' Aanundus was almost jaunty as he made the final adjustments. 'Shall I destroy your hand or your eye? Ah, now there's an elegant thought—an eye for an Eye.' He barked. 'On the other hand, the hand will reveal all. How long can you maintain the illusion of five fingers, I wonder?' The laugh became dry and thin.

'I'm *not* Tamizel.' Reece was sure his bones had liquefied. If he had not been shackled, he would have fallen over. *Tamizel.* The thought was wild and fluttery. *How can I convince him I'm not Tamizel?* The lens caught the reflections from the mirrors and focussed them down into a burning sliver of light. It hit Reece's hand right in the middle of his palm. There was silence. He closed his eyes. *Oh how can I convince him I'm not Tamizel?* More silence. And the smell of burnt skin. Reece's hand twitched violently, but he tried to focus away from it. *Tamizel, why oh why did you leave me?* The aroma of roasting flesh was stronger now, but still he didn't feel anything. *But can't he see I've still got five fingers and so I can't be Tamizel?* Reece opened his eyes and twisted to look at what he thought would be a scorch mark, then realised he could see right through his palm. 'But there's a hole there.' He was momentarily so stupefied he didn't realise he was speaking out loud. 'So how come it doesn't hurt?'

'Because you're in shock.'

Tamizel?! No, not Tamizel. It was that mysterious voice again—the voice Reece had first heard aboard the spaceship. *Or could it be Tamizel? But how?* 'Tamizel?' *No, it's impossible. I've just got Tamizel on the brain.*

'Reece, how did you get yourself into a position like this?'

I'm imagining this. Then, as he saw the startled looks of Aanundus and his guards, and even on the faces of the High Court, he realised they were hearing the voice too.

'Who's that?' Aanundus looked around for the source of the voice. He was frowning, as if uncertain whether it was real or an illusion.

'Reece, this is a tactical blunder of a major order.' There was a sigh that seemed to emanate from heaven itself. 'Well, I'll ask around and see what can be organised to help you.'

'Tamizel, where are you?'

'Safe.'

'Where?'

Silence.

I'm out of my tree. What do they say about grief? Like don't people imagine sometimes that they can hear someone who's dead? But looking at Aanundus as he began to search the metal tree, plainly examining it as if he thought a microphone was hidden inside it, Reece wasn't so sure. At least the Eye was no longer focussed on his hand. *It can't possibly have been Tamizel.* Reece tried to get a grip on his thoughts. *Think it through logically. If that was Tamizel, then it means that, way back on the spaceship, when we first heard about Dreamfall, that would've been Tamizel too—but that's impossible. Because it would mean that, before we'd ever met, we'd been in contact with each other.* And then it hit Reece—an awesome, mind-staggering possibility. *Oh it can't be! Tamizel's outside of time!?*

'I'm sorry, Reece.'

'What? Why?' Reece looked around. *It really is Tamizel.*

'Help's just not available. It's all tied up in trying to prevent an early Unfolding.'

'Huh?'

'It's Hollë—*she who got us into this mess, betraying us to the Invaders for her own purposes, but now realising she can't use them in the way that she had long ago intended to.*' There was another long sigh and the sound of rustling leaves that seemed to come from everywhere and nowhere. '*She's afraid now that Aanundus sees her as a potential threat, and before he makes moves to try to destroy her, she's cutting her losses and abandoning the hive.*'

The sigh became deeper, the susurration of the leaves rising and falling with the sound of Tamizel's breathing. Reece couldn't understand why Tamizel didn't sound jubilant about Hollë's departure. It took him a moment to realise the information was not for him—it was for Aanundus. *Oh, I get the plan. Maybe I should assist with it.* But at that moment, his hand began to throb with pain and within seconds he was in agony. But he gritted his teeth anyway, and asked the sky, 'What's that got to do with the Unfolding?'

'*Hollë's got to get the Sarazen to swarm after her, so that she can set up a new hive.*'

The Sarazen? Reece remembered the high escarpment with its clefts, pinnacles and caves. *Somewhere up behind me is the Star Pool and above it, the Cave of the Sarazen.* He suddenly recalled the sword Holly had found in the Star Pool. *I wonder where it is at the moment. I'd like to see it in Bobenny's hands right about now.* Even as he was imagining the damage the Master of the Hunt would do, there was a cry from the heights.

It was a call, seeking and drawing. It echoed, wild and urgent, down to the City.

'Hollë,' Tamizel said.

All eyes turned upwards, scanning for the source of the resounding voice. High in the apex of the hollow mountain was a huge dark shadow. Suspended in the air just below it was a shimmering iridescent flutter of light, like that of a butterfly first stretching its glistening wings. The iridescent flutter began a slow tremulous circular glide, and behind it, wave upon wave of effulgent wings streamed out of the cave.

The Sarazen had awoken. Hollë was calling, and they were swarming at her command. Quivering awkwardly and trailing slender mist-like threads, they began to spiral, some ascending, some descending. They trilled with high piping voices as they found the warmer air currents of the cavern and began to float upwards.

Aanundus yelled to his guards. The Farafolk cried out in horror as they saw the anti-gravity platforms begin to rise, and the troopers on them ready their weapons, aiming them towards the Sarazen.

But, as the first shot blasted the rock just above the cave, it became clear that the Invaders were firing not at them, but at the writhing monstrous shadow that was Hollë. She howled, calling, calling… and the Sarazen responded instantly.

As the three guards on the nearest platform aimed their weapons, the Sarazen swept in front of Hollë, shielding her corpulent body with their own slender winged forms. More than a dozen fell, plummeting to the ground, some hitting one of the anti-gravity platforms on the way down. Reece was astonished to see it spin out of control, spilling two of the troopers on it overboard as it spiralled downwards. *The Sarazen must have hit the control mechanism.*

A third trooper dived from the platform just before it hit the ground. Slamming into a pair of robots which were patrolling the pens of the prisoners, it tore up rock and turf, piling a mound in front of it before skidding to a halt and flattening the fence of the largest pen. The common people surged forward, clambering over and behind the instant barricade to arm themselves with rocks, twisted metal and weapons taken from the fallen troopers.

Meanwhile the troopers on those platforms still whirring high above divided their fire, targeting both Hollë above them, and the escaping Farafolk below. But Hollë's wild untrammeled song was relentless, and the Sarazen continued to respond to her Music. Some protected Hollë with the shields of their bodies, but many suicided, engulfing the anti-gravity platforms in a shimmer of wings. The platforms veered out of control and exploded as they hit the inside walls of the mountain.

Reece stared. Not all of the platforms swerving into the mountain had been bombarded by falling Sarazen. Or been involved in any other kind of collision. *It's her. Hollë. She doesn't just control the Sarazen, she's got into some of the pilots' minds as well.*

He noticed that the common people, while not immune to Hollë's song, did not set themselves to oppose the Music, but work around it. They defended her by defending themselves. Swarming over two of the robots, they attacked them en masse with rocks and smashing them into immobility. Aanundus shouted orders, but even he seemed distracted and disoriented by Hollë's keening. Several of the remaining troopers somersaulted over the barricade at his command, but this simply proved suicidal.

The Farafolk had the lake at their backs, and were protected by the crashed platform, the ditch behind it, and the wall of earth in front of it. Despite being heavily outweaponed, they had gained a major advantage. Reece watched as Aanundus, standing legs apart, weapon ready, fought to shake off the influence of Hollë's song as he sized up the deteriorating situation. The first thing he did was to remove the Eye from the metal tree. Then he strode away, indicating for some of his remaining troopers to attack from across the lake, while he led the continuing assault on the barricade from the front. As Aanundus' attention was diverted with the combat, one of the High Court, dragging his chains and his brothers with him, struggled forward to Reece. It was the man Reece didn't know—the one he'd decided had to be Haimirel. With only the strength of his bare hands, he tried to pull Reece's shackles apart. 'Forget me,' Reece hissed under his breath, watching Aanundus. 'Quick! If you all rush him and overpower him, you can get the tachyon decelerator back.'

Haimirel's hands were bleeding with the strain of trying to release Reece. It was quite clear he didn't understand a word. 'The armband!' Reece repeated. 'The tachyon decelerator!'

Aanundus whirled abruptly, obviously having overcome Hollë's insidious control at last. He brought his weapon down into a firing position. Perhaps he was only going to use the High Court as a bargaining tool, but they clearly thought they were staring death in the face. Rushing forward as a chained single unit, they cannoned into Aanundus as he fired the first shot. A spear of light spat upwards and a spout of blood sprayed into the air, but Reece couldn't see whose it was. As strong as Aanundus was, the High Court, in their frenzy, were an even match for him. The next moment Reece's water pistol was flung from the midst of the scrabbling pack. *Oh please. Not the water pistol! Don't worry about it. The tachyon decelerator. In one piece.*

The inside of the mountain reverberated with shouts and screams and splashes, the intermittent whoosh and crickle of laser and stazer fire, the clatter of stone on metal, and the bass drumming of stampeding footsteps. But no longer, Reece realised, with Hollë's song.

Then abruptly the members of the High Court ceased struggling, and they stood up one by one, bleeding and torn, two of them shockingly wounded. Aanundus had his arm locked around Varyien's throat and a gun at his temple. 'Aghin!' Aanundus screamed, more than once, and slowly his troopers disengaged from the fighting.

Soon a hush fell. Silence. Hollë had gone. And then there was murmuring, muted and distant. Reece watched the common people as they pointed toward Aanundus and Varyien. He wondered if they really cared about their king or if they were merely interested in the outcome.

Reece became aware of other sounds: from high above came the piping voices of the remaining Sarazen, circling like lost infants. *Hollë has abandoned them.* He was both surprised and unsurprised at the same time.

Aanundus began to speak softly, addressing himself only to the High Court. His voice dropped to a harsh sibilant whisper and sounded, even to Reece's uncomprehending ears, like that of a dragon trying to mesmerise its prey.

'Don't fall for it, guys,' he yelled. 'Whatever he says. It's nothing but lies.'

Aanundus glanced at him and smirked, while Reece glared helplessly back. 'Just don't fall for it,' he repeated. As he watched, the High Court seemed to shake itself free of some strange grip. A moment later, Aanundus fired and one of the metal branches of the tree sheared off, crashing to the ground just in front of him.

Reece gulped, realising that only a last-second jab from Varyien had saved his life. Aanundus tightened his grip on the king but didn't go for a second shot, though he did spare a moment to raise an eyebrow at Reece. The he winked. Reece was bewildered by the gesture.

Then he realised the source of Aanundus' confidence. Varyien's voice rang out across the field and, almost at once, the Farafolk began to lay down their arms.

Aanundus' contemptuous smile barely changed as he nodded in satisfaction and began to push the king ahead of him across the Field of Fountains. No one tried to stop them, not even Bobenny or the members of the Hunt. And so, followed by his troopers, Aanundus and the king passed unhindered through the Farafolk and finally disappeared on one of the pathways leading back to the City. *I don't believe it. They're letting him go. Just like that.*

Eventually Haimirel found the keys to Reece's fetters and released him from his metal bonds. The next thing he knew his wounded hand was being examined by an attendant Haimirel had called.

'Ruēl, Ruēl,' came the whispers, while on-lookers crowded around Reece in awe. Haimirel ushered them away so Reece's injured hand could be treated. But touching it proved to be almost unbearably painful, and he was hard put not to scream. He felt shaky and dazed, and his eyes were watering. His entire arm throbbed from the shoulder to the fingertips.

'Oh, go away,' Reece said between gritted teeth, trying to disengage himself from the examiner's grasp. 'I've got to go to find Holly.' But despite his protests, he was held down firmly by the beaming attendant.

Bobenny finished delivering a whole litany of orders and then came to stand by the attendant's side as the bandaging of Reece's hand began. Filmy white gauze was carefully wrapped across his palm. It stung so much Reece actually did cry out involuntarily.

As the attendant finished, Bobenny held out the water pistol and smiled triumphantly. Reece just stared. *Of all the things you could have rescued, why, oh why, did it have to be the most useless?*

The Tree of 'If'

Holly's escort came out of a winding tunnel and into the bright air of the mountainside. A row of 'copters and vehicles were stationed under an overhang. The escort paused to inspect the surroundings before leading Holly across the terrain to the nearest flyer. Tiny clefts in the wet rocks underfoot harboured clusters of drenched periwinkle-blue flowers and tiny sun-eyed daisies. High in the sky, the distant shrieks of hunting birds could be heard. As the troopers stopped, their leader turned to Holly. 'You will show us where the cliff is.'

Holly was so astonished she couldn't speak. *How can he possibly speak English? Does he come from Earth? Has he been to Earth?*

'Which direction?' The trooper pushed her roughly. 'Don't pretend ignorance.'

Holly looked around, trying to orient herself. She had no idea where she was, not a clue about direction. But as she glanced about, frightened and puzzled, she noticed the shadow of a long taper-thin leg out of the corner of her eye. The next moment, one of the guards was soaring through the air, tumbling head over heels, as an immense thwacking sound echoed across the rocks.

All the guards swivelled, readying their weapons, but the Ettii came from every side—in such swift, numerous packs that the troopers had no chance to fire off more than a few wild shots before they were overwhelmed. A pair of strong, gentle jaws hoisted Holly up out of the pressing throng. It wasn't easy to throw her arms around Glyffy, but she managed it. 'Thank you,' she breathed. 'Oh, thank you. Thank you.'

Glyffy deposited Holly on her neck and with slow, high-stepping movements began to pick her way out of the crowd. Holly held Glyffy tightly. With a sedate pace, the pale green Etus began to descend a treacherous scree-blocked path. Any mis-step would result in the two of them being swept away in an avalanche of pebbles. However the immensely long legs of the Etus were a singular advantage—soon both Glyffy and Holly were at the bottom of the path, treading along the defile of a narrow canyon. A swollen stream, frothing and boiling with mud, swirled round Glyffy's hooves as they followed the ravine downwards. Finally the stream fanned out in a place where the canyon was flatter and broader, disappearing into the sands and leaving only a dark stain as evidence of its passing. 'Where are we going?' Holly felt puzzled and a little uneasy, realising that Glyffy had left everyone far, far behind them. Even the rest of the Ettii.

Without answering, Glyffy kept on strolling, her long legs carrying Holly further away from danger every second. 'Glyffy, Reece is in trouble. Please let's try to help him. We have to go back.'

Still there was no answer. They reached the end of the canyon and, as Holly looked out on the second sun rising over the rim of a landscape like a vast shimmering cauldron, she had an overwhelming sense of home. *The edge of the desert. This is the edge of a desert—just like where Dad took Reece and me camping last year in the Outback.*

Glyffy kept on going. *But there's no cover here. If the 'copters come—and they're sure to, eventually—they'll spot us straight away.*

The crisp clip-clop of hooves on rock soon gave way to soft swish-swashing as they encountered the first sand rise. It didn't take Holly long to realise how much their progress was slowed by the new terrain. Soon she realised she wasn't riding as high as she had been and, as she looked down, she realised that, with each step, Glyffy was past her ankles in sand. As she looked to the dunes ahead of them, she realised the immensity of the task Glyffy had set herself. Perhaps that's why she wasn't talking. *But why is she doing this? Where can we possibly be going? This must be really important.* Holly decided to ignore her inner misgivings. 'Let me get down,' she whispered to Glyffy, tugging gently on the giraffe's ear. 'C'mon, you stubborn old thing, let me down. You're not built with flat feet like a camel.'

Glyffy struggled on a few more paces before relenting. Holly slid down off her back and they set off, side by side, their progress painfully slow. The two suns were climbing to their zenith. Their shadows became shorter and deeper, and the heat beating down on them from the sky and reflecting up from the sand, was almost unbearable. Holly wondered if walking through an oven would be this hot. She felt as if her eyeballs were frying. 'Let's go back,' she rasped through parched lips. 'We'll die here if we go on.' She stopped, and turned, pointing back along the line of their footprints. 'This way,' she pleaded. But Glyffy took her upraised arm between her diamond-sharp teeth and, with incredible gentleness, pulled her around. 'Glyffy, where are we going? Is there anything out here?'

Silence.

Holly's first fall was on the side of a dune so immense that it rose like a towering swell in front of them. Glyffy picked her up and they went on, even more slowly and carefully. *It's a furnace.* And then the sand began to seem strangely familiar. *Maybe the bus will come soon. Mister Jenkins is dreadfully late. He's going to lose this bus run if he doesn't run to schedule.* And then, to her amazement, Holly saw an ice cream van at the crest of the dune. Its bell was chiming and, pied piper-like, its light was winking red and yellow. She hurried then, almost throwing herself towards the van, leaving Glyffy to try to catch up to her. Just as she reached the top of the dune, the ice cream van disappeared, melting away like an evanescent wisp of cloud. Holly stumbled a second time then—falling heavily and skidding down the burning sand in an uncontrolled slide. She was almost at the bottom of the dune when Glyffy caught her. The Etus plucked her up, hurtled on down the dune and then leapt across to the next dune before the avalanche of hot sand that Holly had created buried the two of them. 'Oh, Glyffy!' Holly wanted to cry but found her eyes were so dry no tears would come.

Glyffy put her down carefully and they trudged to the top of the next sandhill. As they finally reached its summit and looked over the side, Holly saw a shimmering smear of silver. *Water. Water.* She was about to dive towards it when she remembered the ice cream van. *Hallucinations*, she realised. And then she fell for a third time.

A moment later—at least it seemed a moment later—a voice as soft as the brush of a moth's wing was whispering close to her ear. 'She'll be awake soon, Glyffy, and then we shall see.'

'I'm awake already,' Holly croaked, opening her eyes. She was astonished to find herself looking up at the waving fronds of a palm tree. The sound of water was bubbling by her elbow and cool shadows slanted across her face. 'Where am I?'

'Between now and forever.'

Holly turned to find a man sitting near her, watching the pool as it bubbled and sang. Glyffy was by his side, her head resting in his lap. 'Who are you?'

'A friend of Glyffy's,' the man answered. 'And of Tamizel's.'

Holly was silent a moment, wondering whether she should tell him about Tamizel's death. But, with an ache, she realised she didn't know for sure whether he was dead or not. 'Well, any friend of theirs is a friend of mine.'

'Are you a friend of theirs?' the man asked.

'Ask Glyffy.' Holly felt suddenly diffident and afraid of the man. She was glad to have a friend beside her. He had a strange face, now that she took the time to observe him closely. It was both stern and kind, gentle and wild, young and old, changeable and changeless—all at once. His eyes seemed to be the colour of amber and he was wearing a white shirt and a suit of a kind of amethyst grey. And his voice no longer reminded Holly of the gentle brush of a moth's wing—it was textured with hurricanes and zephyrs, whispering breezes and fierce firestorms. 'Yes, ask Glyffy,' Holly repeated, a little uneasily. 'She'll tell you.'

'That's just the problem. Glyffy says she has doubts.'

'What?' Holly turned to the Etus and stared in disbelief. *Glyffy doesn't trust me? Impossible!* And then she remembered Glyffy hadn't spoken a single word since rescuing her. With sudden stabbing insight, Holly realised why. *Glyffy took me into the desert to die!* She could scarcely credit it, but the moment she thought of the possibility, she knew it was true. *And she was prepared to sacrifice herself to ensure it. But then why did she save me from the sand avalanche?*

'Glyffy talked Tamizel into giving you his protection.' The man answered her thoughts while all the while stroking the giraffe's head as it lay nestled in his lap. 'And now she feels responsible, not just for breaking his heart, but for urging the Farafolk to trust you when it would appear that it has only brought them ruin.'

'I didn't break Tamizel's heart.' A lump suddenly constricted Holly's throat. 'Honestly.'

'Honestly?' the man asked. 'Well, it's not me you have to reassure, but Glyffy. She seems to have got it into her head that you really are Holly the destroyer, sent to harm the Farafolk. Convincing her that the Invaders would have attacked anyway, regardless of whether or not you were there with the Jewels of Shifting Time, has not been easy.'

'Jewels of Shifting Time?'

'Some of a more scientific mindset call them a tachyon decelerator mesh.' He gestured to her. 'Please move closer to the pool, and perhaps we can convince Glyffy to dispense with this absurd notion once and for all.'

Holly was only too happy to comply with this request. On her hands and knees, she bent over the pool. Scooping up the water quickly, she dashed its coolness into her mouth. Then she stopped, staring, her attention caught by the strangeness of her own reflection. It seemed insubstantial—as if it were embossed on the surface, a mere shadow of a shadow. The man reached into a pocket and flung some dark pepper-coloured flecks towards the pool. 'What's that?' Holly asked, as the water began to ripple.

'Distilling salts,' the man said. 'Now the pool will show us what you are really like.' He raised Glyffy's head, tucking her long face in the crook of his arm and pointing towards the water. 'There you go, my long-legged friend.' He nodded at the Etus. 'Look at that.'

Holly's image on the water was a cimmerian silhouette which abruptly darkened, then just as suddenly lightened again. After a moment, it began shifting between light and dark—but even at its brightest, a deep stain slashed across it. By contrast, both the man's and Glyffy's images shone like sun-washed diamonds. The difference alarmed Holly. 'Why do I look like that?' Her voice dropped to an anxious whisper.

'You have a deep-cracked heart,' the man said.

Deep-cracked heart? 'That's not real good, is it?'

'Fatal,' the man said, peering at the image. 'But not immediately. You have a very nasty splinter there—several in fact, but one especially sharp sliver of ice. Some people's hearts become hollow, eaten out with torment, but others grow cold little by little. When the ice chip reaches your very centre, your heart will be frozen forever.' He looked up at Holly, searching her face.

Holly felt naked under his gaze. 'It was something my gran said.'

'About your father?'

'How did you know?'

'The shape of the splinter.' The man's voice was gentle. 'You need to get rid of it, you know.'

'But I don't want to ask my mum.' Holly was emphatic. 'And anyway, I can't. She's a trillion kilometres away and I'll never see her again.' At this thought, her eyes glazed over with a salty patina of tears.

'Well, perhaps that's so and perhaps it's not. But why don't you ask your dad instead?'

'Because I'd be too scared of hurting him.'

'Really?'

'No,' Holly admitted. 'I'm too scared the answer will hurt me. My dad's not rich, you know—not like…' She hesitated. '*That* man.'

'Your dad has always been rich.' The man shook his head, his eyes twinkling. 'Hasn't he always said so? I'll tell you a secret— one day he won't just be rich, he'll have money to go with it too.' He winked. 'And I'll tell you another secret: your dad will give you the truth, your mother will give you the facts. It's up to you which of those you choose.'

'That's no choice,' Holly said. 'There's no difference between truth and fact.'

'Of course there is. Truth is fact wrapped up as a gift. Truth is deep, while fact is all surface. Truth is a symphony, fact is a melody line.' He patted Glyffy's head. 'Isn't that right, old friend?'

Glyffy nodded. Holly stared at the Etus. 'I wouldn't have hurt the Farafolk, Glyffy.' She felt desperate to ensure Glyffy would trust her again. 'Don't you know that? I wouldn't have hurt Tamizel. I lo…' She broke off, mid-word, realising that she'd never hated Tamizel, even when she'd said she had. 'I did hurt him though, didn't I?'

'Very much so,' the man said. 'It's that heart of yours: how can you feel properly or react properly when it's in such a state?'

'Can it be cured?'

'If you put your life entirely in my hands, yes,' the man said. 'If you give me every moment of your past and every second of your future, then your heart will become whole again.'

'What is this?' Holly demanded sharply. 'Religion, is it? Or just some sort of Magic?' She glared at the man, feeling sudden hostility and suspicion. 'And anyway who are you?' A sudden wild thought occurred to her—ever since Gran had spoken of spending the night on Caer Idris, strange things had been happening. *Could she have called up something?* 'Are you Merlin?'

Laughter was her answer. 'Merlin?' the man asked. 'No. Are you?'

'Me?' Holly asked. 'How could you possibly think I'd be Merlin?'

'Because you've started to live backwards in time. Just like Merlin.'

Holly almost snorted in disbelief. 'Backwards in time?'

'It's really quite common,' the man said, nodding at her. 'There are many Merlins in your world, and in this one, too for that matter—people who live backwards, unable to summon their own future. Their destinies are so dominated by a traumatic moment of their past that they re-live it continually, replaying it over and over again.' The man sighed and looked down at Glyffy. 'All the little Merlins with their frozen hearts, holding on to their pasts and entombed in prisons of their own making because they cannot forgive and let go.' He looked up at Holly once more. 'We've got quite enough of them, you know, without adding you to their number.'

'But I've forgiven Gran.' Holly was indignant as she folded her arms.

'Have you?' the man asked. 'I doubt if you've ever truly forgiven anyone.'

Holly, stung even more by the injustice of the comment, glared at the man. 'That's not true.'

'There are two kinds of people who never forgive.' The man's amber eyes narrowed as he looked at her. 'There are those who are angry and bitter, and there are those who are tolerant and gentle. The tolerant ones excuse malice—they rationalise the cruelty done to them as the actions of someone who didn't know any better. And because they've excused it, there's no need for them to forgive it. The cage door of your esplumoir is swinging shut for you, little tolerant one—what are you going to do about it?'

Holly felt an urgent desire to change the subject. 'I'm really worried about my brother.'

'He *is* in grave trouble.' The man nodded, seeming to reflect on the situation. 'Aanundus delights in inflicting pain.'

'Is there anything you can do?'

The man gestured towards the pool. 'Since we are between now and forever, time is not so rigidly fixed here.' He indicated to Holly that she should gaze in the pool. She looked down and, in its depths, she could see a formless pale swirling which, after a moment, coalesced into sharply-etched shapes. Immediately she recognised Reece—and it took her a moment to realise he wasn't there in front of her. It was just an image. A strange one, though. Reece was tied to the metal tree with mirror leaves. The last time she'd seen it Varyien had once been fettered. His face was taut and sickly white. She could see he was in pain.

But there was something odd about her vision of the Field of Fountains. There seemed to be an enormous translucent hand just in front of Reece, poised protectively over him. Neither Reece nor Aanundus gave any sign of being able to see the shield between them. Holly peered at the image, realising there was a design on the hand. At first it seemed like the moko design from the wheel in the spaceship that had brought her and Reece to Dreamfall.

But then she realised it was a stylised word, a word starting with N. Just as she recognised she was looking at it backwards—as if in a mirror—the hand shifted. It moved its position until it was behind Reece, almost cradling him. *C. The word doesn't start with an N, but a C.* Reece seemed to have become as translucent as the hand. It looked as if he was part of it, as if he were living glass carved out of the hollow of the hand safeguarding him. Then Holly saw more—and wondered how she could have missed something so massive. There was a tree overarching the hand, a tree hung with stars, and from the tree, there came a voice. It was the tree she'd seen at the Starpool.

The voice spoke to Reece, and the more Holly strained to hear it, the more distant and indistinct it became. She felt a sudden desperation to know who the voice belonged to—as if hearing and knowing this were the most important thing in the entire universe.

The image disappeared and Holly found herself looking at nothing more than her own light-slashed reflection on the water. She could almost see the darkness within her consuming the light. She blinked, stunned not just by what she had witnessed, but by the vision of darkness in front of her. She was numb, unable to feel anything. That frightened her still more. 'What is this pool?'

'What you see on the pool here,' the man said, 'is what you would see if you looked in the Eye of Ruēl. The secret of the most destructive power in the universe is on the water below you.'

On the water. Not in? All she could see was her own reflection. '*Me? I'm* the most destructive force in the universe? But that's… that's ridiculous… isn't it?'

The man was silent.

Holly stared. *Not an Evil Eye*, she realised, *the Eye of Truth*. 'It's the ice splinter, isn't it?' She took a deep breath. 'But what if it won't thaw? I'm not sure I can fix it myself.'

'You can't,' the man said. 'It's already lodged too deep. But it's not a question of can or can't, it's whether you want to or not.' He looked at her quizzically. 'Your only task is to ask.'

'Ask what?'

'Ask for help. But bear in mind, to fix the splinter, I need your whole life.'

I'm not sure about handing over my whole life. 'What if I change my mind?'

'What *if* you change your mind?' The man smiled. '*If* is the most dangerous of words. All of the past can be overturned by it, all of the future shaped by it. *If* is the pivot of choice. Yet there are choices that can be undone and others that cannot.' The man looked up at the swaying palm above and smiled. 'The knowledge of good and evil comes not at the moment of disobedience—it's in the act of choosing, either way. Enlightenment comes through the choice.' He looked down at Holly and his smile faded. 'What you choose here and now, Cerylen Morgan, will have repercussions for all worlds, your own included.'

Holly glowered. 'My name's Celyren—that's Welsh for 'Holly'—not Cerylen and my choices are no more important than anyone else's. Everyone's choices, not matter how small, shape the future.'

'Not so dramatically,' the man said. 'As for your name being Celyren—I'd bear in mind that your dad is a notoriously bad speller and that he was responsible for your birth certificate.'

Holly gaped. 'He called me Cerylen?' Instantly she knew it as the truth. Whenever Dad was fooling around, he said her name just like that, with a special twinkle in his eye. He'd say it most often to annoy Gran when she needled him about his lack of education. 'What does it mean?'

'It's Welsh for *my loved one*.'

'My loved one?' Holly repeated, confounded. 'He's not that bad a speller. Did he know? Did he do it deliberately?'

'That's another thing you might want to ask him. Perhaps the first thing.'

Holly was silent for quite some time. She watched the man who, after a little while, began to sing softly to Glyffy. Then she looked at the waving fronds of the palm tree and the tiny wavelets of the pool where her dark image was reflected. 'I think maybe I do want to get my heart fixed after all.' She hesitated. 'Maybe.' She hunched her shoulders. 'Will it hurt?'

'Quite a bit.'

'Oh.' Holly sighed. 'It's why Glyffy brought me here, isn't it?' She scowled at the Etus, feeling that her choices were being made for her. *Maybe I'll go through with it. For Glyffy. And Tamizel. Oh Tamizel...* 'How long's the operation take?'

'Not long. Come with me into the water.' The man stroked Glyffy a moment before getting up and putting one foot on the edge of the pool. 'It's fortunate that we're between now and forever, because it won't even take a moment here.' Holly hesitated a little longer and then with sudden decision she splashed into the pool and stood facing the man. 'Look down,' the man said, 'at your reflection.' Holly did—and saw that the smoky darkness of her reflection was counterpointed by a dazzle of light from the man. Then, as she continued to watch in surprise, the brilliance of the man's image began to flow into the dark murky shape of her reflection, the deep slash in her heart flooded with light, and the shifting pattern of shadows altered to a rainbow interplay of colours.

'When does it start to hurt?' Holly asked uneasily.

'A while back,' the man said. Holly shot a glance upwards at his face and realised he was in tremendous pain. 'I didn't say it was going to hurt *you*,' he whispered.

'Stop!' Holly said. 'Stop! I don't want you to hurt yourself...'

'A little late for that.' The man took a deep breath and looked down at Holly's rainbow image in the pool. 'There!' He smiled. 'Already your heart has become transparent enough to refract the light.'

Holly looked down herself. 'Why is mine coloured and yours blazing white?'

'Because I am the source and you are the lens,' the man said. 'These are the colours of grace.' He stepped out of the pool and slid his hand under Glyffy's jaw, nudging her upwards. The Etus rose unsteadily on her feet, as the man continued, 'It's time, Cerylen, for you to go back to Finddias—you can't stay here. I'll see if there's someone willing to guide you.'

'Why can't Glyffy take me?' Holly asked.

'Because her time of mortality is gone,' the man said.

It took Holly a moment to realise what the man meant. 'She's dead?'

The man nodded. 'She was prepared to die to ensure you did, and then she was prepared to die to save you. And in the end, she did rescue you—with her dying steps, she brought you here.' His smile was sad. 'I have something for you.' Reaching into the pocket of his amethyst grey suit, he pulled out a long white tile.

'That's like the ones on the glass tree,' Holly said.

The man nodded. 'Yes, it comes from the tree of judgment. It's yours, in fact.'

'Mine?' Holly asked, baffled.

'It's a judgment tile—it glowed when Tamizel came to see for himself what the tree might say. He took it for safe-keeping, in case others took it to deface it—and change the judgment.' The man raised his brows at her. 'This tile persuaded Tamizel to trust Glyffy's defence of you. Without this tile, you would have died at that tree—killed by the Master of the Hunt whose duty it is, first and foremost, to protect the secret of Finddias.'

'But why did Glyffy defend us to Tamizel? Especially since she's so obviously regretted it.'

'Because Tamizel asked her to.'

'Tamizel asked her to defend us to Tamizel?' Holly shook her head. 'That doesn't make sense.'

'It will,' the man said. 'Reece will explain it to you.'

Holly frowned, utterly perplexed. 'And what's on the tile? What does it say that made Tamizel trust us?'

'It's only one word.' The man threw the tile to her. 'It is an imprint of the writing inscribed on my own hand,' he said as Holly caught it deftly. Her eyes were drawn, not to the tile, but to the man's hand. She could see something written there, but she could also see sunlight coming straight through the palm.

'You're the Wounded Hand!' She didn't know what to think. *Am I imagining all this?* 'Ever since I made the tree of hands, back home, and Reece made the cut-out of silver foil, I've been seeing signs of you everywhere. If you're not Merlin, who are you?' The man said nothing, and finally Holly turned her attention to the tile in her palm.

There really was a word written on it. Holly almost gasped as she caught her first good glimpse of it: Cerylen. *My loved one.* She looked up in consternation. *Why on earth is my true name on your…?* Her thoughts were cut short by the realisation that neither Glyffy nor the man was there any longer. Nor was the palm tree, nor the shady, refreshing oasis. She was standing in a shrinking pool of water, up to her ankles—in the middle of nowhere.

She looked around, utterly at a loss. Deep within her was the knowledge that the man and the oasis, the palm tree and the pool had welled up from her unconscious, out of the very heart of her imagination. Nevertheless, she knew they were real, not unreal. *Perhaps, they're the only genuine reality I've ever encountered in my whole life. So where does the True come from?*

'Move aside, move aside,' a shrill voice said suddenly. Holly turned, looking for the sound. 'Don't monopolise the whole hole,' the voice went on. 'What are you—a Sarazen or a waterhog?' A massive bird with a flame-coloured crest and outstretched white wings, was tripping across the sand towards her. It was like a giant emu, but with a difference: its wings were long and leathery, like those of a pterodactyl.

'I'm not a Sarazen or a waterhog,' Holly said. 'But what are you?'

'I'm a sharva,' the bird said. 'And this is a very peculiar language we're speaking.' A bright blue tongue flickered inside its ebony beak. 'It feels positively alien.' The bird dipped its head in the water and lapped its tongue rapidly at Holly's toes. 'I'm Sharmika,' it said, as it raised its beak once more and water dribbled down its mouth. 'You're not from round here, are you?'

'No.' Holly shook her head.

'What's that you've got?' The sharva's beady eyes focussed on the white tile in Holly's hand.

'It's just something with my name on it.'

'You've got a white stone with your name on it?' the sharva asked. 'I'll bet it's a secret name, isn't it? Ooooh, you must have a great destiny.' It nodded its head and blinked its eyes like flapping shutters. 'So what are you doing here? This isn't the hub of the universe, you know.'

'I think I'm lost,' Holly said.

'You don't say,' said the sharva. 'I'd never have guessed.' It nodded again. 'Well, you just fly after me—I'll make sure you get safely on your way home.'

'I can't fly.'

'You're not serious?' the sharva asked. 'What sort of Sarazen are you?'

'I told you—I'm not a Sarazen.' Holly stared at the bird. 'Do Sarazen have wings?'

The sharva pouted. 'I knew it,' it snapped. 'I knew it. A message comes to fly out into the middle of nowhere, and I said to myself, if this is another beast-of-burden exercise, I'm going to be very annoyed. I'm going to be stupendously offended.' It screwed up its tiny pebble-like eyes and glowered grimly. 'A talent like mine for organisation and leadership—and it's continually being frittered away in providing the sort of transport service any birdbrain is capable of. I suppose the fate of the cosmos is resting on my willingness to be a taxi—as usual.'

'I wouldn't know,' Holly said. 'But if you could help me, I'd really appreciate it.'

The sharva huffed. 'Oh, jump on,' it said testily, turning around and lowering its haunches so that Holly could sit on its back. 'And you'd better not get airsick or you'll find yourself walking out of this wilderness under your own steam. Got that?'

'I'm sorry to put you to all this trouble.' Holly positioned herself awkwardly behind the sharva's wings. Almost before she knew it, they were in the air. A strong beat of wings, a long slow glide through a wide arc and another flap of the sharva's wings as the bird found an upward thermal of air—soon they were high in the sky, hovering and circling at first, then skimming the wind currents, racing towards a horizon that was glowing pink in the sunset.

They hadn't been flying much more than fifteen minutes

when a wedge of dark silhouettes appeared in the sky ahead of them. 'Hornet 'copters!' Holly exclaimed. 'Stop! Stop! Turn around! Stop, Sharmika, stop!' But the sharva flew on, seemingly oblivious to the danger ahead.

It wasn't long until they were within range of the flying shapes. The closer they got, the more convinced Holly became that the sharva was delivering her right into the hands of the Invaders. 'Ahoy, there!' Sharmika called into the darkening sky. 'Anybody here lost a wingless Sarazen?'

'*Hello*!?' exclaimed an astonished voice. 'Where on earth did you learn to speak…?'

'*Reece*!' Holly squealed, cutting him off. 'Oh, Reece, is that you?'

'Sis?' Reece called.

A little more than a minute later, they were both on the ground and grinning stupidly at each other. Reece had come down on a gondola, towed along by two new-hatched Sarazen. 'I don't know how they do it, sis,' he said to Holly. 'They look so pretty and frail and they've only just been born, you know.'

She was so happy to be reunited and see him safe and well, she hugged him. He thumped her on the back and laughed. 'I guess they're like worker bees—on the job straight away.'

'You're okay?' Holly noticed Reece was keeping his hand up inside his shirt.

Reece nodded. 'I'll live,' he said with conviction as he looked Sharmika up and down. 'Just a bit of a sore hand.' He tilted his head towards the sharva. 'Where did it come from and how come it speaks English?'

Holly shrugged. She peered at Reece closely, wondering about his injury. It seemed to be serious. Normally he acted as if every splinter and pin-prick was a fatal wound but it seemed when something major happened, he could take it in his stride. 'What are you doing out here?' She turned to eye Bobenny and the others accompanying Reece with a degree of uncertainty. She had never entirely lost her fear of the Master of the Hunt.

'Looking for you. And…' Reece hesitated.

'And…?' Holly prompted.

'I think we're doing some reconnoitring as well. The Farafolk are going to attack Aanundus and retake the Citadel that he seized from them. He's got Varyien hostage.'

'Then it doesn't sound like a really good idea to me.'

Sharmika bent her neck until it was level with Holly's shoulder. She nodded at Reece, her beak jodding up and down in total agreement with Holly.

'I'm not so sure,' Reece said. 'You know I don't understand their language very well—Jaizee did translate a little for me, but not everything. But I did gather they don't think there's much of a choice about it.'

'Why not?'

'The Ettii have reported that Aanundus is about to cut his losses and leave this world—and when he does, he plans to leave no trace of his activities here on Dreamfall.'

'So the Farafolk are going to try to take back the Citadel before he can destroy it?'

'It's worse than that,' Reece said. 'He's got the tachyon decelerator. That means he can draw on enough power not only to destroy the Citadel but to obliterate this whole planet.'

'You're sure?' Holly took one look at the desperately worried faces of Bobenny and the Hunt and knew Reece had it right. She didn't need to ask.

Reece took a deep breath and grimaced at her. 'This *whole* planet, sis. And they think he'll have no compunction about doing it.'

The Tree
of
Life

Reece could just make out Holly's aghast expression in the long shadows of sunset.

'What?' She shook her head. 'But what would be the point?'

'If you'd seen what I've just seen, Hol, you'd know there doesn't have to be a point.' Reece shuddered. 'I saw Hollë, Lady Death, using the Sarazen to protect herself. It was senseless slaughter. She could have defended herself without sacrificing them. And on top of that she was the one who told the Invaders all about the Eye in the first place to lure them here—but it seems she now realises they are purveyors of evil, just as she is. She won't be able to manipulate them like she controlled the Farafolk. I'm sure she knows what's about to happen and she wants to escape.'

'What's she like?' Holly asked.

Reece knew that the shadows of dusk effectively hid his face and Holly would hardly be able to see his expression but he still looked down at his feet. 'Don't ask.' His lip curled. 'You don't want to know. I feel sick just thinking about it. She was disgusting. Just this huge ugly monstrous…' Words failed him. '…thing.'

In the momentary silence that followed, he became aware that the members of the Hunt were growing impatient. Bobenny came forward and, tugging at his sleeve to gain his attention, said a few words. 'Now that you've found me,' Holly translated, 'he wants us to go back to the safety of Finddias.'

Reece glared. 'The *safety* of Finddias? What a joke!' He put a hand on his hip. 'I may be scared witless,' he said emphatically to Bobenny, 'but I'm going with you anyway.' He turned to Holly. 'Can you translate that?'

'I doubt if I need to.' Holly smiled to see Bobenny's frown. 'Certain ideas are conveyed by tone alone.' She produced a smile for the Master of the Hunt. 'I'm coming too!' She stamped her foot, but it had much less impact on sand than it would have had on solid ground.

'Well, so am I,' Sharmika piped up. Before immediately adding: 'Oh dear, that was a little precipitous, wasn't it?—just what have I committed myself to?'

A moment later, Bobenny began talking rapidly to the sharva, thumping his fist for emphasis into the palm of his hand. 'Yeah, yeah, sure, sure, Mister Big Shot.' Sharmika nodded after a few sentences, before jodding its beak, and flapping its wings once in an imperious gesture. 'Of course they know all that. Don't concern yourself, dearie. I'll be sure to take care of everything.'

Reece watched as the Master of the Hunt signalled his warriors and they moved off towards the waiting Sarazen. In the meanwhile the sharva turned to Holly and poked at her.

'What's wrong?' Holly asked.

'Wrong?' Sharmika said. 'I've held my tongue all this time waiting for you to introduce me, but you're never going to, are you? Honestly, young people are so thoughtless these days.' She sighed and turned to Reece. 'I'm Sharmika the sharva. You're Reece, I take it?'

Reece nodded as the sharva turned its back to him and humpphed off a short distance to plump its haunches down in the sand. 'Well, come on then,' Sharmika said. 'Don't take all night. They're about to take off without us.'

'What?' Reece demanded. He was flustered. 'What did Bobenny say to you?'

Sharmika flapped her wings. 'Usual stuff,' she sniffed. 'Can't guarantee your safety, that kind of thing. You'll be in everyone's way, they don't have warriors to spare to babysit you…'

'*Babysit*…!' The word nearly exploded out of Reece. He marched over to Bobenny, jerked him around and held up his wounded hand. 'I did not get this…'

'Quiet!' yelled Sharmika, An utterly astonished expression came over the sharva's features as Reece actually did break off, turning silently to give her a questioning look. 'Ooh, I like you,' Sharmika said, obviously forgetting whatever it was she had been going to say in the first place. 'Can I have you all for my very own? You're the first person who's ever shown me the respect I truly deserve. Instant obedience and no argument.'

Reece grimaced as Bobenny broke away from him and mounted the nearest gondola. 'Let me go with you!' he yelled. 'It's important—you just don't understand—I've got to get that tachyon decelerator. The water pistol wasn't important but the tach…' He watched in dismay as Bobenny and the rest of the Hunt rose into the air, towed aloft by the Sarazen.

'They can't just leave us here.' Holly's tone was abject.

'I'll have to go after them.' Reece glared at Sharmika. 'But I suppose you're our escort back to the "safety" of Finddias, and you just won't let us go.' He failed to keep the sarcasm out of his voice.

Sharmika winked. 'Just you hop on.' She raised her beak

towards the flight of Sarazen winging across the desert. 'We'll soon catch them up.'

'Catch them up?' Reece and Holly asked together.

'They're babies, those Sarazen,' Sharmika said. 'They'll have to take rest stops.'

'So we're not going to Finddias?' Holly asked.

'What would we be doing something that silly for?' Sharmika asked. 'They won't let *me* in, so I hardly imagine they'd be allowing riff-raff like you access to their secret City.' She humpphed as she lifted her haunches as soon as Holly had seated herself behind Reece. 'See those oh-so-clever Huntsmen up ahead? They'll be eating humble pie soon enough, you know. They'll be begging us for help. Just mark my words.'

'What do you mean?' Holly bent forward over Reece's shoulder to make sure the sharva could hear her. She couldn't see anything in the whistling darkness, but she was certainly glad Sharmika could.

'No doubt they're thinking they can just glide into the Citadel, under the cover of night, and get into the Old Tower by the secret ways,' Sharmika scoffed. 'What they don't know is that the secret ways have all been found and blocked. They're guarded by robots that shoot at anything they're not programmed to recognise.' The sharva's long leathery wings flapped easily and steadily. 'Which means that if the Hunt intends to rely on glamoure to get them past the sentries, it's not going to work. Robots don't fall for illusions—which is exactly why Aanundus prefers to use them. And doubtless what he used to get through the maze of illusions into Finddias earlier in the day for that matter.' Sharmika sighed and shook her head, as she gazed ahead at the flying Sarazen, that only she could see. 'I don't know, really—an ill-conceived expedition, if ever I saw one. A massacre, just waiting to happen.'

'Is there any way into the Citadel that Aanundus hasn't found?' Reece asked.

Sharmika chuckled. 'That remains to be seen.' Her chuckle deepened. 'And anyway getting into the Citadel is the least of our worries—what we really need to worry about is how to get into Aanundus' private lab.'

'That's sure to be under special guard,' Holly said. 'And what's this "we" business anyway? It's not as if we've got a key.'

Sharmika whistled to herself. 'Rumour is we don't need a key to get in—we need a lock.'

'What?' Reece asked.

'A lock, not a key,' Sharmika repeated, whistling again. 'I like you, kid. So stick with me, and remember to do exactly what I say when the time comes.'

'Have you got a plan?' Reece asked.

'The rudiments of one,' Sharmika said. 'So just be quiet now and let me think.'

Reece lay his head along the sharva's neck and turned to look up at the still-darkening sky. He had been forced to use his hand to hold on to Sharmika when she was taking off, but it had not hurt nearly as much as he had thought it would. *Perhaps things are looking up.* Along the horizon he could see glimmering twilight-touched peaks and ice-bright stars twinkling high above them. *There's Orion the Hunter and Sirius, the Dog Star. An eggcupful of matter from its white dwarf companion, the Pup, is so dense it weighs more than the whole Earth. Earth...* An immense sense of loss and longing threatened to overcome him. *Earth... Don't think about it*, he said sternly to himself. *Look there's the Southern Cross and one of the Pointers. I still can't understand why the other Pointer is never around. It must be...* And then it hit him. He couldn't believe he'd missed the obvious for so long. *Alpha Centauri. Triple star system, one orange, one yellow, one faint red one. Four light years from Earth. The closest star system to the sun. That's why I can't see it. It's not in the night sky anymore because it's in the day sky. We're on a planet circling Alpha Centauri!* Just knowing suddenly where he and Holly were—just being able to name it—filled Reece with a strange sense of relief. *We might be a dreadful long way from home but at least we're in the neighbourhood.*

Flap……… flap……… flap—the sharva hardly seemed to be hurrying at all. 'Can you please go faster, Sharmika?' Holly asked.

'This is the standard flying rate of a lone sharva, idly crossing the desert, minding its own business,' Sharmika said, flapping at the same regular pace. She began singing. 'I'm a little sharva, all alone,' she warbled. 'I'm just finding my way home.' Then she sighed. 'That's a nursery song amongst sharvas. It's a well-established fact, all over Dreamfall, you know, that we sing it often, especially when crossing inhospitable wastelands. Even more especially, now I come to think of it, when those wastelands have Citadels in them which have been conquered by Invaders from the stars.' She sighed again, more deeply still. 'Any lone sharva, not wishing to draw attention to itself, or to cause suspicion which might result in a closer look by the advanced eyes of technological wizardry, would be advised to adhere to this pace and occasionally warble this song. Especially when trying to drown out heavy breathing from anyone who might be accompanying it.'

'Technological wizardry?' Holly asked. 'The Sarazen are flying into a trap?'

'They'll be spotted on what can only be termed "radar" in your atrociously alien language, long before they reach the Citadel. No doubt the Hunt are relying on courage and sheer weight of numbers to carry the day for them. It's a suicide mission of course, which is undoubtedly the real reason why they didn't want you to go with them. Against all evidence to the contrary, it seems Bobenny really might have a conscience after all.'

'But…' Reece began.

'Surprise is not on their side,' Sharmika said, 'but it might be on ours.'

'You have got a plan, haven't you?' Reece asked.

'Patience, patience,' Sharmika said. 'You need to be quiet from now on—we don't want to draw those advanced technological ears in our direction by any injudicious sounds.'

Holly and Reece were both instantly silent. The slow even flapping of the sharva's wings were like the soft straining of oars crossing a lake as they flew on through the night. The rhythmic rise and fall in the bird's movement had an almost hypnotic effect as the horizon dipped and bobbed regularly every few seconds. Sharmika began crooning to herself. Reece couldn't quite make out the words, but he was sure it was the same tune as 'I'm a little sharva, all alone.' The effect of the lullaby-like sound was almost enough to put him to sleep. Every so often behind him he felt Holly jerk back from the edge of unconsciousness.

With an abrupt and electric splash of white, a dozen spotlights splayed across the sky. The Sarazen, descending towards the citadel, were caught in the beams. There seemed to be many more Sarazen than had been with Bobenny and the Hunt. It took Reece a moment to realise that the ranks of the Hunt had been swelled by re-inforcements that had met them en route. *Haimirel and Karuveh and Midíork and probably many of the rest of the Court—and the ordinary people too.*

Laser fire spat into the sky and, with each burst, Sarazen hurtled to the ground. Silhouetted in the dazzling whitefire of the spotlights, they dragged several gondolas to their doom. A groan died in Reece's throat before he could utter it. *Surprise really wasn't on their side. I sure hope Sharmika's right and that it's on ours.*

Flap, flap, flap went the steady motion of the sharva's wings.

Closer and closer they came to the citadel and the searching arcs of the spotlights. As they got nearer, they could hear the screams of the falling Sarazen mingled with sirens, and the uproar of a fight. Down, down, down Sharmika went until she was skimming across the desert at barely the height of a grown man. Reece could feel the sharva's muscles straining. *She's trying to come in under the radar like a stealth bomber.* They were heading straight for the curtain wall of the citadel at a tremendous speed. At the last moment, Sharmika turned her wings. 'Hold on tight now,' she whispered, and they angled crazily, heading vertically up the wall, before diving over it, across the inner courtyard and straight into the re-inforced glassine of a tower window set just above a turreted wall walk on the opposite side. There was a mighty thump as the sharva hit the window and both Holly and Reece were thrown off. At the last second Sharmika had thrown her thick leathery wings in front of them to try and protect them from the full force of the impact. Reece trampolined into Sharmika's wings, and Holly had rolled into Reece, before they both tumbled sideways onto the stones of the walkway.

The noise of the sharva hitting the window at full force was muffled by the noise of the laserfire above them and the clash of hand-to-hand fighting in the courtyard below. Reece got up unsteadily, his hand in agony. He went over to Holly, already at Sharmika's side, who was studying the bird's bleeding head and twisted neck. There was no movement at all from the sharva.

'I think she's dead.' Holly's whisper revealed her misery. 'I can't find any breath or heartbeat. It's just such a stupid, stupid way to die. I thought she knew what she was doing. She said she had a plan.' She began shaking. 'Glyffy's dead too.' She began to cry. 'And Tamizel. He's dead, too. It's stupid to hope he survived the fall when there is no hope.' A sob wracked her body.

Reece grabbed her hand. 'Don't become a blubbering wreck,

Holly. Not now, sis. I need you.' He took a deep breath. 'Look I'm really sorry the bird's dead. And Glyffy too. But we must get the tachyon decelerator back or Tamizel will be stranded forever. He's not dead.'

'Stranded?' Holly looked up and frowned at him. 'Reece, what are you talking about? Stranded where?'

'As near as I understand it, he's between dimensions in the Storm-Tree of Ruēl. He says he's safe, but you know Tamizel. Never tells the whole truth when half of it will do.'

'He's alive?' Holly shook her head. Reece felt her shiver. 'In the Storm-Tree? The Tree of Stars?' She began to cry even harder.

Reece was so startled by her reaction that he kept talking and trying to reassure her. 'He's trapped between time and eternity. Like Merlin, I think, in that esplumoir thing. But I'm sure we can get him out with the tachyon decelerator. I don't know how yet, but first things first. We've got to retrieve the decelerator before we can use it. See, being in the tree and outside of time, is the real explanation, I think, for why Tamizel could speak English—he mistook himself telling himself what we were saying for a "resonance of like minds". And Jaizee was relying on him more than we guessed. It's much harder to communicate with her now she's lost touch with Tamizel.'

'So he's really alive then?' Holly's tears stopped. Kissing the motionless body of the sharva, she stood up and announced with conviction, 'We've got to do it, Reece. You and me. We've got to get the tachyon decelerator.' She stared at him. 'So have you got anything we can use as a weapon?'

Reece reached into the inner pocket of his shirt. He pulled out the water-pistol. Holly's mouth twisted in derision.

'Just my thoughts too.' Reece put it away. 'I suppose we'll just have to wing it, sis, and hope for some sort of miracle.' He pointed then to the far end of the wall walk, indicating a silver hatchway set in a casement in the tower there. The tower housed one of the laser cannons, which was still firing—occasionally—into the sky. 'There's nowhere else to go from here so maybe that's where Sharmika was taking us.' Holly nodded at this. They crept quickly along the wall, staying out of sight of the melee in the courtyard as much as possible. When they reached the door, they could hear a scritching behind it. Reece, with a bound, pulled Holly to one side of the casement jutting out from the tower. The hatch opened. Reece held his breath. A robot trundled out, stopped, saw the sharva lying by the window and, a moment later, babbling to itself and waving its metal arms, it proceeded along the turretway towards the body of the bird. Reece, taking a careful step, slid out from the side of the casement and took a swift look inside the hatchway. *All clear*. He gestured silently to Holly, reaching out to take her hand.

A moment later they were both in the tower. Down—the word seemed to echo in Reece's head. '*Down*,' Reece mouthed to Holly as they found themselves on a tiny landing in the middle of a spiral staircase. As quietly as they could, they descended the steps, tip-toeing all the way. *One good thing*, Reece thought, as they reached the bottom. *The Invaders obviously haven't the resources to install security cameras everywhere. Otherwise the robot would've known about us. It must have just come to investigate the noise, or vibration, of the sharva hitting the window.*

At the base of the stairwell, there were hallways running in three directions. 'Left,' Holly whispered, just as Reece pointed to the right. Instantly compromising, they went straight ahead. They were half-way along the corridor when they heard the sound of running boots coming towards them. There was only one hiding place available to them—a narrow alcove hung with a floor-length tapestry. *Oh, this is dumb.* Reece realised it was a bad idea as soon as they ducked behind the curtain. *How are those troopers ever going miss seeing two bulges as big as we are, especially when they'll be on the lookout for any of the Farafolk who might have fought their way into the Citadel?*

A moment later there was a commotion back at the stairwell. *Wump, wump, wump* came the sound of something thudding down the steps. 'Whoa, whoa, whoa, hic,' came a reeling drunken voice. 'I'm a little sharva, hit a wall—*hic!*—I'm not feeling well at all.'

Reece heard the troopers rush past the tapestry. It seemed they hadn't given it a single glance. He peered out. Six troopers surrounded the unsteady sharva. The bird was clearly in a disoriented and befuddled state. It had a kink in its neck that it seemed to be trying to straighten, but every time it jerked it, it would spin around erratically, wobbling on its feet. 'I'm a little sharva, let me past—*hic!*—or we'll poop on your radio mast. *Hic!*'

The squad of troopers took only seconds to decide the sharva presented no real danger. They then divided into three groups — two went up the stairwell, two to the left, and two to the right. The sharva wove its wavering, but strangely rapid, way straight towards the alcove behind the tapestry. Seconds later it was pecking at the fabric right where Reece's forehead was. Reece whipped the tapestry aside and stared in astonishment at the bird. 'Great plan, huh?' Sharmika asked, straightening the kink in her neck with a wiggle of her shoulders. 'Did you like it? Got that door open and you in here at only the price of a slight headache!'

'But why didn't the troopers shoot you?' Reece whispered as they began to follow Sharmika.

She led them, tip-toe, further along the passage. 'They used to kill us just for fun, you know. So in revenge we started setting up house on their most important installations and toilet-training our nestlings on their interstellar transmitters. They found it was a real nuisance to get us off them without damaging the set-up.

They were bright enough to figure that we'd leave them alone when they left us alone. So now they've got a standing policy not to shoot sharvas.'

Holly ran her hand along Sharmika's feathered flank. 'I was worried about you.'

'Oh!' Sharmika's eyelashes fluttered. 'You know you're almost as likeable as Bozo here.' She indicated Reece. 'Nothing to concern yourself about, though. Knocking myself out was all part of the plan. I couldn't tell you, of course, in case you got captured and the truth came out. I'd have no chance to rescue you then, if it came to that. So I had to rely on your good sense which, thankfully, I see is not altogether lacking.'

'So what do we do now?' Reece asked, as they came to a junction in the hallway.

'We find the main lab.' Sharmika turned right to head deeper into the interior of the Citadel. 'If my reports are accurate, it has been set up adjacent to the old throne room.'

'Sharmika, you have to understand that the most important thing is for us to get the tachyon decelerator back,' Reece said as they hurried on.

'Let me assure you there's nothing tacky in this place.' Sharmika's tone was earnestly as she gazed up at the high vaulted ceiling glowing with topaz light. 'And it's definitely not *decelerating* into tackiness, whatever you may think. Finddias is a hovel in comparison. This was the seat of Farafolk civilisation for a thousand years. Aanundus has let it go to rack and ruin, of course, but even in this dilapidated state you can't miss its original good breeding.' They reached a small stairwell which led up to a gallery overlooking a fountain room inside the Citadel. The ceiling here was held up by groves of columns carved to look like trees.

Reece wasn't looking at the architecture. 'You don't understand,

Sharmika. I didn't say "tacky". I said "tachyon". A tachyon decelerator is an integral part of a time machine.'

'You don't say?' Sharmika asked as they came to the end of the gallery and turned left. 'Time machine, huh?' There was a momentary pause. 'Sounds dangerous.'

'In the wrong hands, anything can be dangerous,' Reece commented.

'Quite so.' Sharmika turned left again as they came to another junction. 'It's incredible, you know, when you think about it. The fate of this entire planet currently rests with me and a couple of young aliens.' She sighed. 'It's a real worry.'

Reece glanced at her. 'Not just this planet. Earth is just the next solar system along and I figure maybe Aanundus will go there next and…' He couldn't finish the sentence.

'Yes, it is a real worry, isn't it?' Sharmika repeated. 'So I think we need to find some security guards right away.'

'Whatever for?' Holly asked.

'To surrender to,' Sharmika said promptly. 'I have to tell you—not that you won't have guessed—but the Farafolk never did make a habit of inviting sharvas to official functions. And so I am forced to confess that I have no idea where we are. We could be going around this place forever trying to find Aanundus' private laboratory.'

'But security guards will just kill us,' Reece said. 'Or maybe throw us in a dungeon. Either way they're not going to take us meekly to their leader.'

'*Go back to the gallery.*' It was a voice out of nowhere, a voice that Reece heard with relief. He saw Holly's hand go straight to her heart.

'Is that you, Tamizel?' Reece looked around to make sure he wasn't being duped.

'Tamizel!' Holly smiled through sudden tears.

'*Holly.*' The word was a liquid caress. '*Sorry to take so long—I've figured* out how to get 'when', but matching the 'when' and the 'where' is extremely complex. Our ability to communicate seems partly tied to how much you need it.'

'Spooks!' Sharmika yipped, taking two steps backwards and frantically rolling her eyes.

'Shhh!' said Holly. 'There's nothing to be frightened of.'

'The gallery.'

Reece grabbed hold of Holly and hurried back the way they'd come. Sharmika trotted along reluctantly after them. 'Now what?' Reece asked, as they looked at the fountain court below.

'Behind you, in the wainscot woodwork, look for a carved panel depicting a king being crowned. He's seated on a throne under a palm tree.'

'This?' Sharmika poked with her beak. 'This one here with these funny long-legged birds wading in a pool?'

'Flamingoes,' Holly identified.

'They're sharvas, carved by someone who'd never seen one. My apologies for any offence.'

'You're a mighty polite spook, I'll say that for you,' Sharmika muttered.

'Do you see the spirals beneath the king's feet? Press on both spirals together as hard as you can.'

Reece held up his hands. The bandaged one was stiff and faintly claw-like.

'Let me do it.' Holly pushed him aside. She placed her thumbs at the centre of the spirals, pressing as hard as she could. *Click!* They could hear a locking mechanism open. Further along the wainscoting a panel slid to one side, revealing a dark stairway.

'The ancient stair goes straight down to the old throne-room. You must hurry now. Everything is ending. And please, try to save Varyien.'

'I'm surprised he's not already dead.' Reece moved to the top of the stairway.

'You *don't get rid of a valuable hostage until you're quite certain his use-by date is up.*'

Reece stood on the first step and peered at the sharva's back as it waddled down the stairwell. Holly pushed him forward and turned to click the door panelling back into place. The walls had a faint luminous sheen. After more than a dozen steps they reached the next level. Patches of light scattered from grids could be seen in the passage to the right.

With distinct caution, Sharmika proceeded to the first of these and placed her beak near the grid. She nodded back to Reece. He moved further along and placed his face against another of the light grids. He found could see straight into the throne room: the grid was a faceted device designed so that by moving the angle of his head, he had a panoramic view of almost the entire chamber. *If it looks, as it probably does, like the diamond tiles in the trellis pattern on the far wall, this is the perfect spy-hole.*

'Is that what I think it is?' Holly groaned, hardly above a whisper, as she pressed her nose against another of the grids. From his own spy-hole, Reece watched Aanundus enter the throne room, carrying a crystal in his gloved hands.

It was the Eye of Ruēl. Walking up to a servo-robot, Aanundus stooped and placed the lens in the clawed hand of the machine. The robot turned and headed for the centre of the room. There, separated from the throne room behind a circular glass partition, was a bank of machinery and controls. 'Oh, no.' Reece bit his lip. 'Tamizel? You still there?'

'Yes, Reece?'

'Do you know the secret of the Eye?'

There was a moment's hesitation. '*I believe I comprehend it—yes.*'

'Can he really destroy this planet with it?'

'The greatest force for evil that exists can be seen in the Eye—and the greatest good also.'

'Is that yes or no?' Reece whispered. He felt testy that Tamizel, even now, was still being evasive. 'Can't you ever give a straight answer?'

'When I met the Wounded Hand...' Holly kept her voice low. '...it became clear to me that the power of the Eye is that it shows you yourself.'

'You met the Wounded Hand?' Tamizel's voice was redolent with delight.

'Don't interrupt. Aanundus has undoubtedly done everything to the Eye, except just look in it. Or maybe he has, and he hasn't understood what he's seen there. There is no greater power for evil, or for good, than an individual.' Holly folded her arms. 'Isn't that right, Tamizel?'

'Yes,' Tamizel said.

'Sounds like humbug to me,' huffed Sharmika.

'Too right!' Reece said. 'But what a relief! I thought we were talking about the ultimate destructive power.'

'We *are*.' Holly stared at him.

'Only in some abstract philosophical sense,' Reece said.

'No,' Holly shook her head. 'But now's not the time to argue.'

Reece watched as the robot with the Eye pressed the metal skeleton of its claw hand against the security panel on the outside of the glass enclave. A light shone through its hand, riffling through the colours of the rainbow, clicking and tumbling like a key in a lock. Then the door opened and it entered. Immediately, it set to work to position the lens within the casing of an optical array. Reece stared at the monitors behind the robot and, although he couldn't understand the script on the screens, he was sure the whole set-up was going through a systems check. And then he saw it—set right in the heart of the optical array—the tachyon decelerator. He almost missed it, almost failed to recognise it. Flat and circular, with tapering curves radiating out from its centre, it was a shimmering silver web, with light pulsing at the crystal nodes where its filaments joined. 'Isn't it magnificent?' Aanundus asked.

For one horrifying heartstopping moment, Reece thought Aanundus was talking directly to him. He thought Aanundus could see through the walls and knew they were there. But he realised Aanundus was not looking at them but towards the throne facing directly away from them.

'He's talking to Varyien,' Holly whispered. 'He's shackled to the throne.'

'A beautiful piece of machinery,' Aanundus went on. 'A shame I will have to leave without the prototype.'

Varyien spoke, his tone pleading.

'What did he say?' Reece nudged Holly.

It was Tamizel who replied. *'You do not have to destroy this world simply to prove that you can.'*

Aanundus replied derisively to Varyien. Tamizel continued to translate. *'But that is exactly the point of destroying it—to prove that it takes no more than a fine-ground lens, a well-tuned tachyon decelerator and a laser accelerator, all in a confined space of zero humidity.'*

I'd like to put you in a confined space of zero humidity with a laser accelerator. The wound Reece had almost forgotten began to ache abominably.

Tamizel continued translating. *'No doubt you're concerned for my safety, but never fear. I have a fast ship waiting. A very fast ship. And the system here won't fire until the coordinates of the array go automatically on-line, which will happen when the orange sun reaches its zenith. In just over ten minutes. And then approximately sixty one minutes and eight seconds later, your second sun will go nova.'* He took a small remote control from his pocket. *'And now to set the final sequence.'*

I should have guessed. He's going to fire the weapon into the sun so that it goes nova. And if Alpha Centauri explodes, this planet will be destroyed, but life on Earth won't survive the radiation either. We've got to stop him. 'Tamizel, how do we get in there?'

'Push!' Tamizel's voice was faint and far-off.

'Push what?' Reece and Holly whispered together.

'The wall. Quick! *Now!*

A grinding screech echoed in the narrow confines of their hiding place as they both leaned forward as hard as they could. A section of the wall moved forward and Sharmika darted out from behind it as Aanundus turned, not to face his intruders, but to hold a gun on Varyien. 'One untoward move,' he warned, 'and your king dies.'

He smiled as he saw Reece and Holly scramble out from behind the wall. 'Oh, it's the little children.' His voice was mocking. 'Did you think you'd succeed where your betters had failed? Did you think you'd be the heroes who saved the day?' He tutted. 'Ah, the perils of reading too many fairy stories!' Holding out the remote control, he activated the destruct sequence by depressing the central button.

Reece lunged towards him.

'Too late, my little chickens.' Aanundus gloated.

Inside the glass-walled laboratory, an arc of light blazed inward from the array to the centre of the tachyon decelerator and then, crackling out over its surface, spearing whirls of radiation began to accelerate around the silver web.

Aanundus had easily evaded Reece's lunge, but he was downed by Sharmika. The huge sharva gave a flying leap, sending him sprawling. 'Mind who you call a chicken,' she squawked angrily, pecking at his forehead. 'And I don't appreciate being called a child, either, come to think of it.'

A sizzle of lightning danced across the pulsing surface of the tachyon decelerator. The rush of sound became so wild and loud that Sharmika was distracted. Aanundus toppled her and scrambled away, his brow covered in blood.

Reece planted himself between Aanundus and the exit, yelling above the noise of the tachyon decelerator: 'You won't get out of here. If you want to stay alive, you'll have to stop the countdown.'

'I can break you like a twig,' Aanundus said, quite unperturbed.

'Let him go, Reece,' Sharmika said. 'He'll only try to stop us reversing the countdown.' She poked out her tongue at Aanundus and growled. 'Shoo!'

'*No!*' Reece shouted vehemently in protest.

'Stand aside *now*,' Sharmika snapped at Reece. 'Didn't I tell you to do exactly what I said?'

'*But…*' Reece said.

'Let him go,' Sharmika repeated, articulating each word carefully. 'Or are you just thinking of something as petty as revenge?'

Aanundus suddenly laughed and threw the remote control to Reece, like a bone to a dog. 'Good luck to you. The programming cannot be altered, the countdown cannot be stopped. But feel free to try. You have less than ten minutes.' He sauntered towards the door.

Reece's face was dark with rage. 'Why did you stop me?' he screamed at Sharmika, as Aanundus closed the door on them.

'Your manners,' Sharmika tutted, 'are sadly lacking at the moment, young man.' She looked around surreptitiously. Seeing only the king still bound to the throne, she went on, 'Wouldn't like to broadcast this, you know, but if the fast ship that he's thinking of is the fast ship I'm thinking of, it's the one I noticed Hollë sneaking aboard.' Sharmika laughed. 'I'd like to be a fly on the wall at that encounter, but unfortunately we have some pressing business with this array thingie here.' She waved her wing towards the lab where the build-up of power in the system was reaching a crescendo. 'In summary, our problem is: a fine-ground lens, a well-tuned tachyon decelerator and a laser accelerator, all in a confined space of zero humidity. And we've got to solve this quandary in the next five minutes or so or a couple of solar systems are going to be wiped off the face of the universe.' She sighed. 'A lock, not a key. Any ideas, folks?'

Hollë and Aanundus—poetic justice. Reece calmed down and turned his mind to the dilemma at hand. *A fine-ground lens, a well-tuned tachyon decelerator and a laser accelerator, all in a confined space of zero humidity. But it's not only that. We'd have to get through the security doors, into the lab, and avoid the robot even before we can think of shutting the system down. Or disrupting it—oh, this is stupid! All I've got is a water pistol that I can't even hold properly because my hand has a hole in...* Reece's eyes widened. *...a hole in it. A lock, not a key. In a confined space of zero humidity.*

'Do it, Reece.'

'No!' Reece said, aware of the only possible answer. 'No!'

'Do it, Reece.'

'No!'

'*Billions of lives are depending on you.*'

'If I destroy the tachyon decelerator, you'll be trapped forever.'

'*I'm safe, Reece. Do it.*'

'I can't.'

'What's going on?' Holly had become agitated as he'd argued with Tamizel. She watched him begin unwrapping the bandage around his hand. 'What's this about destroying the tachyon decelerator? And what're you doing that for?'

Reece's eyes began to glisten. 'Because, damn it, sis...' He couldn't keep the tension out of his voice. '...we need a lock, not a key.' He took a deep breath, and glared in anger at Sharmika. 'You're altogether far too convenient and your information is far too good. Who are you really? Can we trust you? Are you even real?'

'As real as any reality,' Sharmika retorted at once. 'Whatever, of course, "reality" really is.' She grinned. 'Oh, this language of yours is so amusing! Reality *really* is! Now, surely you've learned this lesson before—and you understand the need for just a little deception to get you here.'

Holly's mouth fell open. 'They're Tamizel's words, almost exactly from when we first met, and Reece thought the chair wasn't real.' Her eyes were wide. 'What are you?'

'I'm a sharva,' Sharmika said, 'made from collecting and assembling disconnected fragments of unfinished thoughts, plus the odd couple of interrupted musings. And like Cinderella's coach, which disappears at midnight, I'm on a strict time budget and it's almost up.'

'But you can't just be thoughts,' Holly said.

'All creation originates in thought,' Sharmika said. 'I'm merely a rather nifty exemplar of it.'

'What was the deception to get us here?' Reece asked. 'And why? Who sent you?'

'Kid,' the sharva said, 'this is the moment you were born for. Only you can get in there and do what has to be done—in the next three minutes, I might venture to remind you. But if anyone had told you so, if anyone had suggested to you that the fate of not just two planets, but the entire galaxy was in your hands, you woulda laughed in their face—so that's why I've gone through this little charade. As for who sent me—why the spook did—he worked on me for over a century to be sure Holly would trust me on sight. He made me, so he said, to be everything he was not.'

'So you're nothing but...' Holly began.

'Quit wasting precious seconds,' Sharmika interrupted, scowling at Reece. 'Get moving, buster.' Her eyes widened suddenly. 'Oops, like

Cindy's coach, I hear the clock chimes…' And with that, she began to disappear in a rain of shimmering golden droplets. 'I'm counting on you, kid…' were her fading words as she vanished from sight.

At that moment, there was a commotion at the door. Bobenny, sword in hand and accompanied by a group of warriors, rushed into the throneroom. Varyien shouted at them and, realising there was no sign of Aanundus, several of them raced out again. Bobenny hurried to release the king from his bonds, laying the sword down on the dais beside the throne, as he examined the shackles.

'Quick…' Reece turned to Holly, hearing a discussion between Bobenny and Varyien. 'If they try to stop me, you distract them.'

'Stop you from what?' Holly asked.

Reece didn't answer her. He pulled out his water pistol, shaking it to make sure there was still some water left in it. *Zero humidity, here I come.* He took a deep breath and raised his wounded hand. Going to the lab door, he placed the hand straight on the security plate the servo-robot had accessed. As he pushed against the panel, a light shot out through the hole in his hand, and riffled through the colours of the rainbow, clicking and tumbling like a key in a lock. The door slid open. Reece darted through.

Holly was right there behind him, sword in hand. She'd taken it from Bobenny's side while he was releasing the king. 'What do you think you're doing?' Reece yelled at her as the door slid shut behind them. The servo-robot had already swivelled towards them.

'It's the Sword of Invincibility.' Holly swung the heavy weapon awkwardly over her head. 'It might help.' She lunged forward. 'Duck,' she screamed, as she pulled Reece down.

The servo-robot fired at them. The shot ricocheted off the glass walls, going straight through the beam of the laser accelerator without affecting it, and bouncing wildly off the tachyon decelerator.

'Get out of here, Hol.' Reece felt desperate as the robot

advanced on them.

'I'd never have made a good Lady of the Lake,' Holly shouted. 'But I'd make a great Musketeer. All for one and one for all.' She raised the sword. 'You do what you have to do and I'll keep the robot busy.'

'Hol…' *Why wouldn't she understand the urgency of the situation?* 'Go! Get out of here! You don't understand.'

'Reece, get on with it, there's no time left.' Holly, with an exultant cry and a wild leap, soared upward with the sword in her hand.

Reece blinked. *Was that a tiny stag on her shoulder? Surely it couldn't be. Where had it come from?* The stag kicked with its hoof and she reacted, turning just as the robot fired. The shot missed. She swept around, the sword falling in a long slashing arc. Reece had only a moment to register the stunned faces of Bobenny and Varyien beyond the laboratory as Holly's sword sliced into the robot.

He turned to the tachyon decelerator. Taking careful aim with his water pistol, he fired straight into its heart. He watched as the silver mesh bubbled and ruptured, its gossamer filaments crackling and snapping as it lost cohesion. Then, as the entire system failed and started its shutdown procedure, the decelerator exploded into a million dazzling fragments.

Last Leaf

Reece felt sick. His ears were ringing. When he opened his eyes he found he was blind. A long minute passed and, when he still couldn't see, it didn't particularly concern him. He didn't want to speak to Varyien or Bobenny, and receive their congratulations. All he could think about was Tamizel. *What have I done to you? Why couldn't there have been any other way?*

'Reece?' Holly's uncertain voice came into his ringing darkness as faintly as a shellsong. 'Are you okay?' He felt her scramble to his side. She touched his wounded hand gently, holding it up to examine it. She sighed. 'How are we ever going to explain this?'

'Explain what?' Reece hardly recognised his own voice.

'Your hand. We can hide everything except that.'

But why would we want to hide anything? Fuzzy shapes were starting to form in his line of vision, and the ringing in his ears was ebbing like a tide. He still felt nauseous. *Is this radiation sickness? Already?* 'Hold on, sis. I just need a minute.'

But it was several minutes before he was ready to talk. By

then he could make out the wall of iridescent pastel bubbles in front of him, disintegrating even as he watched. It was exactly the same sort of shimmering wall he and Holly had encountered on board the space carrier—but there was nothing unearthly about it this time. Through the bubbles, he could see a very astonished-looking kangaroo and behind it, a very tall and stately gum. 'We're on *Earth*?!' *But of course we're on Earth! The tachyon decelerator must have, in those few nanoseconds before it self-destructed, tried to repair its disrupted circuitry. It must have defaulted back to its last operational setting and flung us back here. Almost back to where we began. But if its last setting was here, then...* He pondered for a while what that might mean. *Could it have been just chance what happened to us?*

'Yes, Earth.' Holly interrupted his thoughts. Through the shimmer wall, the kangaroo, with a tilt of its head, twitched its nose at them before bounding away.

Together they sat in silence, watching the last of the bubbles waver and fall away in a rippling curtain. Then they continued to sit there, savouring the smell of Earth with its slight, intermittent background sounds and its familiar colours and folds of landscape.

A blue, blue sky and a single sun. I never thought I'd be so thankful for them. 'Holly, we're going to have to find a story and stick to it. We haven't been to Narnia or Oz or met Alice down the rabbit hole. This hasn't been a dream and I've got a bad feeling there's a significant time differential between when we left and now.'

Holly nodded. 'I've already thought of that. Your hand's the only thing we're going to have difficulty explaining.'

Reece looked at it for a moment, then stood up. He felt unsteady for several seconds, but the sensation passed and he extended his good hand to Holly to help her rise. 'I've got an idea.' Suddenly he realised the sword was on the ground beside her and, a little way distant, were the remains of a seriously mangled robot. *Where's the white stag? Or did I just imagine that?*

'What idea?' Holly asked.

'I'll do your washing up from now on.'

Holly stooped down to pick up the sword. 'You don't have to...'

'Hear me out. It's part of a plan I've got. I'll do your washing up, so that you'll have more time for your art—you're good at creating pretty things, good enough to sell. And that way we can save enough money to buy a dishwasher.'

Holly rolled her eyes as she began to pick her way through the bleached brown grass towards the nearest fence. 'A dish*washer*?' She shook her head. 'And here I was thinking you were feeling guilty.'

'But it would give us both more time.' Reece caught up to her just as she placed the sword carefully on the far side of the fence before climbing through it. 'You can then keep on with the artwork, and that will earn us enough money to buy the stuff I need.'

Holly turned and faced him over the divide of the fence in obvious incredulity. 'You want *me* to support *you*?'

'Time and money.' Reece nodded at her. 'If we're going to get Tamizel out of the Storm-Tree, I've got to have both time and money for research.'

Holly stared at him for a moment, before leaning over the fence and planting a huge kiss straight on the forehead. 'Can you do it, Reece?' she breathed. 'Really?'

'I can make that tachyon decelerator, I know I can.'

'Reece, it was an alien device. Maybe Earth doesn't have the materials or technology to construct it.'

'Yes, we do. Or we *will* have.' Reece nodded at her. 'Sis, it's not alien, just advanced. Aanundus has to have found the tachyon decelerator somewhere here on Earth. That's, I'm sure, why he was so fluent in English.'

'If it comes from Earth, then we can save up and buy one.'

'No, we can't,' Reece said. 'We can't buy something that doesn't exist yet. It doesn't exist until I make it. It's a time device—understand?'

It took a moment for Holly to process what he was saying and begin to believe. 'Okay. How long do you think it will take you to make one?'

Reece was clumsy as he climbed through the fence to join her. He winced when he was forced to use his injured hand. Together they crossed over a ditch and onto a dusty road. Reece finished his consideration of the question. 'Ten, maybe twenty years. More even. Maybe it'll take me a whole lifetime.'

Holly stood on the edge of the road and seemed to shrink inside herself. 'Tamizel will be there for years,' she whispered. She bowed her head. '*Years*. He'll be like Merlin, entombed alive, trapped forever.'

'No, he won't.' Reece shook his head. 'Do you know what the difference between Tamizel and Merlin is, sis?'

'No.'

'Merlin doesn't have you and me working on his case.' Reece drew himself up. 'Time doesn't mean anything in this situation, sis. And I'm not fooling around anymore—I'm going to build a real time machine—a *real* time machine, able to go anywhen, if not anywhere. And the nerve heart of it will be the tachyon decelerator.' He grabbed her arm with his good hand and swung it as he pulled her forward along the road. 'Cheer up, Hol. We can do it.' He pointed across a paddock. 'Look, there's Lissa's place. You want to phone home?'

Holly shook her head. 'We *can* do it,' she whispered to herself. Reece smiled as he realised his own determination and cheerfulness was beginning to have its effect on her. 'We can rescue Tamizel. And we won't give up—however long it takes.'

They continued tramping up the slope of the road, when she

sighed. 'But we have other problems to overcome.'

'Like what?'

'Gran's words about Dad. What they really mean. I won't be a Merlin, living backwards in time, and locking up my feelings.'

'Huh?'

'It's something the Wounded Hand said. You know, we've got to deal with this problem of who we are, before we tackle anything else.' She grinned at some private thought. '*Cerylen.*' Her smile broadened. 'Do you want be with me when I ask Dad about what Gran said?'

'No.' Reece didn't mean to be curt.

'Thought so. You really are a Merlin.'

'What's that supposed to mean?'

'It means that when you don't want to face something, you vanish for a while, just like Merlin used to do when he was most needed. When the going gets rough, you disappear, when the going gets tough, your toughness goes. Reece, this didn't start because of the washing up. It started because you're a Merlin. And you've got to stop living backwards in time.'

Reece tried to ignore her. He spotted some old fertiliser sacks at the edge of a field. 'Lissa's dad won't mind if we borrow them. We have to hide that sword somehow.' He reached over the fence and grabbed a sack. And then he gave in. 'Okay, I don't see why you need me, but I'll be with you when you talk to Mum and Dad.' He paused. 'But not a word about Tamizel or Finddias, understand? On that, we have to be internally vigilant.'

'*E*ternally vigilant,' Holly corrected automatically.

'That too.'

Holly smiled. 'I always rise to the bait, don't I? How long does it take you to think of something like that?'

Reece shrugged. 'It just comes. Now what's our story? We've got to figure out a very satisfactory collusion.'

'Satisfactory *conclusion*,' Holly corrected.

A yellow bus hurtled over the hill, swerved wildly to avoid them and then came to a screeching halt.

'Put that sword behind your back,' Reece muttered through his teeth at Holly as the door swung open.

'Is it ghosts I'm seeing?' Mr Jenkins peered out, white-faced.

'Oh, Mr Jenkins!' Reece shoved his hands in his pockets. 'Are we ever glad to see you!'

'Not 'alf as glad as your father'll be.' Mr Jenkins grinned. His pale face was recovering its colour with every passing moment. 'You know he's been arrested for your murder?'

'*Murder*?!' Holly and Reece exclaimed together. They exchanged horrified glances. Reece shook his head, remembering Gran's prediction.

'Yes, murder!' Mr Jenkins was staring at their Farafolk court clothes, his expression a mix of curiosity and suspicion. 'Well, come on then...' He ushered them into the bus. 'We'd better hurry to set those detectives straight and get your father out of jail.' He glared at them, looking them up and down, his attention caught by the oddly shaped sack in Holly's hands. 'I'll bet you two have a story to tell.' His fierce gaze softened. 'You're all right, aren't you? Have you been kidnapped?'

For a moment, when there was no answer and they threw sidelong glances at each other, he grew almost angry, as if suddenly convinced they'd organised their own disappearance. 'Where on earth have you been for the last fortnight? Have you any idea of the uproar you've caused?'

Still neither of them answered. Reece realised they hadn't agreed on a story. They sat down, brows raised at each other.

Mr Jenkins sidled back into the driver's seat and revved the engine. Then he began laughing—a loud, uproarious sound. He turned back to Reece and stopped his cackling long enough to say, 'You were right, you know, Reece. History *will* remember my name. I'll be a legend. If we're real quick, I can get you both to the memorial service just in time for the two of you to make it to your own funeral.' A huge smile almost threatened to split his face.

Reece could see he was contemplating being able to tell the story of the dash into town with the missing twins for the next twenty years or more. 'Our funeral? That should be fun!'

Mr Jenkins turned back to the wheel, but the bus—almost, it seemed, by itself—had already taken off in a flurry of dust, like a hornet released from a trap.

Other books by Anne Hamilton

Daystar

'What's to stop me killing you and taking the Powers?' The giant raised the sword. 'All I see is a dwarf, a pony and seven children, none of whom is even remotely capable of resisting the might of Uller Princekiller.'

For centuries, the knights, dwarves, giants and sages of Auberon-Zamberg have been intent on a single quest. They're all searching for 'The King Who Guards the Gate'. Prophecy speaks of him as one of seven protectors who will defeat the armies of night and overcome the Dark Sleeper.

The last thing anyone is expecting is that these seven protectors are ordinary children.

ISBN: 978-1925139518
CBCA Notable Book 2017
Available at
www.booksinstock.com.au

Other books by Anne Hamilton

Many-Coloured Realm

Love, faith and the theory of relativity.

Many-Coloured Realm is a children's and YA fantasy in numerical literary style—a rigorous mathematical design underpins the text. It's got 1 nice girl, 2 bad boys, 3 tortuous tasks and 4 strange ambassadors. After that, it's hard to keep count. Dozens of elves, hundreds of goblins and legions of demons all converge on the colourless goblin realm for the king's birthday party. Robby and Chris enter a world where time is relative—can they name the king and rescue Stephen before they're all trapped?

Finalist in International Book Award 2011 (Fantasy)

ISBN 978-1921633065

Available at

www.booksinstock.com.au

www.ingramcontent.com/pod-product-compliance
Lightning Source LLC
Chambersburg PA
CBHW050513190726

48284CB00003B/798